The Clan Records

The Clan Records
FIVE STORIES OF KOREA

Kajiyama Toshiyuki

Translated by Yoshiko Dykstra
with an introduction by
George Akita and Yong-ho Choe

UNIVERSITY OF HAWAI'I PRESS
Honolulu

In memory of
Ryōzō and Mitsue Ariyoshi

00 99 98 97 96 95   5 4 3 2 1

Library of Congress Cataloging-in-Publication Data
Kajiyama, Toshiyuki, 1930–1975.
  [Richō zan'ei. English]
  The clan records : five stories of Korea / Kajiyama Toshiyuki ;
translated by Yoshiko Dykstra, with an introduction by George Akita
and Yong-ho Choe.
    p. cm.
  ISBN 0–8248–1532–7
  I. Dykstra, Yoshiko Kurata.   II. Title.
PL835.A35R5313   1995
895.6'35—dc20   94–42476
                                                              CIP

**Publication of this book has been assisted by a generous grant from
George R. Ariyoshi.**

Designed by Kenneth Miyamoto

Contents

Introduction

George Akita and Yong-ho Choe

Toshiyuki Kajiyama (January 2, 1930–May 11, 1975), one of postwar Japan's most prolific writers, is but little known in the West. This volume offers a sampling of his work in English for the first time.

Kajiyama was born in Seoul, Korea, where his father, Yūichi, was a civil engineer in Japan's administration of Korea. Yūichi was born in Hiroshima and had served in the same capacity as civil engineer in Taiwan before he was transferred to Korea with his wife, Nobuyo. Nobuyo had been born in Kahuku on the island of Oahu in what was then the Territory of Hawaii but was sent alone to Hiroshima at age nine to be raised by her relatives. The Kajiyamas had four children: a girl and three boys. Toshiyuki was the second son. He attended Japanese schools in Seoul and was a fifteen-year-old student at Keijō (Seoul) High School when the Pacific War ended in 1945.

Following the Japanese defeat, the family was repatriated to Japan. Toshiyuki attended the Hiroshima Higher Normal School (now Hiroshima National University), majoring in Japanese language and literature. He graduated in 1952, writing his undergraduate dissertation on the *shishōsetsu* ("I-novels") of Kamura

Isota. He moved to Tokyo in 1953, intending to be a journalist, but taught high school instead for two trimesters. He supplemented his income by writing children's stories after marrying Minae Kobayashi of Hiroshima. A daughter, Miki, was born in 1961.

Kajiyama's fortunes improved when he became a freelance writer in the forefront of young contributors to the popular weeklies and monthlies that were enjoying an unprecedented postwar boom. His abilities found their fullest expression, however, in his twenty-year career as a novelist. That active career was punctuated with best sellers. The first was *"Kuro no shisōsha"* (Black test car, 1961), which dealt presciently with espionage in Japan's developing automobile industry. Set in an atmosphere of vicious, cutthroat competition, it recalled medieval Japan's *sengoku jidai* (period of warring states).

Kajiyama's collected works sold more than sixteen million copies during his lifetime. His literary output was reprinted as the *Kajiyama Toshiyuki Collection* and has sold an additional seventeen million volumes since his death in 1975. His popularity may be attributed to his finely tuned sense of what his readers felt but could not quite articulate: the sense that Japan was rising to economic greatness after exhaustion and defeat in 1945 but might be losing something irreplaceable in the process. Kajiyama was a sharp-eyed analyst who took on subjects such as the travails of urbanization, the many-sided possibilities of feminism, and the hidden hypocriscy, falseness, corruption, and immorality of Japan's financial, industrial, and political worlds during spectacular economic growth.

Before his death, Kajiyama had outlined his "lifework," a tour de force that was to have focused on three interlocking landscapes: Korea, the place of his birth and early upbringing; Hawaii, his mother's birthplace and the setting for the Japanese immigration experience; and Hiroshima, his father's birthplace and the site of the atomic bombing. He had even selected a title: *Sekiran'un* (Beneath the storm clouds). In preparation, he had accumulated more than eight thousand items, including government documents, reports, diaries, memoirs, biographies, and out-of-print books. He purchased these items with royalties from his best-sellers; after his death, they were donated to the University of Hawaii in 1977 and housed in the Kajiyama Toshiyuki Collection of Hamilton Library for use by scholars and writers.

Kajiyama's Korean tales, five of which make up this volume, were to have made up one of the components of his planned trilogy. The first of these to appear was *Zokufu* (The clan records, 1961). It was made into a movie in 1978 in Korea and was nominated for a grand prize. It fell short of the prize, however, because the original work was by a Japanese. The second story to appear was *Richō zan'ei* (The remembered shadow of the Yi dynasty, 1963). This was nominated for Japan's prestigious Naoki Prize and in 1967 was also made into a highly acclaimed movie in Korea. It is significant that these and the other three short stories collected here are the first English translations from the Japanese that deal with Korea under Japanese rule.

Japan was the first country to induce Korea to sign a modern treaty in 1876, thus forcing Yi dynasty (1392–1910) Korea to open its doors to the modern world. Japan eliminated Korea's close tie with China in the Sino-Japanese War (1894–1895), clearly demonstrating its imperialistic designs. The increased influence of the Japanese was challenged by Russia, which was also interested in Korea, and the Russo-Japanese War (1904–1905) erupted. Following Russia's defeat, Japan made deft diplomatic moves to win the support of the United States and England to advance Japanese interests in Korea. Japan established a protectorate (1905) and then eventually annexed Korea in 1910. Enraged over the aggression of Japan, many Korean nationalists, known as the Righteous Armies (Ŭibyŏng), took up arms to resist the seizure, but their resistance was unsuccessful.

Japan ruled Korea from 1910 to 1945. The period from 1910 to 1919 was characterized by its extremely harsh military rule, known as *budan seiji*. The resentment of the Korean people against the Japanese exploded in the March First Movement, also known as the Mansei Incident or Mansei Agitation of 1919. Inspired by Woodrow Wilson's peace proposals in Europe, Koreans of all ranks joined in the proclamation of Korean independence and staged peaceful demonstrations throughout the country. Caught by surprise, the Japanese authorities resorted to extreme brutality to suppress the movement. One of the most gruesome events took place at the village of Cheam-ni, a scene depicted in *Richō zan'ei,* where more than twenty villagers were murdered.

The March First Movement, however, forced Japan to adopt a more conciliatory policy toward Korea and grant more press freedom, allow more emphasis on education, and provide greater economic opportunities. At the same time Japan reinforced its security apparatus. Known as *bunka seiji,* this conciliatory policy lasted until power shifted to the military in Japan in the 1930s.

The effect of this shift was felt in Korea, where the governor-general, Minami Jirō (1936–1942), and his successors imposed a

The Kajiyama family, Seoul, 1937. *Left to right:* Nobuyo; *standing,* Yūichi, holding Hiroko (one year old), and the Kajiyamas' Korean housekeeper; Hisashi (ten years old); Toshiyuki (eight years old); Sadao (five years old).

Kajiyama Toshiyuki in his personal library, Tokyo, 1971. The documents pictured now comprise the Kajiyama Toshiyuki Collection, Hamilton Library, University of Hawai'i.

heavy-handed rule aimed at the total eradication of Korean culture and tradition. In the name of *naisen ittai* (unity of Japan and Korea), all Koreans were required to recite daily the Oath of Imperial Subjects, every Korean was compelled to bow before a Shinto shrine, many Korean youths were forced into the Japanese army, the use of Korean language was prohibited, and every Korean was required to adopt a Japanese name (as described in *The Clan Records*). In addition, to aid the Japanese war cause, about one and a half million Korean laborers were forced to work in mines, munitions factories, and military installations under extreme hardship. A large number of young Korean women—perhaps as many as three hundred thousand—many still in their early teens, were mobilized to serve as prostitutes under the name of "comfort women."

The Korean people resented Japanese rule and celebrated the termination of that control in 1945 as a day of national liberation. The heart of Kajiyama's stories is located in this difficult period of recent Korean history. Kajiyama was affected by contradictory influences: he recognized that the Koreans were rightly antagonistic to everything Japanese while they were under Japanese rule; yet, as a Japanese himself whose father had worked to improve Korea's infrastructure, he took pride in Japan's accomplishments. Despite these pressures, Kajiyama succeeded in infusing his Korean protagonists with dignity and courage and depicted subjects understandably sensitive for Koreans in an unusually subtle, sensitive, and empathetic manner without being patronizing. In these stories, too, Kajiyama avoided the temptation to whitewash the inhumanity and the brutality of the Japanese occupation.

The stories ring true on another level as well. Kajiyama's narrative is laced with local expressions, historical terminology, and accurate descriptions of Korean culture. Kajiyama accomplished this through his basic sympathy and love for Korea and the Koreans.

Kajiyama, in these stories, has managed the most difficult of feats. He has succeeded in winning the critical approval of both Koreans and Japanese. It is a final irony that these most sympathetic introductions to Korea's rich cultural heritage came from the pen of a Japanese author illuminating a period during which his own government was attempting to eradicate that heritage.

The Clan Records

IN THOSE DAYS I held a job in a government office because of a cowardly desire to avoid the draft. It came about this way. . . .

As a result of my physical examination I was classified as unfit for military service, but since my weak constitution had led me to enter the school of fine arts, and in those critical times oil painting was a trivial activity, I was clearly in danger of being called up for some kind of labor service. Sure enough, in that summer of 1940, just at the beginning of August, I was ordered to report for ten days of labor on the height called Namsan, where the "Korea Shrine" stood—a shrine the Japanese had erected to their own Shinto deities in an attempt to extend those deities' potency to Korea.

On the continent the summers are hot and the winters are cold. Summer that year was especially hot; the burning heat continued for days. Japanese soldiers were constructing an antiaircraft position on Namsan. We laborers were to clear the mountainside. There was no protective shade. I was quickly exhausted.

The work was simple, crushing rocks and carting away the

sandy soil. A group of middle-school students had been summoned to help, but it was our group of some two hundred
men who were abused by the soldiers. "You don't work hard
enough," they railed. "Compared to the students, you grown
men are slackers." Most of us were artistic or literary types,
weak and pale like me. We knew nothing about laboring
together, and we were not energetic.

I ignored the soldiers' goading, but one day I passed out in
the sun. "Go rest in the shade," a soldier scolded, and then he
shouted, "By tomorrow every one of you will crop his hair!
Long hair causes sunstroke!"

That was ridiculous. Almost all of us had long hair, but the
sun had prostrated me because my straw hat had blown away. I
was incensed. I dodged work for two days using sunstroke as
my excuse. I heard that on the last day they would give us from
three to five yen as transportation money, so like a model
laborer I went back to work. It took me an hour to climb the
steep slope. Unexpectedly I was summoned by the commanding
officer, an artillery captain. "Why didn't you report before you
took leave?" he barked. "Taking leave without permission
shows no sense of responsibility."

He was so pompous that I couldn't suppress a grim smile.
That was a mistake. He ordered me to go down the mountain,
get a doctor's diagnosis and an excuse for my absence, and
report back within two hours. It was preposterous to make
such demands in the labor service, but the consequences could
be terrible if I disobeyed. I glanced at my watch and rushed
down the mountain. There was no time to return to where I
was living in Sŏsomun, so I burst into a small clinic at the
foot of the mountain, explained my situation to the doctor,
hurried his diagnosis, and wrote an excuse for absence on his
stationery.

The climb up the mountain was hot. I ran the rocky path,
gasping and dripping sweat. Still I was five minutes late. The
captain read the diagnosis and asked my address. I said that the
diagnosis was made by my family doctor.

"Clever, huh," he said, clicking his tongue. Then he

grabbed my collar and shouted, "So you were not sick! You were faking to avoid work! Tell the truth!"

The whole experience was bitter. Once was more than enough, but I was sure I would be summoned again. My anxiety increased when I heard from the head of my district that every district was required to provide five more men for labor service.

It was not that I was averse to physical labor. But to have my body abused while my mind was deadened—to swing a heavy pick and shovel in the burning heat while soldiers reviled me—was intolerable. My life would turn to ashes. Hastily I looked for regular work.

It was arranged by my brother-in-law, who was a section head in the governor-general's office. I readily accepted, since it required no special skills, but in the end I found it unendurable.

Every morning I put the lunch prepared by my elder sister into an old briefcase given to me by my brother-in-law and went to the office. I was a punctual machine. A chauffeured car picked up my brother-in-law every morning, but he never offered me a ride. My sister was busy raising two children and had no time to look after me. I thought of moving to a lodging house, but just the idea of looking for a place tired me. I resigned myself to the situation.

From the official residences at Sŏsomun I went down the slope to the Paejae Middle School, passed the courthouse, and reached T'aep'yŏng Avenue, where Tŏksu Palace stood on the left and the prefectural office building was on the right. I walked north along the tram line toward the imposing white headquarters of the governor-general. Just before it, on the right, was the brick building that housed the Kyŏnggi Provincial Office, where I worked.

Fall turned quickly toward winter. The big leaves of the plane trees along the avenue fell in the wind. In the swirl of the leaves along the pavement each morning I heard the footfall of approaching winter and saw the sad image of myself. I was not doing well in my job.

The war in China was deadlocked. Reflecting the frustration of the war, Seoul was restless. There were air-raid drills, people wore the drab national uniform, and the "volunteer soldier system" was imposed. Every phase of our daily life was affected.

When my work stalled I went to the window for a cigarette. Through the faded autumn foliage I could see the propaganda slogans hung on the white walls of the governor-general's headquarters: "Japan and Korea Unified" and "A Hundred Million People of One Mind."

"'Japan and Korea Unified,'" I would say to myself. "Governor-general Minami Jirō must like the sound of that." But it gave me no inspiration at all.

"Mr. Tani!"

The voice of the chief made me turn. I knew he disliked me because I still wore a civilian suit handed down from my father, while the rest of the section were in the national uniform. I heard that behind my back he had slandered me as a traitor. But I had something on him: an artist friend had told me that he was secretly keeping a mistress, a waitress in a Meiji Street coffee shop.

I stubbed out my cigarette, left the window, and walked slowly to the chief's desk. He knew very well that I was there because he had just called me, but he pretended to be so deeply engrossed in the document on his desk that he was unaware of me. I knew it was a report from the Suwŏn county. "I know, chief, you are a very busy man and the model for our section," I said to myself as I stood silently before his desk.

"Oh, Mr. Tani." He raised his head as if he had just noticed me. A small man, the shine on his face betrayed his heavy drinking at nightly parties. As usual, he pushed up his spectacles with his right index finger and frowned deeply.

"So, how is your work going? Well, I suppose."

I was prepared for criticism, but his sarcasm nettled me.

"Yes, mostly. . . ."

"Hah. Mostly, you say. But according to this report, your district is only thirty-seven percent. Do you call that 'mostly'?"

"But chief, a step like changing one's family name can't be taken in one day."

"Wait a second. 'One day' you say. But Mr. Wakuta, who has the counties of P'och'ŏn, Kap'yŏng, and Yangju, and Mr. Ninomiya, who has Yangp'yŏng and Kwangju, have both achieved seventy percent. Why have you only thirty-seven percent? Do you think Mr. Wakuta managed this in one day?"

"Chief, that's because Mr. Wakuta and Mr. Ninomiya have forced the people. The directive says that family names should be changed voluntarily. I've been trying to get them to change their names willingly."

"Don't talk nonsense. Of course that's what the directive says. But Koreans won't move until they're forced to. How in the world can you make them change their names by sitting at your desk and writing letters to the district office! At our last meeting we carefully laid out the tricks to get the job done. Yet you . . . fellows like you are no good!"

"Fellows like you." I suppose he meant my young artist friends who gathered at the Domino Bar on Meiji Street. Recently one of my buddies had had too much to drink there and got into an argument with an offensive military police-man posing as a civilian. My friend landed in jail. I had to bail him out and assume custody. The chief must have heard about it.

"In any case, you must achieve one hundred percent by next March. Understand?"

Without replying, I dipped my head and left him.

As many of you already know, name conversion was a policy of assimilation that the Japanese imposed in the colonies of Korea and Taiwan. It was an attempt to make Japanese out of their populations by forcing them to take Japanese names. It was part of the scheme heralded under the slogan "Japan and Korea Unified." It was one of the most arrogant measures carried out in Korea.

When I began my job it never occurred to me that this conversion-of-names program had ulterior motives. On the contrary, I regarded it as a boon to the Koreans, who had suffered from discrimination. When I was assigned to this duty I thought, "This is certainly more meaningful than building an antiaircraft position."

I was truly innocent, ignorant of reality. My father was a government official. When I was five we moved to Seoul, where I went through primary and middle schools. When we returned to Japan I went to a school of fine arts. But I missed Korea and returned to Seoul, relying on my elder sister and her husband.

I thought I knew something about the Korean people and their lives, and I sincerely believed that the conversion of names would help them. In those days the Koreans were oppressed into a condition of slavery. As a child I pitied them, but I never questioned how or why they had been tyrannized. Only after I went to art school did I become aware of the cruel methods used in the Japanese occupation of Korea. Even then, what I was told was only superficial.

Despite the slogan "Japan and Korea Unified," the Japanese scorned the Koreans. Even Japanese children showed contempt, using expressions like *yobo,* which the Koreans deeply resented. A Korean word, *yobo* originally meant "hello," but in the mouths of the Japanese it implied "you slave." By taking Japanese names the Koreans could speak and be spoken to as equals, and longtime Japanese residents of Korea did not welcome this: they would not so easily shed the contempt they had cultivated for thirty years.

My job was to enforce the conversion of names in Kyŏnggi Province, the capital district. I had no interest in politics and neither did my comrades at the Domino Bar. When I told them about my job, one of them said, "Huh! Do you think that changing Korean names like Kim and Pak into Japanese names like Kaneda and Kinoshita will unify Japan and Korea? What nonsense!" My friends were cynical about everything, and in their negative attitude demonstrated their sense of futility by hanging out in a colonial bar.

Kyŏnggi Province was divided into five areas parceled out to the five members of our section. I was assigned the counties of Sihŭng, Suwŏn, and Chinwi. My area was the smallest in size but the largest in population.

There were no Koreans working in either the First (mine) or Second Sections of our office, which was called General

Authority and which was under the General Affairs Department, which reported to the provincial governor, who took orders directly from the governor-general. My chief constantly bragged about this. After a month in the office I understood why our position in the organization was so close to the governor-general. We were charged with publicizing and enforcing policies in a manner that would give the Koreans no choice but to comply. In the conversion of names, for example, this was typical of our propaganda: "The Korean people have strong aspirations to work side by side with the citizens of Japan, who today lead the world. And every Japanese hopes that Korea will be unified with Japan. However, the Koreans have suffered discrimination because they are judged by their names. The Japanese and the Koreans share the same ancestors and physical features; the only difference between them lies in their names. Until now, complicated qualifications and procedures have made it very difficult for Koreans to become naturalized Japanese. But now, in response to urgent requests from the Korean people, the governor-general has made the momentous decision to implement the conversion of names in order to solve burdensome problems for the Koreans, including discrimination."

What was the real intention behind honeyed propaganda about equal rights? It was to put the Koreans in the same position as the Japanese, subject to military conscription, labor service, payment of taxes, and delivery of rice quotas. It was nothing but a change from voluntary to compulsory service. (Significantly, the Pacific War soon erupted, consuming enormous numbers of soldiers.) When I became aware of this, I was appalled. I finally realized the nature of politics.

Naturally, I didn't want to go to the front, and neither did the young men of Korea. They hadn't started the war. How would they feel when they were told, "You are now Japanese in mind and body. Take your physical examination!"? They would have to stand naked in line and sign for the draft on red paper. Shocked, they would realize that the conversion of names concealed a hook and that equality with the Japanese meant battlefields for them. As this dawned on me, I became depressed. To urge name conversion in glowing terms was to deceive the Koreans.

"We Japanese men face conscription. When Koreans change their names, of course they should be drafted as we Japanese are. They can't have the rights and reject the duties." That was Ninomiya speaking. He and I had joined our section at the same time. There was logic in what he said, but to me the method was unfair. Instead of using sweet words to disguise the hook, I thought we should expose it. That would prevent both criticism from the Japanese, who thought the governor-general was spoiling the Koreans, and misunderstanding by the Koreans, who thought only of the equal rights offered.

When I looked into it, I found that the Japanese had been very shrewd in promoting name change. Some wealthy and influential Koreans were given Japanese names as though they were ranks or titles. Some of these Koreans put both their Japanese and their Korean names on their business cards; the newspapers used their Japanese names. Respect for government officials and condescension toward commoners and civilians was ingrained among Koreans, and the authorities took advantage of this trait. They first aroused a desire for Japanese names by giving them to prominent figures, and then they began to promote name conversion.

At first the Koreans, out of caution, did not comply. Then other means were devised. Special benefits were given to those who changed their names. For instance, only students with Japanese names passed the entrance examinations to get into the university. Suddenly the number of applicants for name change increased among the Korean intelligentsia. A desire for benefits is characteristic of the masses. Name conversion increased in popularity.

About that time, the Japanese authorities abandoned their soft approach and became forceful. A fisherman doesn't offer bait to a fish already caught. After the preparatory phase in which Koreans themselves requested conversion, Governor-General Minami Jirō issued orders to each provincial governor,

and government officials began to coerce name changes in
every district of Korea.

According to the norm imposed by my chief, I was supposed to complete eighty percent of my assignment by the end
of the year and to finish by the end of the following March.
Once I knew their devices, I didn't feel like doing my job, yet
what could I do? I felt like a minister of justice who hesitates to
sign an order for an execution.

To evade the draft I had no choice but to perform my duties
faithfully, unless I found another job. Rumor was that Koreans
were being routed out of bed in the middle of the night or
seized while they worked in their fields and shipped away to
labor in the mines of Hokkaidō or Kyūshū. If the authorities
waited for the Koreans to volunteer, the quotas would never be
filled, so the labor sections of the district offices began to use
force. "No work, no food."

"It's not a joke," I told myself. "Who can guarantee that I'll
be safe from the draft if I leave this position?" I was still young
and self-absorbed. Under the circumstances I wanted not a
studio and French brushes to paint with, but just a conven-
tional attitude toward my job. If one brings no conviction or
passion to his work, what can keep him going but a formal
sense of proper behavior? Should a mountain climber taking
shelter behind a rock in violent storm be called a coward? I
wrestled these questions as I watched my friends being shipped
to the front or to labor in factories.

Sŏl Chin-yŏng was the reason my district was behind in
name conversion. He was the greatest landlord in the area, and
his clan had a long and illustrious lineage. Because of that, he
refused to change his name. He said, "If I change my family
name, what excuse can I offer to my ancestors?" Since the Sŏl
clan would not change their name, neither would thousands of
other families in the district. When the greatest landholder
refused, why should small tenants comply?

It would have been easier for us if Sŏl Chin-yŏng had
refused to change his name because of Korean patriotism or
feelings against Japan. I could have converted hatred of Japan

toward the righteous cause. But he was staunchly pro-Japanese
and had been making annual donations of a hundred thousand
bushels of rice to the Japanese army in Korea.

A year after the war with China began, Sŏl heard that the
Japanese army needed rice. His offer to donate rice was greeted
with skepticism, but the next day the quantity of rice delivered
to the Yongsan depot left Chief of Staff Ohara breathless. A
hundred thousand bushels of rice would feed three divisions for
a year. A surprised journalist asked Sŏl, "How can you manage
if you give up the tenant fees for the whole year?" He answered,
"I can pay my taxes and cover my living expenses out of my
savings. The soldiers are risking their lives. I am just doing my
part." Because he was so clearly pro-Japanese, even the district
office could not force him to change his name. Not knowing
how to handle him, they had to accept the situation.

Respect for one's ancestors was easy to understand. It was
doubtful that taking Japanese names would make the Koreans
happier. Had the situation been reversed, would the Japanese
have changed their names to Yi or Pak and been loyal to
Korea? Would the feelings of a people robbed of their country,
their language, and even their names be so easily pacified?

It seemed to me that the Koreans' blood and emotions
were thicker and deeper than my section chief could fathom.
Governor-General Minami had given a party to honor the aged.
He had invited some influential elderly Koreans and attended
in Korean costume. The newspapers played it up with photos
of him under banner headlines like "He Himself Demonstrates
the Unification of Japan and Korea."

I realized that the unification of Japan and Korea was not
going to be achieved by Governor-General Minami's attending
a party in Korean costume or by the Koreans' speaking Japanese and taking Japanese names, but to my profound regret I
was engaged in polluting this nation by enforcing those policies. Yet though I was clearly aware of the misfortunes that
would result from the conversion of names, I hesitated to leave
my job. The mountain climber seeking shelter behind a rock in
a storm finds an unexpected obstacle; to save himself he must

close his eyes and kick the obstacle to the bottom of the valley. It was really not my fault. Working in First Section, General Authority, I was just following orders. Still, I wandered in a dark valley of doubt, frustrated and feeling guilty. I was under tremendous pressure. A leaf fallen into a rushing stream has no chance to stop, think, or look back; it is just tumbled down the stream, hoping that it will not be crushed by rocks or sucked into a whirlpool. When I left the chief's desk I felt like such a leaf, helpless to escape the current. I made a decision: "I will visit Sŏl Chin-yŏng. He can't be so obstinate if he is so pro-Japanese."

The next day I took the Kyŏngbu line from Seoul, my first trip in the line of duty. To get to Sŏl Chin-yŏng's I was told to get off at a small station called Pyŏngjŏm and walk for half an hour along the highway.

The dusty road ran along a small stream lined with poplar trees. The leaves of the poplars and the grass on the banks were turning brown, and the hands of the peasant women washing their laundry in the cold stream were red. In the weak sun of early winter the white jackets and skirts spread on the dry grass looked chill. The broad rice fields were striking, stretched along the highway with their neatly stacked rows of straw. I should have come earlier, I thought, visualizing golden rice rippling in the autumn breeze as far as the eye could see, red dragonflies gliding over the noisy locusts. The half hour stretched to an hour, and I began to feel uneasy among these endless fields. Finally, at the foot of the mountain on my right, I saw a village. At its center there was no mistaking the big Sŏl residence, old, stately, surrounded by an earthen wall.

As I came closer, the earthen wall turned out to be a row of small houses, tenements built around the main building. I stepped inside the gate. White-bearded old men sat on the thresholds of their houses, leisurely smoking in the sun. In a clump of trees there was a spring, rare in this landscape, and to the rear were persimmon trees hung with ripe fruit.

The old men ignored me, an intruder. Without changing their position, one knee drawn up, they continued to smoke. In this country it was customary for a rich family to take care of their relatives within the family compound. The little houses were for the dependents of Sŏl Chin-yŏng. The indifference of these old hangers-on amused me. They reminded me of the relaxed old Korea, untouched by the war outside.

I pushed open the squeaking, moss-covered doors of the inner gate and mounted stone steps to the main building. I gave my name card to a man who looked like a butler and told him I wanted to see Sŏl Chin-yŏng.

Sŏl Chin-yŏng was, I suppose, about fifty-four or fifty-five, a gentle-looking man whose round face and mild manner told me that the people of his area placed great trust in him. He introduced the young woman who brought us ginseng tea. "This is my daughter Ok-sun. She graduated from a girls' school just last spring." Still holding my name card, he went on, "Excuse me, Mr. Tani, but aren't you an artist?"

His question, coming before I had stated my business, disconcerted me. For the past few years I had been painting scenes of Korea. One of my works had received an award in the Korean Exhibition, and it must have caught his attention. At that moment I hated the title on my name card: Tani Rokurō, First Section, General Authority.

With a smile, Sŏl Chin-yŏng said that, since his Japanese was not very good, his daughter would act as interpreter. The outer appearance of the house was traditionally Korean, but the drawing room where we sat was as modern as a fine hotel. The floor was covered with a thick carpet, and a costly leather sofa had been placed casually in the middle of the room. Somehow the father and daughter in their Korean costumes fit beautifully in that room.

"My daughter likes to paint, and the art teacher at her school, Mr. Hayashi, has encouraged her. Thanks to her, I often go to art exhibitions. If I remember correctly, Mr. Tani, you painted a scene of nŏlttwigi last year."

Nŏlttwigi is a kind of seesaw game that Korean girls play on a long board balanced on a bundle of straw. Young girls in colorful New Year's dress, jumping up and down with their long skirts flying in the cold air, are an ideal subject. I had painted such a scene and entered it in the exhibition.

"You remember it well," I replied, and felt a little happier. I turned to Ok-sun. "You must be a graduate of F Girls' High School since you studied with Mr. Hayashi." Hayashi had attended my alma mater.

Sŏl Chin-yŏng put his hands on his gray hair and looked at his daughter with deep affection. Quietly, I took time to savor the flavor and fragrance of the tea. For a moment I relaxed, but then my mood darkened. I had presented my official name card: I couldn't leave without discussing official business.

"The fact is," I began, in a voice that seemed to stick in my throat, "that I came here to ask a favor with regard to the conversion of names." It seemed that both Sŏl Chin-yŏng and Ok-sun had already guessed why I was there, yet they appeared to listen carefully.

I began to speak. My memory has faded and I can't recall exactly what I said. I must have been very tense, trying to be persuasive. I could only put forth government propaganda, and I was too poor a salesman to sell inferior merchandise.

Sŏl Chin-yŏng listened, nodding. Ok-sun's calm brown eyes seemed to see through me, and I couldn't hide my distraction. I concentrated my gaze on the master of the house; words tumbled out in a frenzy. My heart pounded. I sounded as if I were trying to persuade myself rather than Sŏl Chin-yŏng. I told how in European hotels even Chinese guests signed their names in Japanese to make it appear that they were Japanese; how Koreans and Japanese shared blood and ancestors although the Japan Sea lying between us made us feel different; and how Koreans everywhere now wished for conversion of names, for, as the proverb put it, "Names reveal physique." I sounded possessed.

"Mr. Tani, I quite understand you, but no matter what you say I cannot change my family name of Sŏl. If I change my given name to Japanese, won't that do? If in my generation the family name is abandoned, I can give no excuse to my ancestors. . . ." As he spoke he left the room, soon returning with a large box of documents: the clan records.

In Korea the first son, the senior member of the clan, was obliged to record in detail every event concerning clan members, including marriages, births, and deaths. Those documents chronicled the noble history of the Sŏl over seven hundred years. I had heard of clan records, but for the first time I saw them.

As I thought of how those records had been diligently kept for the past seven hundred years and how they would be continued into the future, the history of the Sŏl clan swelled in my mind. I had heard that the royal clan, the Yi, many of whose records had been destroyed in warfare, had documents for only three hundred years. Sŏl Chin-yŏng said that the box before me held the records for only the past hundred and fifty years. Four more boxes were stored away.

"You see, Mr. Tani, . . ." Sŏl Chin-yŏng opened parts of the documents and explained that he was showing me only the records that he had compiled since becoming head of the clan. "My father, my grandfather, and my great-grandfather faithfully maintained these records with pride in the tradition of our clan. If I change my family name, no longer will anything be recorded under the name of Sŏl, which means that the Sŏl clan will end with my generation. I cannot do that, Mr. Tani. Please allow us to keep the surname Sŏl."

"Do you mean that the Chinese character for Sŏl should remain unchanged? If so, that is not changing your name, Mr. Sŏl."

"Some Japanese names are written with one character. Yours is, Mr. Tani. The character for the name Sŏl cannot be changed."

"I'm afraid that won't do, Mr. Sŏl. The Japanese authorities do not have a sense of humor. They will not magnanimously permit you to keep the single character of your Korean name but pronounce it in the Japanese way."

"In that case, Mr. Tani, I cannot change my family name or my given name. It may sound ridiculous to you, but my ancestors are very important to me. I cannot permit myself to put an end to seven hundred years of clan history. I won't do it. I will do anything else—I will donate rice and money. But not change my name. My ancestors would lament and my descendants would be embittered. When I think of this I must refuse . . . I can do nothing but refuse. . . ." His voice broke and there were tears in his eyes.

Grasping the old records with both hands, this notably pro-Japanese Korean landholder silently wept and shook his head. I was speechless. I wanted to find words to console him, but I wavered. Unless he changed his name, his tenants and neighbors would not change theirs. Once more I appealed, rubbing my hands so hard I chafed them.

"I understand, Mr. Tani. I will speak to my tenants and tell my relatives to change their names. But please excuse my case. Exempt the main family of the Sŏl clan." Sŏl Chin-yŏng wiped away his tears.

I had no confidence that he could carry out his aim. If he could prevail upon his tenants to change their names, the district officials who were close to the situation could have done it long ago. It was understood that he cherished his clan records, but no one in this area was going to change his name unless Sŏl Chin-yŏng did. "He is a cancer in this effort," I said to myself.

I tried to convince. I whispered to my conscience: "I can't let sympathy sway me. I must carry out my mission to survive. I must be a heartless government official, dedicated to duty." Straightening my back to hide my lack of confidence, I focused on Sŏl Chin-yŏng's lowered countenance and began again. "The conversion of names is a benefit especially designed for the Koreans," I repeated as if reciting an incantation. It was no use. Every empty word turned on me like an arrow in my heart.

Must I survive by harming others and deceiving myself? I felt a spiritual pain sharper than the torment of forced labor.

Although I mistrusted the conversion of names, I had a duty to enforce it. Step by step I was approaching tragedy. Loneliness invaded my heart. I was seized by an impulse to scream like a madman. I was utterly miserable.

Suddenly the room was lighted. Unconsciously I sighed. I was weary. With the lamps lighted the room seemed darker. I thought I should leave. I would give in. I would let him go through the procedure of changing his name by retaining the character for Sŏl but pronouncing it Japanese-style, as Masaki. But though I came to this decision I was dejected, not from a sense of failure but from a premonition of disaster.

When Sŏl Chin-yŏng refused to change his name, the seeds of disaster were planted in his family; but the pretext that the conversion of names was voluntary on the part of the Koreans robbed me of power to coerce him. Letting him keep the character for Sŏl but pronounce it in the Japanese fashion was my only way of paying respect to this father and daughter who had liked my painting. Perhaps it was also the only way I could show resistance to the conversion of names.

When I was about to say goodbye, Sŏl Chin-yŏng held me back, and presently Ok-sun, who had left, returned. "It's nothing special," she said, "but some Korean dishes are ready. You might find them interesting." I could easily have refused, but that might have hurt their feelings. Besides, I was drawn to these people. I accepted, something unusual for me, because I had always been reserved, even unsociable.

I was led into a small, Korean-style room with a heated floor. The simple decoration was a red carpet. A variety of dishes was laid out on the table. The liquor was rice wine, and the cups held almost three ounces. As I ate dishes of braised meat and dried fish I emptied several cups. The drink went to my head, and I began to feel a dull ache.

Sŏl Chin-yŏng began to hum an old Korean folk song. A sense that I was really in Korea crept over me. His song was a familiar one, about young women in springtime gathering the white flowers called toraji for their edible roots. The simple song somehow troubled me, and I drank more.

"I have never seen my father like this," said Ok-sun, who seemed straightforward in expressing her feelings. She poured me another cup of the hot liquor, and almost under her breath said, "Please don't torture my father. I feel so sorry for him."

I felt as though I were being whipped. As she watched her tipsy father I stared at her pleasing face. I was not torturing Sŏl Chin-yŏng, but what could I say? I nodded and finished my cup. Why were these Korean songs so sad? Were these melancholy tunes telling me the fate of this race? Heightened by her appeal, the pathos of the melodies overwhelmed me. My corruption tormented my conscience. . . .

Almost three months passed. Winter was severe. Outside, the wind from the northern mountains blasted the frozen streets. In our office, the limit on coal consumption meant that we were always cold. Standing in front of the chief's desk, I tried to warm my toes by wriggling them in my shoes. As usual, the chief looked severe, furrowing his brow as he studied some papers. I knew that they were reports from my districts.

He raised his head. "Ah, Mr. Tani." His tone was cold. By this time I had learned to ignore his affectations and, besides, I had been working diligently. I made schedules, visited district offices, and met, encouraged, and persuaded influential Koreans in my territory. My weapon was to state, "Even Mr. Sŏl Chin-yŏng has presented an application to change his name." It worked. Many landholders in the district decided to comply. By the New Year season almost eighty percent of the Koreans in my districts had applied for Japanese names. The change was remarkable. I concentrated only on my job. The chief seemed surprised at my success and appeared to have a higher opinion of me. Complacently I told myself, "Now you see what you can do if you really try."

"One of your districts has sent me this report. You know Sŏl Chin-yŏng, do you not?"

A sense of foreboding sobered me. "So," I thought, "it didn't work." I had known that Sŏl Chin-yŏng's application would not be easily accepted. That was why I had met with the chief clerk of the district office, explained the situation, and sought his understanding.

"Yes, I do. He is very pro-Japanese. Is something wrong?"

"Yes, something is wrong. He has not changed his name."

"That can't be true. I know that his papers have been filed. I remember that he changed his name to Masaki Eiichi."

"Do you really think that is a proper change? Did you permit him to use that name?"

Then I remembered the greed on the face of the district chief clerk as he repeatedly said, "Sŏl Chin-yŏng is the richest landowner around here. They say he can go from Pyŏngjŏm to Suwŏn without leaving his own land. He owns so much land . . ." Why didn't I realize that he was hinting at a bribe? Maybe I should have alerted the Sŏl family. Seeing me wordless, the chief was about to continue. Hastily I began.

"But chief, the Sŏl family has a remarkable clan record stretching back seven hundred years. In this family-oriented country, landed families have kept detailed clan records to hand down to their descendants. Most of their precious records were destroyed in Hideyoshi's invasion. The survival of the Sŏl records is very rare. Changing the way their name is written will extinguish the records of the Sŏl clan. That is why Sŏl Chin-yŏng resisted so strongly. So I tried—"

"So you permitted him to change Sŏl to Masaki without changing the way his name is written. Is that what you are saying, Mr. Tani?"

"Was I wrong? Since I understood his situation I thought an exception could be made in his case. Some Japanese have a one-character name. I thought it was interesting to keep his character and read it in the Japanese way."

"What? What do you think you are doing? Are you Japanese or Korean? You thought it *interesting!* You must be joking. The conversion of names is not for amusement. You had no right to do this. Go and have him change his name at once!"

"But chief, Mr. Sŏl is highly regarded by the military headquarters because he donated rice. So I thought that for him an exception might be made."

"What are you talking about? Such an exception can be

made only by the governor-general. Besides, according to this report, all of his tenants have taken one-character names like Kin for Kim or Boku for Pak. I'm sure it's his idea."

"No, chief. Sŏl Chin-yŏng is not that kind of man."

"You really stick up for him, don't you? At a time like this, no one should be concerned about such things as family records. You must force him. That's the only way."

"But chief, I understand that the royal family, the Yi, have not changed their name."

"Don't speak disrespectfully. I don't want to send you to the military police for this. The Yi family are the royal family. Sŏl Chin-yŏng is a mere commoner. If he is so pro-Japanese he should be happy to create a new clan record with his generation. Make him change his name. Do you understand, Mr. Tani?"

"I will do my best." I bowed angrily.

"Wait. Look at this." His voice was harsh. He pushed a paper in front of me. It was from one of my districts.

"This is about the conversion of names. What's wrong?"

"Read the name."

"Hirokawa Hitoshi. Isn't it acceptable?"

"For an artist you're not very sensitive, are you? It's not a mere name. He dared to ridicule the name of our Emperor Hirohito. He has inserted *kawa* between *hiro* and *hito* using the same characters as emperor's name. This is apparently a case of lese majesty."

"But chief, that's too far-fetched."

"You always talk back with a 'but.' That's not good. Only liberals use that word. Go to the military police immediately."

"The military police?"

"Yes, to the military police, where the one who called himself Hirokawa Hitoshi is being interrogated. They want one of us to be present at the interrogation. Go and tell them very politely that since your chief is in conference with the governor, you have come in his place. Be sure to apologize. Say that we did not know about the name and that nothing like it will happen again."

"You mean I have to apologize?"

"Of course. As my representative."

"I see."

"They're irate. They say that this Korean has insulted our imperial family, so take care with your language."

"I understand." I was imagining the interrogation by the military police. I recalled the insane brutality suffered at their hands by my Domino Bar friend. When I bailed him out he couldn't stand by himself. He was half dead. His face was bloody and swollen, his breath came in harsh gasps, he could scarcely speak. The military police said arrogantly that they had given him "a little kick" because of his erroneous ideology, and glared at me for looking angry. "Little kicks" were games they played to spice their daily routine. The only way to avoid such interrogation was to make a false confession; then one would either land in a cold jail or be forced to enlist for immediate shipment to the battlefield. I knew that that poor Korean would be beaten senseless.

From Pyŏngjŏm Station I again walked along the highway. It was frozen white. The bare branches of the poplar trees trembled in the piercing north wind. My toes were numb in their thick boots. My ears ached, and the cold blasts penetrated my coat. The snow-covered rice fields were a frigid expanse. There would be more snow.

As soon as I had returned from the military police, the chief had ordered me to go to Sŏl Chin-yŏng's. It was already late; I told him I couldn't get back that day.

"You fool!" he shouted. "Stay there until he changes his mind. No matter how many days it takes, make him change his name. Otherwise, don't come back."

Walking the frozen road I became more depressed, more reluctant to face Sŏl Chin-yŏng. "Why do I have to go through this ordeal? It's only to bring credit on the chief." I dragged my heavy boots.

Finally the village came in sight. I stood for a moment. The face of the district chief clerk came back to me. He had got even with me by sending that report to my chief. If only I had been alert enough to tell Sŏl Chin-yŏng that he was greedy. Sŏl Chin-yŏng would have done anything to protect his seven-century-old records. He would have bribed the man lavishly with entertainment and expensive gifts. Why didn't I realize what had to be done? Now Sŏl Chin-yŏng and I must suffer.

Again I was amazed by the chicanery of bureaucracy. Its gears were corroded, but a secret application of golden oil would smooth its operation. My chief coveted that oil.

It was dark when I reached the village. As I walked through it I looked at the names on the tenants' houses. Just as the chief had said, the surnames had all been changed to one-character names like Ch'oe—which in Japanese could be read as Sai—or Chŏng—Japanese, Tei—or Hong—Japanese, Kō. Only the given names were truly Japanese.

The villagers watched me suspiciously. There was menace in the air. In my head a gear spun futilely. I seemed to be walking through a distorted scene in a distorted time.

Sŏl Chin-yŏng was in bed with a cold. Ok-sun helped him to the drawing room. He said he had caught cold five days earlier from waiting in the cold corridors of our provincial office building. He attempted a smile as he coughed painfully.

"How are you now?" I asked.

"I'm all right now." Then he tried to make light of his illness: "My cold must depart because my daughter is to be married next month."

So Ok-sun would soon marry. Early marriage was customary among the Koreans. Rich families usually selected marriage partners when their children were born.

I learned that Ok-sun's fiancé, Kaneda Hokuman, was a relative, the son of a doctor and himself a medical student. Although his family was prominent, they had long since changed their name from the Korean Kim to the Japanese Kaneda; they had no clan records to concern them, and the name change was an advantage to them in running their hospital.

Kaneda Hokuman was now an intern. "Maybe that's why she takes such good care of me," Sŏl Chin-yŏng said with a happy smile, but his cough was painful. Ok-sun put a fur vest on her father and blushed as she gently stroked his back.

The affection they displayed almost softened my resolve,

but I reminded myself that I was no longer an artist; I worked in a government office. I waited desperately for an opening to state my business. I could not be too sympathetic.

"Mr. Sŏl," I began formally, "Mr. Sŏl, your Japanese name Masaki Eiichi has been disapproved. I was chastised by my superior and I have come back to ask you to change your name again."

"I know why you have come tonight," he said drily. "I too was called in and castigated."

"I truly understand how you feel about your lineage. But Mr. Sŏl, I am only a worker in a government office. I can't help you; neither do I intend to force you. But since you have filed one application to change your name, can't you reconsider and take a different name?" I felt tongue-tied, threatened by the chief's livid face and grim edict.

"Is that so . . . just as I thought."

"I explained your special circumstances to my superior. But all of your neighbors have imitated you, Mr. Sŏl."

He remained silent. Wiping the perspiration from my forehead, I asked him not to complicate matters any further. I wanted him to survive this ordeal with as little pain as possible, yet I could not bring myself to suggest that he bribe my chief. Would that be only a cowardly way to protect myself? There seemed to be a strange beast inside me, coldly watching my behavior, scornfully telling me not to let sympathy supplant justice.

With a hopeful voice, Sŏl Chin-yŏng told me that a professor of history at Keijō Imperial University (Keijō was the Japanese name for Seoul and hence the name of the university the Japanese founded there) had urged him to preserve the clan records as precious documents. "Mr. Tani, what do you think of my asking the professor to speak to your chief on my behalf?"

For an instant I thought, "That's a way out." In the next instant I knew that such action would only provoke my chief to more cruelty against the Sŏl clan. The seven hundred years of history in the clan records had no interest for the chief. All he cared about was carrying out the orders of the governor-general.

I had failed. I had failed to be heartless. I had exposed my weakness to Sŏl Chin-yŏng. I felt like crying.

"Mr. Sŏl, my chief told me not to return until you were persuaded."

For a moment his face went hard, but he quickly regained his composure. In the instant that he showed anger I forgot my resentment against the conversion of names and the unification of Japan and Korea. I no longer felt guilty. I just wanted Sŏl Chin-yŏng to change his name without more trouble. Or should we, at the risk of being thought cowardly, actuate the machine with oil?

I remembered the miserable figure of the young Korean who had called himself Hirokawa Hitoshi. His bloody, swollen face, the forehead torn by hobnailed boots, was superimposed on the gentle face before me. Instead of Sŏl Chin-yŏng I saw the tortured young Korean. I wondered if Sŏl Chin-yŏng could stand up to that hellish brutality. I sank into irritation and frustration.

Sŏl Chin-yŏng did not give in. He insisted that he was not anti-Japanese. He declared that his patriotic loyalty to Japan was genuine. He was humble but he refused to change his name.

"Unless you change your name the consequences may be terrible. I can foresee . . ." My voice had become strident. Sŏl Chin-yŏng stared and mocked me with deliberate calm.

"I have sincerely contributed to the welfare of Japan. I don't believe that the Japanese government will treat me badly just because I won't change my name. You say 'the consequences will be terrible'! Do you mean they will impose higher taxes and a bigger rice quota? Japan is at war: I don't mind paying higher taxes and donating more rice. Besides, the conversion of names is not required by law. If it were, I might have to reconsider."

I realized that we Japanese had nothing to match the faith and trust of the Korean. I was utterly baffled. My head sank.

I spent the night at Sŏl's. The room with the heated floor
was warm and comfortable. I was confused and worn out. I
slept the sleep of exhaustion.

I stayed for three days. When we met at every meal I tried
to persuade him. Finally I gave up.

The next morning I received a telegram from my chief:
"Return immediately." I took my leave.

"Next time, Mr. Tani, come for pleasure, not business." Sŏl
Chin-yŏng shook hands and bowed to express his sadness.

Ok-sun insisted on accompanying me to the station though
I repeatedly asked her not to. The sky was clear and blue and
empty. The wind across the frozen fields shook the poplars.

"My father is obstinate, Mr. Tani. Please don't feel bad."
She saw my black expression and apologized, but she added
that her father was right.

"Do you know the Japanese expression that it's safer to go
with the strong one?" Again I tried to explain that refusing to
change their name would hurt their family. The governor-
general was trying to transform the Koreans into Japanese by
changing their names. In actuality the intent was to destroy the
strong nationalism of the Korean people. That meant destroying their clan records. The Sŏl family would soon find that
refusing to change their name would bring greater tragedy than
changing their name.

"Do you want your father in jail?"

"In jail?" It was as though she were whispering to herself.

After that she walked in silence. Repeatedly I told myself
that this was a chance to tell her that her father could escape
this dilemma if he would just bribe the chief. I tried to speak
before we reached the station, but her silence stopped me. I
could not speak of bribery. I couldn't let her think that I too
wanted a bribe. Lamely, I said, "I may look like a devil to you.
I don't like this kind of job. But there are times when one can't
paint. I want to produce one good painting. But I can't."

As I gazed out the train window on the way back, anger
grew in me. Sŏl Chin-yŏng's firm determination was admirable,
but I was stung by his refusal to take my advice. Doubts

assailed me. I felt disgusted with myself. The motion of the
train numbed me. It seemed that only the shell of Tani Rokurō
swayed there.

The chief was impatient to hear my report. My four days'
effort was of no concern. When he heard the bad news his voice
rose. "What? That man pro-Japanese? He must be a nationalist." He called the chief clerk and dismissed me. "We'll handle
this now, in a different way. It's a good case. Leave this affair to
us and go on with your other duties." His tone indicated that I
had failed because I was weak.

I was relieved that I would not have to face Sŏl Chin-yŏng
again, but when I saw the chief wearing the same expression I
had seen on the faces of the military police as they tortured the
poor Korean, relief turned to worry.

Name conversion had stalled at about ninety percent. Most
of those who had refused to change their names were persons
of influence—landowners, ministers, doctors. The chief saw the
case of Sŏl Chin-yŏng as a chance to teach them a lesson.

Ten days later an official letter summoned Sŏl Chin-yŏng to
the office of the provincial governor. After careful investigation,
ranking officials had decided that his case was delicate and that
the governor should see him personally. And my chief must
have thought that this Korean with his strong sense of pro-
priety would bow to the governor.

At the office I was told that someone had come to see me.
In the hallway I found Sŏl Chin-yŏng in traditional Korean
dress, his gentle face pale and taut after the long walk in the
bitter wind. I took him to the janitor's room downstairs and
again pleaded with him.

"Mr. Sŏl, I am going to ask you one more time. The conversion of names has almost legal force now. If you will take a
two-character Japanese name, everything will go smoothly.
You can still maintain your clan records, can't you?" I was
desperate to persuade him. Tragedy was already casting its dark
shadow over him. I couldn't bear to see this pure-spirited man
fall into disaster. The harder he fought, the more tragic would
be the consequences.

"So it's about that," he muttered. "Just as I thought." But I saw the same determination in his eyes.

That morning the chief clerk had secretly told me their scheme. If Sŏl Chin-yŏng did not change his name that day, his daughter's fiancé, Kaneda Hokuman, intern at the Severance Medical School, was to be arrested as a political criminal. Sŏl Chin-yŏng couldn't know this and I could not tell him, but I wanted to grab his shoulders and shake him as hard as I could. I wanted to call him "Fool!" I wanted to force him to change his name.

He was politely led to the governor's office. There he had lunch with the governor, who tried his best to change his mind. It was no use. I knew the attempt was futile, but when I heard the result I shuddered. Now I could only look on. But hadn't I brought him to this? Wasn't my naiveté the cause of it all—my ignorance of the ways of the world?

I was in despair, but about four o'clock in the afternoon the chief returned from the governor's office gleeful and smelling of liquor. Smiling and talkative, he rattled on to the chief clerk. "It was the governor's decision to go rather slowly with Sŏl Chin-yŏng, since he has been so pro-Japanese and we didn't want to irritate military headquarters. We have various options. You know, it is thanks to Sŏl Chin-yŏng that I, only a section chief, could talk with the governor on intimate terms. He seems to like me. He invited me to go with him to Shimmachi tonight." Shimmachi was the entertainment district.

I was disgusted—disgusted that he was happy to promote himself through the misfortunes of others, disgusted by the chief clerk's fawning on him. I looked at my watch. It was about time for the military police to arrest Ok-sun's fiancé and take him away to be tortured in a cold prison cell. I went to the window to suppress my anger. Mount Pukhan soared in the late afternoon light. The governor-general's slogan, "Japan and Korea Unified," was carved on the side of the mountain, but I could see only splotches of white snow on its rocky surface.

I wanted to scream. Every nerve throbbed. I had fallen into a bottomless swamp. I could do nothing. I could not save Sŏl Chin-yŏng.

Two days later, the seventh of February, Ok-sun came into town; she had learned of her fiancé's arrest. She went to the military police but was coldly refused permission to see him. Not knowing what to do, she came to see me at the office. She was pale with anger and tension. Her eyes were accusing. I could not escape consciousness of guilt.

She told me that her father had been ill since his return from Seoul. "I don't want to trouble him, so I came myself." She was tearful. She must have been treated badly by the military police. I could find no words to console her. I got permission to leave and went out with her.

"I will go to the military police myself," I said abruptly. I knew it would do no good, but I wanted to show Ok-sun that I had nothing to do with the arrest. She must have already realized that it was linked to her father's refusal to change his name.

Amenities were growing scarce in Seoul, but there were still a few taxis. I hailed one, dropped her off at her uncle's, and went on to the military police headquarters. It was my third visit to the red brick building in front of Yongsan Station.

I stated that I had come concerning the prisoner Kaneda Hokuman. The man in charge of the case glanced at my name card. Seeing that I was from a government office, he relaxed and grinned. "He's under arrest for subversive ideas."

When I explained that I was there because his fiancée was very worried about him, he was delighted. "That's exactly what we want. When she comes tomorrow, we'll kick him in front of her. Koreans hate the sight of blood. When she sees his nose bleeding she'll moan and faint. Then she'll appeal to her father to help him and in no time at all he'll cave in."

Suddenly I was dizzy. Things went black and I almost fell. I broke out in a cold sweat. Lightning flashed in my head, rainbow circles throbbed at my temples, my stomach contracted and bile rose in my throat. I managed to say, "I will return tomorrow," and headed for the door.

The military policeman escorted me outside to a stream of sadistic boasting. His skin was dark, and he had that repugnant odor peculiar to soldiers. "Tomorrow Sŏl Chin-yŏng is coming

too. We told Kaneda's father that his son would be released if
he had good surety. He was delighted to learn that Sŏl Chin-
yŏng could stand surety. He's gone to get him."

"Is that so?" I thought I replied, though in fact I said
nothing at all. I turned up the collar of my coat and walked
headlong through the windy streets. My dizziness left in the
cold air. The streets of Seoul were bleak under a gray sky. The
passersby looked tired. "They have no dreams," I mumbled to
myself. "They're dried up, exhausted." I shunned the trams,
kept walking.

As expected, Sŏl Chin-yŏng, despite a high fever, appeared
at the military police headquarters the following morning. His
daughter was supposed to be married in a week. He presented
the necessary paper with his signature. The military police
officer looked at it and handed it back. "You must sign with
your Japanese name on an official document." He refused to
listen to Sŏl Chin-yŏng's reasons, pushed another paper at him.
"If you love your daughter, file this application to change your
name at once. Otherwise we cannot process your document to
release her fiancé." At last Sŏl Chin-yŏng realized what they
were doing. He sighed deeply but, still obstinate, said, "Let me
think about it for a day."

I stayed home from work that day because I was afraid that
Sŏl Chin-yŏng and his daughter might come to the office to
see me. But I could not avoid them. That afternoon one of my
sister's children called to me, "Uncle, you have guests."

I went to the vestibule and found them both there, looking
miserable. I almost choked. "We went to your office, but
learned that you were absent because of a cold. We are sorry
to bother you when you are ill, but. . ." Sŏl Chin-yŏng spoke
timidly; he had lost his usual composure.

I invited them to the parlor and lit the gas heater. I felt like
a criminal dragged to court for a hearing, but I couldn't help
being pleased that, after all, they had come to see me.

Sŏl Chin-yŏng gravely explained what had happened at the
military police headquarters and asked if he really had to
change his name to obtain Kaneda's release. He was almost
pleading.

"Do you know anyone," I asked, "who has already changed his name and who can qualify as surety?"

Sŏl Chin-yŏng answered that Kaneda's father had already done his best to find another guarantor for his son but in vain.

"Of course," I thought, "all this has been prearranged solely to make Sŏl Chin-yŏng change his name."

"Mr. Tani, you have been very kind to us in this matter, and I am sorry to trouble you further. But we have no one else to turn to. Please . . ."

I was grateful to him for thinking well of me, but the situation was out of my control. Now that the military police were involved, bribery was out; if only I had suggested a bribe earlier! I blamed myself and, feeling guilty, I repeatedly left them to go to the kitchen, though I had no business in the kitchen.

There was only one way out: to obtain special dispensation from the governor-general exempting Sŏl from changing his name. Sŏl Chin-yŏng had thought of that, of course, and his reply was quick. "That won't do. Governor-General Minami has gone to Tokyo, hasn't he? He won't be back before the date for the wedding." He added that the Keijō Imperial University professor of history who had pressed him to preserve his records had petitioned the governor-general to allow him to keep his Korean name but had not received an answer.

His hair had grown whiter since our first meeting the previous November. Because of his high fever he seemed to have some difficulty breathing; sometimes his shoulders shuddered. His cheeks had become hollow. Yet even in torment, he retained the dignity that bespoke the seven-hundred-year history of his clan.

"I no longer know what to do," he murmured, almost to himself. "So I will let my daughter decide. I will do whatever Ok-sun says."

Ok-sun had been trying to suppress her tears. Now her body was racked with sobs so loud that my surprised sister came into the room.

Sŏl Chin-yŏng's voice trembled. "Ok-sun, Hokuman is your future husband. Choose either him or me. I will abide by your decision."

I was shocked. What was going through his mind? Was he not moved by his pride in Korean nationalism, now even more precious to him than his concern for his ancestors and the clan records? Was his anger not directed at the cunning and cowardice of the Japanese government? As he watched his sobbing daughter his eyes became vacant but his lips were pressed tight. Ok-sun's sobs pierced my heart.

The daily torture of Kaneda Hokuman increased. In their judo hall the military police kicked and whipped him until he lost consciousness. His family cursed Sŏl Chin-yŏng. Hokuman was their only son. His mother screamed at Sŏl Chin-yŏng: "Are you going to kill our only son?" But for Kaneda Hokuman there was no deliverance. Ok-sun chose her father instead of her fiancé.

Kaneda Hokuman was a slight, spoiled young man. He had nothing at all to confess. He had not the slightest idea why he was being tortured, why the military police shouted, "You must be a nationalist! You want to make Korea independent!"

He wanted only to sleep, but he was kicked, hit, and choked. When he passed out they brought him to with buckets of cold water, and the torture went on. At last, to escape his suffering he pressed his thumbprint as his signature on a confession. Only then did one military policeman show some pity and tell him he had been used to make Sŏl Chin-yŏng change his name. At that moment was born his fury against Sŏl Chin-yŏng, Ok-sun, the hated military police, and Japan. Wrapped in a thin blanket, shaking in his cold cell, he cursed all Japanese. A passionate nationalist was born.

On the same afternoon he was released by the military police, he was forced to enlist and was put in a training camp in the suburbs. A red mark was placed by his name in the roll book, and the instructors kicked him as often as they wished. He was constantly injured, and he was not allowed to see his family or even to write to them. But he was no longer the weakling he had been. There were many young Koreans in camp who had been abused as he had been and who shared his bitter-

ness. They plotted together and tried to escape. He was caught
and eventually died in prison.

The second scheme to coerce Sŏl Chin-yŏng was quickly
put in motion: to draft his beloved daughter for labor in the
arsenal at Inchŏn. Since they could not call up only Ok-sun,
they would conscript all the young unmarried women in the
area. I learned of this quite accidentally. During the chief clerk's
absence I took some papers to his desk and among them saw
"A Plan to Draft Seventy Persons for Labor Service, Including
Sŏl Ok-sun." I didn't need to read it to know what was
intended.

That evening I sent a special delivery letter to Ok-sun telling
her to find a job right away. She wrote back that she had no
idea where to find work. We had no time to waste. What came
to mind was the military warehouse where Sŏl Chin-yŏng had
donated rice. Fortunately, some of my high-school classmates
were working there. With an introduction from them, I met the
officer in charge. "Sŏl Chin-yŏng's daughter would like to serve
by working here," I told him.

"Is that the Sŏl Chin-yŏng who donated a hundred thousand bushels of rice?" The officer remembered him, and since
the warehouse needed many people, Ok-sun went to work the
following Monday. I was pleased that one thing had gone well.
I heard that the young women who were sent to the Inchŏn
arsenal were making the Model 38 rifles. I knew little about the
place, but since Ok-sun had been slated to go there it was clear
that the work would be anything but easy. Even I could not
endure labor service for more than ten days. I couldn't bear to
have Ok-sun suffer and come to hate the Japanese government
as a result.

Ok-sun commuted to work from her uncle's home on
Hamaguri Street in Seoul. One day she came to thank me for
arranging the job. She felt fortunate because she had been
assigned to secretarial work at the warehouse, while the girls
who had been drafted slaved in miserable conditions at the
arsenal. "They can't go home even when they get sick," she
said. She knew that those young women were victims because

of her father. "Why are they treating him like an enemy?" she asked sharply. "Has he done anything wrong?"

I felt good because I had been able to block their second maneuver. Imagining the crestfallen faces of my chief and the chief clerk when Ok-sun's name was not among those drafted made me feel at last revenged.

By that time the conversion of names was being enforced in all of Korea as though it were mandatory under law. When the police found Korean names on doors or gates, they walked right into the houses and told the residents they'd be jailed if they didn't change their names. Influential local figures, earlier reluctant, had given up when they were threatened with being labeled anti-Japanese and assessed higher taxes and rice quotas. What had happened to Ok-sun's fiancé was widely known.

However, Sŏl Chin-yŏng knew that name conversion was not yet law. The Japanese could not promulgate a law solely to cover cases like his without admitting failure in their campaign for voluntary compliance and facing loss of prestige as a result. They were desperately trying to sway the holdouts. Sŏl Chin-yŏng was not the only one. Song Yŏng-mok, the governor of Chŏnbuk, and Kim Tae-u, the governor of Kyŏngbuk, had not changed their names, but they held high government rank, while Sŏl Chin-yŏng was an ordinary civilian.

Meanwhile, I was confused and without hope, plagued by self-doubt. My days were meaningless. As I worked on complicated documents I sometimes raised my head and looked at my fellow workers, next to me and across from me. We were like machines, following without question the chief's orders as relayed by the chief clerk. "I cannot be a machine," I muttered to myself, but I knew I was only a cog. Sometimes I seemed to be in a black whirlpool that spun me slowly and heavily, then swiftly and violently.

"One could go mad if he tried to think logically in a situation like this," I said to myself, and tried to accept things as they were. At times I wished to be merely a faithful government official.

Despite the holdouts, the conversion of names was considered complete at the end of May and we were given a new assignment: "Use Japanese." The objective was to make the use of Japanese universal by abolishing publications in Korean: newspapers, magazines, and, of course, elementary-school textbooks. All people under the Japanese emperor had to use the Japanese language. To speak Korean would mark one as anti-Japanese and a shirker in the war effort.

Ridiculous slogans in Japanese were to be recited like incantations: "Pledges to the Imperial Nation." Elementary-school children were required to chant "We are subjects of Great Imperial Japan. We will cooperate loyally to serve our emperor. We will become good Japanese for the sake of our country." The pledge for adults began "We are subjects of the Imperial Nation and we serve our country loyally."

We were ordered to promote the recitation of these pledges by any gathering of five or more people and at all ceremonial occasions. The authorities hoped that repetition of these vows would inculcate loyalty among the Koreans. I found this job distasteful, too.

Around the middle of June I received a letter in beautiful calligraphy from Sŏl Chin-yŏng: "I am truly grateful for the kind consideration you have shown my daughter. Your favor is unmatched in our lives and will never be forgotten."

Reading his letter I wondered how he had been doing. I wanted to help him if I could, but since I was no longer involved in name conversion I had no idea what was being done about him.

When I was a child I saw some children cruelly skinning a live snake. The skinned snake writhed in agony in the grass by the roadside. It finally crawled onto the dirt road and died struggling in the mud. I was reminded of that snake as I thought of Sŏl Chin-yŏng. He was suffering and I was merely watching with clenched fists and bated breath just as in my childhood I had stared at that poor snake.

If only Sŏl Chin-yŏng would change his name—but he wouldn't unless a law was enacted. All that remained to him was his pride in the seven-hundred-year history of his clan. Five thousand years of his nation's history and the language and letters used by three hundred thousand Korean people were being systematically nullified. Now he faced final defeat: loss of his clan name and legacy.

Sŏl Chin-yŏng's obstinacy, his insistence that he would not change his name voluntarily, inflamed the Japanese authorities. Short of a miracle, the outcome was obvious. I sensed that the gray shadow of death was approaching Sŏl Chin-yŏng, its color darkening to mourning black. He was like a terminally ill patient. I had prolonged his life with injections, but shouldn't I have insisted on a radical operation?

Yet all through the summer I received fine melons and pears, with no hint that things were not going well. And so my foreboding came to pass with unexpected suddenness.

On October 2, 1941, a telegram arrived. "Father died. Funeral will be on the sixth. Sŏl family." As I took the telegram from my brother-in-law and read it, my hands trembled.

"How excitable," my brother-in-law laughed, "to send a telegram on the second about a funeral on the sixth." Ignoring him, I opened the curtain of my window. It was raining. Summer had ended; the city of Seoul was at rest. The big, purple grapes in the garden looked cool in the rain.

"Maybe he has been ill," I said to myself, shaking off black thoughts. A man as stubborn as Sŏl Chin-yŏng could not have committed suicide. If he had, why would his daughter send a telegram to me? I was part of the cause.

I walked to the office in the rain. The chief appeared in the office about ten o'clock with a hangover. In the afternoon I was supposed to go to Kaesŏng to attend a lecture on propagating the Japanese language. I put my seal on a paper authorizing my trip and took it to the chief to get my travel expenses. While he brushed his seal to clean it, he smiled and said, "Mr. Tani, you're working hard, aren't you?" And putting his seal on my voucher, he answered himself. "Oh yes."

He leaned back in his chair, his favorite pose when telling section members about his successes.

"Yes?" I asked.

"You know the one who gave you so much trouble—the one who made the rice donation?"

I couldn't believe what I was hearing. How could he already know about Sŏl Chin-yŏng?

"You mean Mr. Sŏl Chin-yŏng?"

"Yes, that Sŏl Chin-yŏng. He finally changed his name on September 30. He gave us so much trouble but at last we have achieved one hundred percent in name conversion!"

"Mr. Sŏl Chin-yŏng has changed his name?" I swallowed and thought to myself, "How could it be possible?"

"So you too are surprised, Mr. Tani? This is what I accomplished by asking the governor's assistance. You thought I couldn't do it, right?" Narrowing his eyes, he sipped the tea that had been brought to him.

Again I felt dizzy. I gripped his desk to steady myself, and insisted, "Chief, it can't be possible. Sŏl Chin-yŏng is dead."

"What? He's dead?" He started half out of his chair. "Are you sure? What was the cause? Suicide?"

Seeing his confusion, I thought that I understood everything. The chief clerk came over and asked in a low voice, "Sŏl Chin-yŏng? Really?" And to himself he muttered, "I'm amazed."

"Yes," I said firmly. "It is true that he is dead but I do not know the cause, accident or illness." But instinctively I knew. "These men have killed him. They hatched one more plot against him."

The accusation was written on my face. The chief sneered and stared back. Again he leaned back in his chair, looked at the ceiling, and said arrogantly, "So, the traitor is dead. We cannot offer him even a stick of incense, can we, chief clerk?"

I was furious. I trembled with anger. White heat struck me like lightning. My fists shook. I could stand no more.

"Chief, take that back! Sŏl Chin-yŏng was a finer man than many Japanese. At least, finer than us . . ." I couldn't control my voice. It grew louder as my feelings overcame me.

"Mr. Tani, when you say 'us' do you include me?"

"Don't criticize the dead! He was not a traitor."

The fury in my voice appalled the people around us. They seemed about to stand. The chief, too, half raised himself from his chair but then got a grip on himself and sat down with a thud. He smiled, trying to appear calm, but the blue veins in his forehead swelled and his lips quivered.

"I see. If he was such a fine man, why did he give us so much trouble over changing his name? Should a fine man act like that?"

I resented his evading the issue. A voice inside me said, "Don't lose your temper; don't say something you'll regret!" I knew that what I was doing could get me into serious trouble. But it was obvious that an underhanded plot had brought down Sŏl Chin-yŏng. I wanted to say so, but I couldn't find the words.

The chief looked hard at all the staff. Taking out his handkerchief, he began to polish his eyeglasses, as if to ignore me. Again I was attacked by disgusting dizziness. My vision darkened and the blood throbbed at the back of my head.

"Chief, you talk about him like that because your only concern is name conversion and you have never seen his clan records. How can you call him a traitor? Would a traitor donate to the army a year's supply of rice without being asked? To me a traitor is a man who keeps a mistress on Meiji Street at a critical time like this and who cares for nothing but his own success. Compared with such a shameful man, Sŏl Chin-yŏng was a far better person. That's what I mean."

The dismayed chief clerk put a restraining hand on my shoulder, trying to stop me. "What are you saying, Mr. Tani?" He looked anxiously at the chief.

"So, I've said it," I thought. And as suddenly as I realized that I was finished in this office, my dizziness disappeared and I was clearheaded. I calmly shook off the chief clerk's hand. The chief was pale, trying to find words to defend himself.

"Chief clerk," I said, "you misunderstand. Was I speaking about our chief? Do you mean to say that he is the traitor who keeps a mistress on Meiji Street? I'm sure our chief is not that kind of man. He must be an honorable man, or he couldn't defame as a traitor a man who gives a hundred thousand bushels of rice to our army." My fluency surprised me.

It seemed that in our office only the chief clerk and I had known the chief's secret. Now it was out. I couldn't see the chief's face, but his clenched hands were shaking and the veins in his forehead stood out.

"In any case, I am going to the Sŏls' house now. I will take leave from my work today." I bowed slightly, returned to my desk, and began to clear it. The chief clerk stared at me blankly, at a loss. Everyone else in the room was very quiet.

"Mr. Tani," the chief called harshly.

I smiled. "I know, chief. I don't think I'll be coming back here. You're going to call me a traitor because I spoke ill of you. You want me to leave because I am a traitor, right?"

The chief clerk rushed toward me. "Apologize at once!"

I shook my head. I felt tears coming to my eyes. "I have cleaned out my desk. You can send Mr. Ninomiya to the lecture in Kaesŏng." I took my briefcase, pushed open the door, and quietly left the room. Carefully, step by step, I descended the stairs.

"I've done something stupid," I thought, and began to feel uneasy. I had cut the ropes with which I had been trying to control my gnawing frustration. I tried to console myself, thinking that those ropes would sooner or later have burst, and that I was better off to cut them.

I looked back at the red brick building. Everybody in the section must be talking about me, calling me a fool. "Yes, I am a fool," I said, but I felt well and relaxed. It was not as though I had lost everything but as though a heavy burden had been lifted from my back. I walked leisurely in the quiet rain.

I recalled that Ok-sun had burst into tears when she had had to choose between her father and her fiancé. Now the father she had chosen was dead. As I thought of her grief the rain became depressing.

Just as I had feared, Sŏl Chin-yŏng had committed suicide. The conversion of names had killed him. As I listened to

Ok-sun tell of her father's death, I was truly ashamed to be a Japanese.

The third plot against Sŏl Chin-yŏng had involved his five grandchildren, all in elementary school. To hurt them, the authorities had used their teachers, who told their students, "Some in this class are not yet Japanese. Those who have not changed their names are not Japanese. They need not come to school after tomorrow." They shamed Sŏl Chin-yŏng's grandchildren. Their classmates had never before dared to tease them, but now they were taunted unmercifully.

The grandchildren had rushed to Sŏl Chin-yŏng as soon as they returned from school, asking why he had not changed their names. He told them it wasn't necessary, but the next day the children came home in tears, saying they couldn't go to school any more because their teachers had told them not to come unless their names were changed. For a day or two, their parents soothed them and sent them to school, but then they all refused to go, saying that the other children were terribly mean to them.

They were too young to understand their grandfather's pride or to appreciate their clan records. All they knew was that their grandfather was wrong, because their teachers had told them so. Daily they pressed him, wearing him down. He loved them and knew from their begging and crying how badly they were being treated. When he found that they had not gone to school for three straight days, he stayed up all night, busy in his room. In the morning he gathered his grandchildren to him. "I am going now to do what you want me to," he told them, "so now you can go to school."

The happy children set off for school, and Sŏl Chin-yŏng went to the district office and presented his application for change of name. When the official examined the application he found that every member of the family had been given a Japanese name, Kusakabe (Grass wall), except the head of the family, Sŏl Chin-yŏng. He asked, "What is your Japanese name, Mr. Sŏl?"

Sŏl Chin-yŏng smiled and gestured apologetically. "I

haven't thought of it yet. I'll do it tonight. Please accept the change for the members of my family today."

He went home forlorn. He stayed in his room until dinner time. After dinner he talked happily with his family and played with his grandchildren. He went to bed at his usual time. At midnight he rose, dressed in clean clothing, went outside, and weighted by a rock plunged into an old well behind the main building.

His body was discovered the next morning when a dog barked unceasingly, circling the well. Telegrams were sent to Ok-sun and to his sons. At home, Ok-sun cradled his cold body and wept bitterly. When his testament addressed to me was found, they telegraphed me.

At their home I opened the letter in the presence of Ok-sun and the other members of the family. I trembled, certain that I faced judgment. But the letter was not at all what I expected. He began by expressing his gratitude for our relationship and asked me to laugh at his foolish behavior in following his ancestors. He continued: "It would be most regrettable to put an end to the Sŏl clan records in my generation. Destroying them would be a shameful waste. I would like to leave them in your hands since you have so well understood and appreciated them. I would be most grateful if you could arrange to donate them to Keijō Imperial University."

The entire letter was written in classical Chinese. As his intent became clear my eyes filled with tears. The letter concluded: "On the twenty-ninth of September, 1941, because the Japanese government has enforced the conversion of names, the clan records of the Sŏl are herewith discontinued. The head of the clan, Chin-yŏng, to express his shame and to apologize to his descendants, now terminates his life along with the clan records."

His body was formally dressed and laid before the family altar. The elaborate rites of the Korean tradition continued for three days. More than six thousand people gathered for the funeral. The casket was carried on a flower-covered ox cart. Dancers performed to console his spirit. Professional mourners, women whose heads were bound with hemp cords, keened their lamentations over the sobbing of family members walking close beside the casket in funeral robes of hemp. The long line slowly advanced to the graveyard. The elderly of the neighborhood said there had never been a funeral like it, but the newspapers gave only a few lines to Sŏl Chin-yŏng's passing. As if on cue from the authorities, the cause of death was reported as "neurotic exhaustion."

I stayed with the family that night to help with the afterburdens of the funeral. I did not sleep well, brooding that my chief had made no appearance and that the wreath sent by the governor seemed somehow insincere.

During the night I heard footsteps in the courtyard. Getting up, I saw Ok-sun bent in exhaustion. When she noticed me she said with a slight smile, "I can't sleep for grieving over my father."

I joined her and slowly began to tell her how I had quit my government job. I didn't mean it as self-defense, but in reply her voice was harsh and loud. "It's too late. Everything is too late!"

Her anger at having lost both her father and her fiancé was so intense that I could find no words in reply. I could only whisper, "Yes, everything is too late now." She said there was no word from Kaneda Hokuman and that she was not permitted to see him. I murmured, "You must find me detestable. Please don't hate me."

Three months passed. I was drafted. The Pacific War had begun. I asked my sister's family and my artist friends not to see me off at the station. I boarded the train and sat alone in a third-class seat, waiting for the train to start. The platform was crowded with people saying good-bye to draftees. All alone, I said to myself, "This is as I wish it to be." I was not lonely. I felt that I was atoning for my mistakes.

Seeking Life amidst Death:
The Last Day of the War

REMEMBERING the last day of the war, August fifteenth of 1945, still fills me with guilt and frustration. On that fateful day I was an insolent, cheating student who went boating on the Han River and enjoyed lascivious fantasies in the darkness of a movie theater while all my classmates in the national labor service were being dazed by the news of Japan's collapse and confused by the meaning of their tears, which flowed without being summoned. Furthermore, on my way home that day, I dealt a hard blow to my friend Hisatake, when he told me about Japan's unconditional surrender.

Why was I so excessively excited as to abuse my good friend? Since this event happened more than ten years ago, my memories of it are not clear; but I can still see most vividly the profile of Hisatake, lying on the pavement of Shōwa Street, while the sky above us glowed with the vermilion light of the setting sun. Even now the memory of this scene makes me writhe with regret. More than once I've tried to find the reason for my conduct, usually deciding that I must have reacted so foolishly simply because I could not really believe that Japan had lost the war. But such a conclusion sounds like the excuse of a pretentious patriot and, even worse, lacks honesty.

Somehow, on the morning of the fifteenth, I suspected that the war had reached its final stage. During the previous night, my father, an official in Japan's government-general of Korea, received a phone call from a subordinate at about three o'clock in the morning. Our telephone was close to my room. The maidservant seemed to be sound asleep, and no one else got up. So I answered the phone and went upstairs to call my father. Covering my head with a sheet, I was trying to go back to sleep, but the surprise in my father's voice reached me now and again. After a while a government car came to pick him up. With a worried look, my father said to my mother and me, standing on the porch to see him off, "Something serious has happened!" and hastened down the stairs.

According to contemporary records, the news about Japan's acceptance of the Potsdam Declaration and the country's unconditional surrender arrived at the Seoul branch office of the Dōmei News Agency at twelve o'clock midnight, at the start of August fifteenth. Of course the news was kept secret until it could be released officially. My father, strictly observing regulations, would not tell us anything at all; he revealed his distress only by admitting, "Something serious has happened!"

However, judging from the agitation of my father, a man I knew to be always calm and quiet, I could imagine that something very important worried the governor-general's staff. That's why, when later in the day Hisatake told me about the surrender, I was neither surprised nor excited.

If anything, I had been a delinquent student since my junior-high-school days. Although I lacked the courage to write love letters to girls (or to dare to buy the comforts of prostitutes), I did frequent movie houses, and I smoked my father's cigarettes as often as I could steal some. Yet I absolutely detested fighting and physical violence. I was one of those gentler types who considered as stupid and brutal those students who, pretending to be patriots, wanted to beat up other classmates whose small faults they disliked. Given those circumstances, I must have had some reason to strike Hisatake.

I wonder if, by such wild behavior, I was trying to cover up

my guilty conscience for neglecting my duties in the labor
service. Or did a personal grudge against Hisatake, scarcely
recognized, cause anger to explode so suddenly? This explanation sounds more plausible than others but, judging from the
actual situation that day, I cannot help but think that some
extraordinary impulse existed other than those relatively superficial reasons. If so, what was the underlying cause of such an
outburst? I have spent many years in endless fretting over this
puzzle without reaching any answer. And, of course, the human
tendency to reject all unpleasant explanations for past errors
has extended beyond comfort this nagging concern with that
event.

Quite recently, while engaged in a game called the Association Test with a friend who is interested in psychoanalysis, I
quickly said "cow!" in answer to the phrase "end of the war."
In this game, one says the first word or words to enter his mind
that he associates with the idea presented. Five minutes later,
when the same challenge is repeated, he may or may not give
the same response. The analyst obtains some clues to the
respondent's psychological processes by observing how his
mind has shifted between the first association and the last.
Naturally, the first response is the key to the whole game, and I
answered "cow." My friend burst into laughter. "Why did you
associate it with a cow? What in the world does a cow have
to do with the end of the war?" My unexpected association
surprised even me, but thanks to that answer the very cause of
the impulse that made me hit Hisatake finally became clear—it
was a cow! In fact, *the* cow.

Toward the end of the war all the students at my high
school were drafted into the labor service and assigned to work
at the S Glider Factory at the foot of a mountain about two and
a half miles from the Noryangjin Station in a suburb of Seoul.
The factory, which had been built in the early spring and identified by an overlarge signboard stating "Commissioned by the
Ministry of the Army," was a shabby plant with rows of poorly
assembled sheds set in a wide lot. The cheapness of the place,
with its camouflaged tin roofs painted green and brown to

deceive enemy planes, immediately demolished our interest in
working there.

In the office of the supervisor who received reports on our
absence and tardiness hung a framed motto: Seeking Life
amidst Death. But we saw that the latest of the gliders, which
had been assembled after repeated tests, looked ridiculously
heavy, like a snake swallowing a frog, instead of being stream-
lined and capable of flight. We began to wonder if it really
could be the promised secret weapon that was supposed to help
us in seeking life amidst death by improving our country's
condition. We were told that this type of glider, with a half-ton
cargo capacity, would be towed in a linked group of several
gliders, much like a goldfish trailing bubbles behind it. These
gliders were supposed to make their great contribution at the
time when enemy troops dared to invade Japan. Our valiant
warriors, carried in those gliders, would rush out and attack
the enemy's headquarters and also take food supplies to our
country's brave defenders.

Most unfortunately, only the night before the dedication
ceremony for the seven new gliders we'd just made, the pride of
the Japanese army, and before they had the chance to play their
part in the meritorious operations of the army in the endeavors
of the Greater East Asian War, they were irreparably crushed
under the very sheds in which they'd been assembled. Those
flimsy buildings were blown down by the violent rain and wind
storm that blasted southern Korea during a single night. From
that day until the last day of the war, we students had to clear
away the wreckage left by that divine wind.

While working with Korean laborers to carry those broken
beams and the remnants of seven gliders, we anxiously listened
for the siren at whose warning we were privileged to run into
the air-raid shelters dug in the corner of the compound. Those
shelters reminded me of octopus traps—narrow at the mouth,
widening toward the rear. The muskmelon patch beyond the
barbed-wire fence was very attractive, and we could enter it by
crawling though the summer grasses grown high around the
shelters.

Even though the inside of an octopus trap was terribly hot, we had a much better time there, during breaks, than outside. Above ground we were yelled at by old retired captains or forced to listen to harangues on the Hagakure samurai spirit.

What bothered me most in those days was neither the hard labor under the blazing sun nor the boring lectures on moral precepts, but commuting from my home to the glider factory. The trip from our house on the hill of Sindang-dong to the Noryangjin Station took at least an hour and forty minutes. Buses had once run to Changch'undan Park. After gasoline became scarce, they were fueled by charcoal, than by acetylene. Long before war's end they were discontinued. The tram that had run between Changch'undang and the sixth block of Koganechō was also discontinued.

So every morning I had to get up at six o'clock, wrap on puttees while eating cold rice, and rush out of the house clutching my book bag. By the time I reached the sixth block of Koganechō, a long line of people stood waiting for the train. Except on rainy days, I always had to wait more than ten minutes to board it.

Riding in a crowded car for more than an hour was all but unbearable. I learned to relieve boredom by directing amorous glances at the girls of F Girls High School or by discreetly chewing roasted peas drawn from my bag. What annoyed me most about those suffocating rides was the stink of garlic that wafted from the lunch boxes of the many Korean laborers who were bound for Noryangjin Station. It was less nauseous in winter, but very potent during summer days. When someone shoved an odorous lunch box under my nose, while another kicked my legs and stepped on my toes, I had no way to escape. Bruises were bad enough, but the smells—of garlic and sweating bodies—were the worst afflictions of all.

At the factory, two punishments fell upon those who missed the shuttle truck that picked us up at eight o'clock in front of Noryangjin Station. Those who were late had to run along a lonely mountain path and through several pumpkin fields to reach the factory and report in by eight-thirty. If an unfortunate student stepped through the gate after eight-thirty, he had to submit to a most unpleasant first ordeal—listening to the scolding of the old captain. The second punishment deprived him of the rice gruel served at the three o'clock break. In those days, everyone was hungry every day, all day long, and even rice gruel with a touch a salt tasted delicious. To watch one's workmates slurping up hot gruel, their noses perspiring, while one suffered from hunger pangs, was very painful.

Going through the Korean village that had grown up in front of the station would take me to the newly opened red clay road up the mountainside. On a rainy day the road, marked by trucks' tire tracks, became extremely slippery along the steep incline. But on dry days, in the clear morning air, the ascent was as pleasant as one could wish. And yet the chirping cicadas, sounding from the pine trees that bordered the road, were just as irritating as were the old captain's screechings. Hoping to stop them, I used to throw pebbles into the pine groves. Needless to say, the cicadas paid not the slightest attention.

After surviving the cicadas and the wearying climb, I descended the mountain to be confronted by an expanse of pumpkin fields. The rolling fields looked more extensive than they actually were, and just the thought that running across them would bring me at last to the factory was thoroughly depressing. Truly, one could never describe the misery of the youth running alone under the blazing August sun along the dusty path through the vast fields where innumerable pumpkins lay, one after the identical other, monstrously swollen zeros, images of nothing.

The trial of pushing past those entangling vines, with their watching golden eyes; the clammy heat; the weariness; and the old captain's shrill scoldings were enough to make me withdraw from the whole dismal experience and drive me to choose an easy, immoral, and yet rather daring alternative: sneaky sabotage. Yet I must confess that I discovered another fact that encouraged my delinquency. This was a map of the city of Seoul and its vicinity, posted on a wall in my father's study.

One Sunday, when I went into the study to steal some cigarettes, I saw the map and, looking at it for the first time, learned something discouraging. The glider factory to which I had journeyed every morning in the week, spending so much time along the way, was practically in my backyard—on the map, that is. With a ruler, I measured the distance and found that it was less than four kilometers from my home on the map. I had been going the long way around, when I could have gone directly to the factory! My surprise at the fact completely discouraged me. But then reality put everything back in scale.

Namsan Park, squatting blatantly in the central part of Seoul, was one sinister cause of my wasted time and effort. Mount Taeyŏn, a thousand meters high, and the wide, blue Han River also obstructed my beckoning four-kilometer shortcut. So, to tell the truth, my morning ride was forced on me by the inconsiderate gods who made Korea. After realizing this, I conceived a satisfying grievance. Each time I faced those pumpkin fields because I was late for the truck, I excused myself, thinking, "This is not my fault after all. It's the fault of Seoul's topography. Besides, does my being late once in a while really affect Japan's ability to win—or lose—the war?"

However, I was not late on the morning of August fifteenth. On the contrary, I arrived at Noryangjin Station two hours earlier than usual. Of course I had my own reason for doing that. Our newspapers and radio stations had been announcing for two days that news "unparalleled in history" would be released at noon on August fifteenth. If I had been more mature, or less self-indulgent, I could have fathomed that the phrase "unparalleled in history" implied Japan's defeat, but I was just a young schoolboy who had been raised and trained to believe that Japan was the invincible country of its guardian gods.

I certainly had detected anxiety in my father's manner earlier that morning, but I never associated the "serious matter" he mentioned with the unconditional surrender of Japan. Besides, I cannot deny that at the bottom of my heart lay an ingrained need to reject such an unimaginable thought. In

spite of the sad succession of terrible defeats our government
had admitted, such as the fall of Okinawa, the powerful new
kinds of bombs dropped only a few days before on Hiroshima
and Nagasaki, and, most recently, the Russian invasion of
Manchukuo, I probably expected another boastful new
dispatch of the sort usually released from Japanese military
headquarters to the bouncing accompaniment of the battleship
marching song.

On the previous day, we students had engaged in silly
conversation on our way home. "Our commandos must have
attacked Washington, D.C.," said one. "No," countered
another, "we'll hear news about the final battle on the main
islands of Japan." And I said, "I wonder if the news will tell us
that the Russians are coming into northern Korea." But none
of us predicted the surrender of Japan, the Divine Country.
Mentioning the surrender of Japan was not taboo, nor would
doing so have made us fear being arrested by military policemen. But the thought alone would have frightened us. We were
like well-trained, faithful dogs, and the idea of Japan's sur-
rendering was beyond the reach of our imagining.

Shichijima, the second son of an obstetrician, peered at
me. "They're saying something 'unparalleled in history.' What
kind of news will that be, do you suppose?" The phrase
"unparalleled in history" hung in the air above us, causing a
foreboding, the awareness that we lived upon the very edge of
tremendous change.

A few minutes later, while hanging on to a bamboo strap in
the train, I thought up a plan for the next morning. I was well
known for habitually arriving late. But now I decided to be at
the gathering place earlier than anyone else on the following
morning, mostly to be able to impress them with a witty greeting. They would be absolutely amazed to find me there before
them and would certainly throw sarcastic remarks at me. Then
I would straighten my shoulders and retort, "Oh yes. Something unparalleled in history . . ." This unordinary expression
would be so fitting for the time that I would be applauded with
cheers and laughter not only by my fellows but also by students
from other schools. The plan was well developed in my mind,

and by the time I left Shichijima at Eirakuchō Station, I was so
taken with it that I even forgot his agreement to show me one
of his father's films on the delivery of babies. In olden times,
Priest Nōin strove to give reality to poems he had created. Now
I was falling into the same pit. Content with my scheme, I went
to bed early, as soon as I had finished eating supper.

During the night father was called by his office and, thanks
to that emergency, I got up early and left home an hour earlier
than usual. I ran through the fresh morning air to the sixth
block of Koganechō. Hardly anyone waited at the tram stop,
usually so packed with a long line of people. The strange
emptiness made the place look weird. When I arrived at
Noryangjin Station, the sun was tinting the summit of Mount
Kwanak a light purple.

Our gathering place was under a huge elm tree at the
entrance to the Korean village. Leaning against the elm, waiting
for my friends, I gazed at the effects of the rising sun, changing
the color of the world at almost every second. When the light of
day took over, I followed the movements of the black ants busy
on the ground.

The time, which had passed so rapidly in the train, flowed
very slowly under the elm tree. I felt uneasy as I recalled a
mistake I'd made about a meeting place during grade-school
days. I rushed back into the station to see if my wristwatch was
correct. None of my fellow workers appeared at seven o'clock,
not even at ten minutes after seven. Irritated by then, and more
than slightly disappointed, I was experiencing the same frustration that the striving poet, Priest Nōin [998–1050?, a well-
known poet of the late Heian period], must have felt.

About the time the sun lifted its fullness above the mountain, lighting the thatched roofs of the Korean houses, some
old women carrying their laundry baskets appeared, heading
toward the Han River. I was completely bored. Finally, a figure
that looked like it might belong to a classmate came in sight.
Immediately my spirits brightened, my heart pounded with
excitement. But as the figure came closer, my elation subsided.
He was Kanemoto Kōshoku, nicknamed "The Fool."

Kanemoto was said to be a son of a very rich and famous

Korean family. He was well known among us for his unusual height and his perfect English score in the entrance examination. Wearing capes and wooden clogs was not permitted in our school, else he would have worn them. In our decadent group, we cherished the stranger habit of wearing worn-out clothes and shapeless caps. Kanemoto was the exception, of course, always dressed properly in uniform and wearing a cap, both of which looked like they had just been bought. Such formality made the rest of us feel suffocated. He was the only one who did not wipe away sweat with the hand towel that hung from the belt of everyone else. He alone drew a linen handkerchief from his pocket and carefully wiped his face and neck. Perhaps because of my antipathy toward him, based upon my inferiority in foreign languages and physical training, I really despised him. "With this fool, the wit of my remark will be reduced by half!" Utterly disgusted, I decided to withhold my greeting, as if I were a miser clutching his gold.

As he approached, I just said, "Hi," assuming an unpleasant air. Kanemoto walked up to me, smiling. In the manner typical of a shy and rejected youth, he blinked, and said, as if seeing into my mind, "You are so early today. We might call this something like an event 'unparalleled in history,' not so?" I doubted my ears. I winced! This was turnabout with a vengeance! Why had I troubled to get up so soon and come to this station a whole hour earlier? If I'd known that the game was going to turn out like this, I should never have withheld my greetings.

I recalled the sight of a wretched sumo wrestler being flipped to the ground by his opponent and crawling out of the ring tilting his head in shame. My pride had been dealt a comparable hurt by this Kanemoto, whom I had been despising all along as an undoubted fool, with no sense of humor. His unexpected attack left me reeling inwardly. My face, instead of showing scorn, froze into the shit-eater's smile. Chagrin never tasted so vile!

Sensing that I was not being at all friendly, Kanemoto slowly sat down upon a raised root of the elm tree and took a small English-Japanese dictionary from his pocket. Growing angrier by the second, I stared at his broad shoulders and straight back. Self-disgust churned in me as I realized that, unless I gave him a witty reply now, I would spend a most unpleasant day. But in the next instant I recognized that I'd lost the chance. The match was decisively his—and he'd scored a perfect victory! Disgust turned to rage. "Stop studying the enemy's language!" I snarled.

Kanemoto looked up at me. "Is that so bad?"

"Sure! I don't like it! You don't need to study English when you come for labor duty!"

Kanemoto, plainly bewildered, quietly put the dictionary back into his pocket. But I felt indescribably defeated and ashamed.

Did Kanemoto, showing no resistance, not even annoyance, yield to my unreasonable order simply because I was a Japanese? Or did some emotion, more fundamental, more hidden, tell him how to respond? As far as physical strength was concerned, I was no match for him. And, of course, he could not know or even guess the reason for my anger. Under these circumstances, if I were he, would I obey another's harsh order so calmly? As an oppressed Korean, shouldn't he have tried to oppose me as a brutal member of the hated ruling class? If Kanemoto had shown any sign at all of resistance, I would not have been so troubled. But his complete acceptance made me feel unhappy and sick with regret that he should be so weak in the presence of this bullying Japanese. To him, I saw most clearly, being a Korean meant being at the bottom in everything. Always a loser, never a winner.

We Japanese children brought up in colonial Korea knew a very convenient expression: "Being Korean, how dare you. . . ?" This cruel question possessed an unopposable power until almost the very end of the Pacific War. In spite of all the propaganda about the "unification" of Korea and Japan or about the equality of the two countries, the scornful attitude of the Japanese toward the Koreans had been nurtured in us since childhood and was not easy to change, even if Korean names, like Kim and Pak, were changed into Japanese versions, such as Kanemoto and Kinoshita. Besides, we Japanese had been brought up without knowing how cruelly and severely Japan had attacked, exploited, and suppressed the Koreans: discrimination against them had been practiced in every area, including education and employment.

During my junior-high-school days, I began to feel a degree of sympathy toward the Koreans—which I kept well hidden, of course. Once a year, on a certain day, all the students in the city of Seoul, except for elementary-school children, gathered in groups under their school flags in the great square before the building of the governor-general of Korea to hear a reading of the new Imperial Rescript for students. After the edict was read, we marched to the Namdaemun Gate and visited the Korea Shrine, which was halfway up Mount Namsan.

On that occasion, I clearly saw proof of the insulting discrimination between Japanese and Korean students when we were ordered to present arms by lifting our rifles in salute to the governor-general, up there on his high stage. The rifles that we Japanese students held were genuine weapons, made of shiny black steel; the things held by Korean students were made of wood. The contrast between the steel weapons and those wooden "rifles," all held up at the command "Present arms!" created a tragicomic effect that made many Japanese students giggle and terribly shamed all Korean students. Shocked at this display of arrogance, I looked at nearby classmates to see how they reacted. Most assumed obviously superior looks, proud of being Japanese, while, like true warriors of Dai Nippon, they straightened their backs and squared their shoulders. An overwhelming depression seeped through me. That evening, at home, I talked about my responses with my father. When I asked the reason behind our cruel discrimination, father immediately said, "Don't be a fool! Don't you know those Koreans will cause riots and rise in rebellion as soon as they get their hands on real rifles?" "But aren't they Japanese, just as we are?" I asked. Father made a strange reply: "Don't you realize that Japan is now at war?" But he did not really answer my questions.

As I became more attentive to everything, I found many more contradictions between the true state of affairs and the official pronouncements about Japan's relationships with Korea. This discovery forced me into looking at things from Koreans' point of view. I realized that just as I was having innumerable contradictory experiences, so must Kanemoto have gone through countless humiliating ordeals. Yet, I confess, I was not always sympathetic to the Koreans. Just as water flows from higher to lower levels, sympathy is given only by those in higher positions. For example, I used to feel annoyed whenever our Korean maidservants spoke insolently to us after they'd become familiar with our household manners or when father's occasional Korean guests addressed him as if they were his equals. "How dare you?" I wanted to ask them. In such instances, my antagonism was based only on the fact that they were Korean. So the emotion that welled up in me when Kanemoto obediently put his dictionary away must have come from the disgust with myself that had been building up in me as a result of Japan's policy of oppression.

Even then my self-torment did not end. I looked down at Kanemoto, sitting at my feet, chin resting on his knees, gazing into space as if he could think of nothing except obeying me. The awkwardness between us that I had provoked was hardening into a virtual wall. Stubborn still, refusing to admit that I was the troublemaker, I remained silent, awaiting the arrival of our classmates.

A new military road cut through the Korean village. While I surveyed the place disapprovingly, a number of villagers darted across the road into the right section of the village. Soon more villagers hurried after them. "What's going on?" I muttered, hoping that Kanemoto would hear me.

He was guiding ants along, with a dried leaf held in his scholar's hand. Again I spoke, louder this time: "I wonder what's happening?" Kanemoto looked toward the village but immediately turned back to the ants. The tension between us reached its peak. Then I understood: his silence was evidence not of deference to me, the lordly Japanese, but rather of anger carefully controlled. I understood, in a flash, how in every moment of his life he must keep up that guard over every thought and act. With that discovery the hardness in my heart cracked, and pity for Kanemoto, for all Koreans, flowed out from it. Aware that I had been relieved of a heavy burden, I walked toward the village. My footsteps resounded as I clopped along in my untied shoes. I wanted to free myself from the weight of Kanemoto's sorrows and to exchange our uncomfortable antagonism for the lighter affairs of a whole village. I checked my watch to see if I could get back in time to meet the truck.

The village was quite large, sprawling across a wide valley. Many people had gathered in a circle around a cultivated field beyond a peasant's house at the far end of the village. By standing on tiptoe, I could see two brown beasts violently crashing against each other within a temporary corral. At first I thought it was a bullfight. But when I found a space that afforded a better view, I saw a magnificent sight worthy of the saying "Flesh beating against flesh."

Those two creatures, which usually moved so slowly, pulling heavy carts while drooling and coughing up their cud, were madly jumping about within the enclosure in an entirely unexpected manner. Where had the stolid cow hidden the agility and the coyness that now tantalized the bull?

She kicked out with her heavy hind hooves, striking hard blows to the neck and chest of the bull, who was fiercely attacking her rear. The harder he was kicked and rejected, the more he seemed to be aroused. The cow's refusals were repeated, but the bull blindly continued to thrust at her with his smooth, extended penis. After a while he appeared to tire, but the cow stood there, quite serene. A man among the onlookers urged the bull on with a vulgar expression uttered in shrieks imitative of a woman's voice. At the villagers' loud laughter, the bull jumped again at the cow, who delivered another kick to his side.

My ears became hot, my cheeks flushed. A mixture of feelings—rising lust in me, the curiosity that held my eyes fixed on the lustful animals, and shame because of my insistence upon seeing everything—disturbed me. As I became more absorbed in the struggle—an absorption that hastened my swelling excitement—I completely forgot about the time. Drooling like any aroused bull, I swallowed my saliva as fast as it flowed.

Inasmuch as I was a grown boy, I had acquired a good theoretical knowledge about the principles of sex, but I had never seen anything like this. Clenching my fists, I tried to quiet my feelings. My brain seemed to fill with blood, so that I saw everything through a red haze. My stomach churned, and the pressure on my bladder made me want to urinate. Then, suddenly, I had a marvelous fantasy: I became the bull, persistently thrusting his hard pizzle at the cow.

When the bull's chest was kicked, I instantly felt the pain in my chest, and my blood seemed to spurt through my skin because of my humiliation. Stumbling forward, I glared at the cow with bloodshot eyes. "You've fooled me enough!" I shouted to myself. Exhausted by her whorish teasing, I ground my teeth.

"No, I won't let you go!" I yelled to myself. My heart began to pound in rhythm with the panting bull's, and my legs, like his, were ready to collapse. Yet the cow, still teasing, lay close to the ground, writhing with desire. I lost my head. Trembling with excitement, I went completely mad. An insane and violent impulse made me forget everything else. I attacked frantically and violently, my mind screaming, "Damn you! Remember, no matter how much you struggle, you are mine now!"

I completely forgot the time for the truck to arrive. Only the wild sexual excitement possessed me. Staring at that heroic mating, I myself felt the desire of that bull. And when he mounted her, conquered her with a quick thrust of that hard penis, I too enjoyed that triumph as my seed poured forth upon my crotch. Although no one in the crowd could possibly have known, I was ashamed. But even then, my excitement did not end. As I left the circle, still stiff and hard, I marveled that I managed to walk at all.

The spectators did not cheer the victorious bull. Only the sounds of the animals' hard breathing followed me as I reeled away, still in my lascivious dream.

The image of the two humped animals, lathered with sweat and vaginal froth, made me dizzy. I had to stop to catch my breath. A reddish-black lump seemed to swell in the pit of my belly, demanding another exquisite release.

I ran, desperate to prevent that second shaming. Hoping that the faster I ran the sooner I would forget those copulating creatures, I stumbled along crazily in a frenzy. Throwing myself down in the shade of the elm tree, I stretched out my legs, pulling at the crotch of my trousers to ease the tightness there. I was not eased. After a long while, I realized that no other students shared the shade of the tree. "Damn it!" I groaned. "The truck must have left already."

My watch read ten minutes after eight. The sun, promising another hot day, was already dazzling in the cloudless sky. The sunlight cast the dark shadow of the tree on the dry ground. I clicked my tongue with disgust and tried to find some comfort in my favorite expression, "Tardiness 'unparalleled in history!' " But that helped not at all.

I was too depressed to get up and start walking to the glider factory. If nobody had seen me here earlier in the morning, I would have been in a safe position. But that fool Kanemoto had seen me. Now I could not avoid reporting for duty. Looking up at the glaring sun, sweating in the increasing heat, I moaned at the thought of the pumpkin fields that lay between me and honorable duty. Who had caused me to be such an idiot? Who else but Kanemoto? That fool Kanemoto had done it! I ground my teeth with rage.

After all, I had arrived here an hour earlier than usual. And before I could express my brilliant witticism, which I had thought up all by myself, he had said it so casually—and, even

worse!—without my permission. Everything was his fault!
Kanemoto Kōshoku, that damned, that most arrogant fool!
Dejected and furious at the same time, I cursed him under my
breath.

"So the truck seems to have gone already, eh?" The good-
natured voice, coming from above, interrupted my soliloquy of
hate. Because of his unmistakable accent, I didn't need to see
his face to identify him. The very Kanemoto about whom I was
complaining towered above me.

Fearing that a fox-spirit was tricking me, I sprang to my
feet. Trying to hide my surprise, I asked, "Did you too see that
business with the bull and the cow?"

"Well . . . maybe." Ambiguous as always, he blushed
slightly. At this my whole body was filled with a swirling joy
that exploded in high spirits, a rush of goodwill. Laughing, I
said, "So in commemoration of our tardiness 'unparalleled in
history,' let's go boating!" "I'm willing," he said, with a big
smile. "I don't feel like working today."

Whistling as we went, we walked toward the great iron
bridge over the Han River. I was so happy. The pleasure of
having the fool Kanemoto as my companion—and accom-
plice—made my heart beat faster. It was almost like the thrill
that comes with violating something that is sacred. Like pissing
on the grave of someone else's ancestor.

To ease the memory of that earlier tension between us, and
to bind him even more closely to me as a companion in treason
to our duty, I quickly described the mating scene. But it was
quite unnecessary, because he was far more acquainted with
such country matters than I expected.

As soon as we'd boarded the boat, he took a cigarette from
a pocket, skillfully lighted it, inhaled deeply, and said, narrowing his eyes, "Ah, how delicious this Chienmen is."

Chienmen were high-class Chinese cigarettes, hard to
obtain. Kanemoto told me how he had fooled his officer-in-
charge during junior-high-school days. Once, when the officer-
in-charge who inspected his clothing found some Chienmen
cigarettes in a pocket, Kanemoto said that his father wanted

him to offer them to this very officer. Nodding happily, the
officer-in-charge released him immediately, saying, "I see," and
accepted the cigarettes.

"That was because of the quality of those Chienmen.
Another brand of cigarettes wouldn't have done it."

I was impressed by this further evidence of his quick wit
and by his talent for being more than he pretended to be. If he
was smart enough to bribe the officer with forbidden cigarettes,
then his formal style of dress must be a trick intended to
deceive our teachers. He was no weak-minded fool. He was
instead a clever trickster, smarter than all our fellow students
and than I, too. Later he said, "You know, when I do something
forbidden, I usually do it alone. A crime committed without
accomplices is harder to detect, you see. You didn't know that I
smoked, did you? And went to movies when I cut class?"

In his opinion, among all the districts of Seoul, Ch'anggyŏngwŏn was the part least controlled by police. Indeed, one
could do almost anything, unnoticed, in the spacious gardens
of the Yi dynasty palace and fully amuse oneself at the zoo, the
botanical garden, and the museum.

Yet in being impressed by his ingenuity, I must not allow
myself to devalue my own ego. Intending to deflate his ego, I
asked with the sincerest of faces, "Do you know the taste of a
woman?" If he replied no, as I honestly expected, I was going
to display all of my knowledge of sex and women—gained
from reading books, seeing the films made by Dr. Shichijima
the obstetrician, and watching the mating of a bull with a
cow—to even the score between us.

And so much for deviousness. Kanemoto simply grinned,
a mixture of embarrassment and shyness. My face changed
color. Intuition told me that he knew all about that greatest of
mysteries.

Overwhelmed with envy, I didn't know what to say. Then
sourest jealousy replaced mere envy. I studied his complexion,
no longer that of a schoolboy. The more I looked at him, the
more mature and confident he was. In him I saw neither
desperate frustration about sex nor strong curiosity about the

experience for which I hungered. Blushing, I mumbled, "At a brothel or. . . ?"

Blinking rapidly as usual, Kanemoto did not give me the self-satisfied smirk I expected. "Just between you and me, I am already married," he said sadly. He was not lying.

In Korea the first wife for the heir in an aristocratic, or yangban, family was usually chosen before he was born. Kanemoto said he was born into such a situation. Because even a grown bachelor, a ch'onggak, was never treated like an adult, men tended to marry young. Kanemoto's parents had followed the custom and married him to an eighteen-year-old girl when he was thirteen. His first wife had had to serve her husband faithfully when he was still a sixth grader in elementary school!

As he talked so casually, I was again overcome with jealousy. Suddenly, his whole long body seemed to swell, to become as tumescent as the bull's pizzle had been. As if to overpower me . . .

"When did you lose your virginity?" I asked, eager to hear details.

"Oh, let's quit talking about this stuff," said Kanemoto, bored with it all. Only a man who has already enjoyed the mysteries of sex could have dismissed them so easily. As if hushing me for proposing so childish a question, he did not bother to say anything more about the most fascinating subject in the world.

About midday, we parted company at the Yongsan Station. I was exhausted, as we'd been rowing most of the morning. I went to Hommachi by tram, walked along the road despite the heat, and finally decided to go into a movie theater called Kirakukan. (It was my last visit to that theater, later destroyed by a young kamikaze pilot who committed suicide by diving his plane into the building. And I never saw Kanemoto again, because he and his family, which was pro-Japanese, were killed by rioters soon after the war ended.)

The interior of the theater was cool and quiet. The film, with its prescribed theme of loyalty to the emperor, stopped several times because of electrical shortages. I did not mind those interruptions much, because I could not concentrate very well on the screen as I recalled Kanemoto's quiet, sensuous smile and the violent impact of flesh against flesh as those beasts rutted in the farmer's field.

In the darkness of the theater, I saw again the copulating animals. Every movement of the mating appeared at fantastic speed in my mind. Inexorably those scenes progressed to lewd visions of Kanemoto copulating with his wife.

Whenever the film stopped, I sank back in my seat, closed my eyes, and enjoyed lascivious fantasies about animals. In their world they had no fears of being expelled from school, no worries about morality, no laws, no shame, only the freedom of instinct. I wished that I could be transformed by a magician's wand into a bull or a stallion.

I could hear the animals' hoarse panting. The private parts of that cunning and sensuous cow opened crimson petals in the theater's darkness and released a maddeningly tempting fragrance. "Oh, how I wish I could know what it's like!" Just because it was something unknown to me, something like forbidden fruit, my burning desire raged beyond control, hurting my private parts. A lust possessed me that never let go. It pulled me into its burning world, where I fell into the pit of torment and anguish.

Being unable to control the urges within my healthy body, with its desires stronger than those of anyone else, I cursed it. Yet when I thought about them, I perceived that my fantasies were caused not so much by merely physical pressures but by the lurid visions I deliberately invoked. My need to make love to a warm female body was like the appetite of a hungry fox greedy to devour a tender chick.

In those times, when I might be sent to the front the very next day, who could promise me that I would not die within an hour of reaching the line? Rumors told us that the Russians had already invaded northern Manchukuo and were fighting Japan's troops near the border. How could I expect to escape that bloody fate?

I recalled father's words when he left home so hurriedly

that morning. What would happen to the Japanese there if
the Russians occupied all of Manchukuo? My imagination
increased my frustration. Dark-bearded and gigantic Russian
soldiers swarmed into my fantasy, wearing high, black Cossack
hats and long, blood-stained capes. I could hear the neighing
and the hoofbeats of their powerful stallions.

"That's right! I have no time!" I convinced myself as, with
swelling desire, I summoned up a new scene: the long line of
soldiers waiting in front of one Seoul's whorehouses. . . .

On the slope rising from the fifth block of Hommachi to
Tōgokenchō, the great Buddhist temple of Kōyasan backed
up on the pleasure quarter offering hundreds of Korean prostitutes. People in Seoul used to call the area Paradise Slope
because of that paradoxical arrangement of temple and
brothels.

One Sunday afternoon, when I went out to hunt for books,
I saw the usual long lines of soldiers on Paradise Slope. Since it
was not a rare scene, I paid no attention to the soldiers as I
walked down the slope—until I saw the one at the end of the
line and, shocked, stopped to stare at him.

He was a young pilot, little more than a boy, wearing a
flier's brown jacket with the white silk scarf hung loosely
around his neck. He stood with legs apart, his small feet shod
in low boots. His smooth, pink cheeks, reminding me of roses,
told me that he was a few years younger than I. *Younger than
I!* He must have come in to Seoul from Kimp'o Airport, the
base for the kamikaze pilots of the Imperial Special Air
Commandos.

In the line of older and middle-aged reserve soldiers, slop-
pily clad in their wrinkled uniforms, the young pilot stood out
gallantly, looking pathetically young and fresh. I felt an instant
antipathy toward him. Envy of this mere boy, insolently joining
the older men in their need for prostitutes. The sight of him
filled me with rage. As if sensing my antagonism, the boy-pilot
turned and gave me a challenging look. With a contemptuous
smile, he almost left the line to challenge me and my obvious
dislike. The reflected sunlight seemed to set his eyes afire,

making him look even more like a young hero from the Age of
the Gods. The legendary Yamato Takeru must have looked like
him, I thought. Quickly I shifted my gaze, afraid of his power.
Then he became human again. Stepping out of the line, he
yelled to everyone ahead, "What's happening up there? Do it
faster! Faster!"

A reply drifted back. "When one gets older," said a voice,
very courteously, "it takes longer, *sir!*" The other soldiers burst
into ribald laughter, in which I detected a mixture of scorn and
tolerance. The boy ran toward the head of the line. Suddenly
he stopped. His back showing fierce indignation, he shouted,
"You fools! I haven't got time to wait!"

At that my dislike vanished. Pity took its place. They
should not be laughing at him. He was so honest, so desperate
in his anxiety. He reminded me of a candle flame about to die
out, flaring up in its last moment, using all the energy left in its
frail wick. From this augury I knew the boy would die on his
first mission. He would give his life for the emperor, just as
Yamato Takeru did so long ago.

"Was he a virgin?" I asked myself, in the darkness of the
theater, recalling the young pilot's blazing eyes, the daring
smile, the youth in his rosy cheeks, and his shouts, full of
energy, full of life.

"I haven't got time!" Wasn't this the uppermost thought
in all of us during those days of our dying empire? I felt
immensely frustrated as I stared at the screen floating pale and
ghostly in the dark. I did not fear death, if I could face it with
a gun in my hands. But thinking about death in the abstract,
finding the meaning in it, troubled me. To me, death should be
like a strong blast of wind. When, at the moment of dying, I
would close my eyes, the wind would blow right through my
body, carrying away my spirit. Strangely enough, thought of
the suffering that comes with dying always conveyed to me the
picture of a beautiful woman's body trembling in the ecstasy of
love. I might well have taken the young pilot's words—and his
message—into my subconscious, just as I shared his wish to
visit a brothel on Paradise Slope.

The steadily deteriorating conditions in those last days of

the war made me feel like a leaf being blown about in a
typhoon. Instinctively I knew the vanity of analyzing the nature
and the direction of the storm. If I could neither stop it nor
change its course, I might just as well hope for the least distress
and the most pleasure in whatever was left of my life. There
were so many things that I had not yet experienced, and the
need for women and the sexual pleasures they promised was
my most urgent concern. I thought of little else. I, I, I, me, me,
me—those were the only notes in the song of my life.

In those days, the ordinary course of courtship and
marriage was not possible for us who were young Japanese
men being prepared for war. The only approved alternative
was to avoid sentimental involvements entirely. In theory, the
brothels on Paradise Slope were available. To many men, and
to me, they were the most attractive, but in reality I was always
afraid whenever I passed them, and I never had the courage to
enter one. My high hopes sank every time I smelled the stench
of that area, and, to make matters worse, at night it was
darkened because of the danger of air raids.

I would never act decisively unless placed under the same
kind of stress that gripped the young pilot. I was afraid of
being put in such a situation, but my interest in exploring the
unknown was greater than my fear and encouraged me to
venture ahead. Closing my eyes and resting my feet on the back
of the seat in front, I tried to imagine such a situation as realis-
tically as possible, but I always became confused exactly at the
point where my imagination stopped. Then only an abstract
image appeared before me: against the tremulous darkness,
overlapping red folds quivered like lips opening to enclose—
to enwrap—to suck me in to a warm, wet death.

Oh, how I wished I had been that bull! Panting hard, sweating, I had to know what that apparition meant, even if I died.
Wanting to gain the strength of the bull of the morning, I
yearned to leave shame and morality behind, to throw myself
completely into the world of Eros, to see and to touch the
unknown beauty with my eyes and my fingers and my—

Each time the film stopped, the dream of delusion beckoned
me into it. The frenzied breathing of the animals lingered in my

ears, and Kanemoto's face, showing ecstasy at the moment of climax, filled the vacant screen. Damn it! Even Kanemoto—that fool Kanemoto!—had known a woman! Shit! The fantasy ended, like a pricked bubble. I sank into a morass of irritation and gloom. The furious tyrant in my crotch convinced me that the time had come to enter a brothel on Paradise Slope.

My decision became firmer with every second, and by the time I left the movie theater it had become an unchangeable supreme command. Fortunately I had a hundred-yen note that my mother had put in my billfold for use during an emergency, such as an air raid. The Russian soldiers were coming. Tomorrow, my class might be called up to fight. I should not hesitate a minute longer. I must boldly stand in line on Paradise Slope along with all those other horny men. Relieving myself with a helping hand was not possible now: that forbidden release was for boys, not for grown men. Not for us who were about to die. I felt that my body was flying away to Paradise Slope, dyed crimson by the rays of the setting sun.

When I left the movie house, I was transformed into a wild man, a hunting animal. Repeatedly I had to control the urge to shoulder aside anyone passing near me. Just like a soldier heading toward the front, I marched with my shoulders squared. But my hand gripped the hundred-yen note that would buy my peace in Paradise.

Just then I met Hisatake at the Shōwa intersection. "Hi!" I said. "How was it today?" My greeting held a variety of meanings. Most of all I was trying to hide my embarrassment over shirking work at the factory, while also checking to see if he knew about the unpatriotic way in which Kanemoto and I had spent much of that day. But Hisatake, ignoring my greeting, just stared at me, as unfriendly as a cranky child. His coldness reminded me of an unpleasant incident several months before.

The junior high school that Hisatake and I attended had an unusual tradition: everybody, including the principal, exercised every day for fifteen minutes during the noon recess, wearing no other clothing than underwear.

In the fall of our third year, just as we'd finished exercising, sharp-eyed Hisatake, pointing at me, bawled for the entire class to hear, "Hey, look everybody! He had a wet dream last night!" That was a natural event in the life of any healthy junior-high-school boy, but when Hisatake called everyone's attention to the telltale stains on my underwear, I was very embarrassed. In fact, I had been worrying about those stains all morning, because I was too ashamed to put the underwear in the laundry hamper at home. So when Hisatake pointed at me, I reacted in the natural way, turning attention from me to him. "Hah!" I shouted. "For Hisatake, wet dreams seem to be unusual. Let's get him! Let's check him!"

We chased Hisatake up the hill to the firing range behind the school and there stripped him of his one garment. As my hands pinned his shoulders to the ground and others held his legs and arms, he stopped resisting and glared up at me, in his anger showing the whites of his eyes.

On that last day of the war, then, when we met by accident at Shōwa intersection, Hisatake did not reply to my greeting. He might have been annoyed by my stupid chatter, which revealed complete ignorance of Japan's defeat. He looked pale, depressed. After a long moment he said, "Because we have fellows like you around, Japan has lost!"

I was more than startled. "What? Say that again!" I even managed a laugh, because I thought he was telling a bad joke.

"Since you always fail to show up at work, you miss such important news! The war is ended!"

A violent fury boiled up in me, exploding in clouds of red swirling before my eyes. Screeching at him, I blamed poor Hisatake for all my disappointments. "You traitor!" I bellowed. "The war never ends!" I snarled. I was much more upset by the news that the war had ended than by the even more appalling fact that Japan had lost the war. Because Japan's collapse meant the breakdown of my little hugely personal world, of all that had happened to me during that day, beginning with the thrilling mating of bull and cow, the evolution of my sexual fantasies in the darkness of the movie theater, leading finally to my decision to lie with a prostitute, the supreme culmination of lust to which I had been so furiously driven.

When I recovered from my spell, I saw Hisatake sprawled on the pavement, touching his chin. I didn't remember seeing him fall. Why was he lying there? The setting sun cast long shadows of the plane trees upon the street and upon the pale profile of Hisatake. Confounded by everything, I shouted at him, "Hey, you!" Hisatake was too surprised to talk, but anger shot up at me from those blazing eyes. Squaring my shoulders like a true warrior of the emperor, I demanded, "How does the war dare to end?"

But even to me my voice trembled, my words, intended to be heroic, came out like the squeaking of bats. At last I began to understand the meaning of father's words, "something serious," and of the radio stations' preparations for "an announcement 'unparalleled in history.' " Even so, the news of Japan's surrender neither especially moved nor saddened me. But surprise that the war was over, that everything in the world I had known since I began to think about it was finished, did overwhelm me. Regret poured in from all sides like an enormous wave: Regret for the future so foolishly planned and now so irrevocably lost. Regret for Japan, for my father, for me the center of my world. And, underlying all else, but closest of all to my hopes, intense regret that I had been cheated of the chance I wanted most passionately to take, in one of those brothels on Paradise Slope. The embers of the burning need that had tormented me so exquisitely during the long afternoon still smoldered.

Close to my ears I heard the snorting of the aroused bull. Against my thighs I felt the cow's kicks, violent and exciting. Thinking of the brothels of Paradise Slope, with their unreachable delights, recalling the faces of Kanemoto and the boy-pilot, so much more manly than mine, I mumbled to the sinking sun, "The war would never dare to end."

But how faintly my voice sounded. . . .

When the Hibiscus Blooms

I

GOING TO CHINA, Manchuria, or Korea in the hope of making a fortune attracted many Japanese in the 1930s. The trend was encouraged by Japan's government, which had had ambitions in Manchuria even before it annexed Korea. In addition, Japan's economy had deteriorated during the Great Depression, and many Japanese wished to leave their home country.

Responding to the circumstances, Ikeda Shinkichi took a teaching position at Keijō High School in Seoul after he graduated from Tokyo Imperial University.

Shinkichi was the youngest of five brothers. According to the eldest brother, his career had been "somewhat delayed." All his brothers had advanced to the so-called elite courses by graduating from the First High School and Tokyo Imperial University. Shinkichi chose an irregular course, attending the Third High School and Kyoto Imperial University, then taking a leave of absence, and finally graduating from Tokyo Imperial University at the age of twenty-eight, with a major in English literature. Accordingly, his eldest brother's remark about him sounds reasonable.

Yet one important man wanted to employ slow-paced Shinkichi. Principal S of Keijō High School twice traveled all the way from Seoul to recruit Shinkichi while he was still at the university. Shinkichi was impressed by the principal's enthusiasm for Korea, as well as by his interest in the dilatory student himself. Shinkichi had already made an informal arrangement to take a position at Taisei High School in Tokyo upon his eldest brother's recommendation. But when he met the principal from Keijō on his second visit to Tokyo, he was much moved by S's talk about Korea. "You may feel that I am trying to trick you, but just come once to Seoul and see for yourself. You will like Korea. It is a beautiful place! I love the hibiscus. That's the Korean national flower. Of course, we have many primitive places, too, in Korea, and the beauty of the kisaeng, the court dancers, is incomparable! They are nothing like the Japanese geisha."

The hibiscus, now cultivated in many other countries (in some of which it is called the Rose of Sharon), blooms from spring to fall. This large, five-petaled flower, about fifteen centimeters in diameter, comes in several colors, including white, lavender, pink, and red, and is much appreciated for its cool beauty. Just as Shinkichi had heard, Principal S—who talked about Korea in the same breath with hibiscus and kisaeng—was a wonderfully open-minded man. Shinkichi thought, "If my life is to take another course, why not in Korea?" Besides, he wanted to get away from home and be independent from his fussy eldest brother, an official in the Ministry of Internal Affairs. So he accepted the position in Seoul.

After the farewell party given by his four elder brothers, Shinkichi arrived in Seoul in April. Principal S and his wife welcomed him at the railroad station and took him by rickshaw to his lodging house in Takezoechō. Shinkichi's new life in Seoul had begun.

Everything in Seoul looked strange to Shinkichi, who had grown up in Tokyo and traveled only to Kyoto. In Seoul he felt he was in a really foreign land. First of all, the scenery was

different. The mountains, including Mount Pukhan, seemed
raw and stern, not elegant, as are Japanese mountains. The
Korean people, dressed in their characteristic white clothing,
walked leisurely in the streets, with slow, easy movements.
They had a somewhat pathetic air, a characteristic of a people
deprived of their country, and that shocked Shinkichi. Most of
what he saw and heard was new to him and different. He could
scarcely control the rush of curiosity and excitement.

His landlady, Itoman Tane, who had arrived in Korea from
Japan during the fourth decade of the Meiji era, expressed her
strong dislike for Koreans by calling them yobo. Later he
learned that her husband, a policeman born in Okinawa, had
been killed by Korean rioters in the Mansei Incident (March
First Movement) during the eighth year of Taishō (1919), in
which the Koreans held nationwide demonstrations for their
independence. Many settlers from northern Japan and southern
Kyūshū preferred to become policemen or military men during
those days. Shinkichi's eldest brother explained this in simplest
terms: "Coming from poor prefectures, they want power and a
comfortable living." Probably he is right, thought Shinkichi.

His landlady might have treated Koreans badly just to
cover her distress at being an Okinawan. Yet she was very fond
of a young Korean servant girl named Kim, caring for her as if
she were a daughter. Shinkichi found her contradictory attitude
interesting.

Keijō High School was famous for its excellent applicants,
who came from all parts of Korea to take the entrance examinations. However, few Korean students, perhaps only one
could pass the examinations for each class room, and the
school appeared to be intended for outstanding Japanese
students rather than for Koreans.

At the welcoming party for Shinkichi, held at Tenshinro at
the foot of Namsan, an old headmaster named Nitta told him,
"When a student asks a question, never say you don't know the
answer, because if you do that you will lose his respect. You
should give a temporary or even an arbitrary answer. And if
it should be wrong, tell him later another interpretation is

possible besides the one you gave. This is a valuable teaching technique!" At the same party Aoyagi, a math teacher, informed Shinkichi, "Among your fourth-year students is a Korean called Cho Ch'ŏr-in, who is excellent in English and mathematics. You should notice him."

According to Aoyagi, Koreans were brilliant at learning foreign languages. Adaptation to foreign languages had become a national trait because for centuries outsiders constantly invaded and occupied their peninsula. Shinkichi did not agree with this opinion, but he looked forward to meeting Cho Ch'ŏr-in.

Keijō High School had been founded in April 1911, the forty-third year of Meiji, two years after the Keijō First Girls High School was established. Shinkichi did not know the details of its beginnings, but he was sure that his school was a famous one in Korea.

Shinkichi was tense as he stood before his first class in the middle of April. On the blackboard, he wrote his name, Ikeda Shinkichi, in large Chinese characters and asked the class how to say it in English.

Some, translating rather than thinking, said "pond" for *ike;* others said, "rice field" for *da.* Shinkichi smiled sourly. But later in the morning a student in another class raised his hand and said, "It is Mister Shinkichi Ikeda." Shinkichi replied "Good!" and asked him, in English, "May I know your name?" The student stood up and replied, "My name is Cho. Or Patto in the Japanese style." "So he is the one," thought Shinkichi, studying him. Smiling, Shinkichi commented, "You are good." Completely ignoring this praise, Cho kept his blank expression. That was their first encounter. Cho's father, a plantation owner in Suwŏn, was so concerned about his son's education that he moved the family's residence to Seoul for the boy's sake. Cho Ch'ŏr-in was the eldest son of this great landlord from Suwŏn.

II

One Sunday Shinkichi visited the principal's home on the hillside behind the school. The many blooming hibiscus competed with one another for attention. Spreading a straw mat under a flowering bush, the principal said, "Come, sit here, Mr. Ikeda." Soon his wife and daughter brought them flasks of hot sake and side dishes arranged on a tray.

"You know, I have come to Korea to bury my bones." The principal sipped the sake and spoke in his local dialect as he stroked the tips of his mustache. "These hibiscus bushes have large and full blossoms, but sometimes to me they appear very sad and lonely. I love these flowers precisely because of that effect of loneliness. Other kinds of flowers bloom unknown, even unseen, in wild, far-off places. But these hibiscus bushes grow as high as three meters and bear large blossoms. Their faces are big, but their hearts are lonely." The principal lowered his voice, as if afraid the thought police would hear him. "Japanese want to live like cherry blossoms, which bloom all at one time and then scatter their petals quickly, in a rush. By comparison, Koreans are very tenacious. Like these hibiscus flowers." The principal's poetic metaphor caught Shinkichi's attention.

Before he had been in Korea a month, Shinkichi, through his student Cho Ch'ŏr-in, began to discover the tenacity of Korea's people. He wondered if being tenacious meant having guts. Unlike the jinchoge blossoms and the sweet osmanthus with their strong fragrance, the large, beautiful blossoms of the hibiscus had hardly any scent at all.

The two Japanese teachers exchanged sake cups and immensely enjoyed drinking in the warm sunshine of the quiet afternoon. Then a visitor, the father of Cho Ch'ŏr-in, called upon the principal, bringing fresh plums from his plantation. "Ahh, you are enjoying each other's company," he said, standing at the garden entrance. "And who is this gentleman?" he asked. "A newcomer?"

"I am the new teacher, Ikeda."

"Well, well. I've heard about you from my son. He says your English pronunciation is excellent."

"Only my pronunciation?"

Mr. Cho heard the sarcasm. "Oh, pronunciation I think is most important in learning a foreign language. One may learn the words and the grammar of a language, but even so cannot make himself understood because of his poor pronunciation."

In contrast to the slim son, the father was a stately, large-framed man, looking every inch the yangban, or aristocrat. Yangban, usually rich and belonging to one or the other of the famous clans, were like Japan's daimyo, the warlords of samurai. For centuries yangban had been directly involved in the nation's politics; more recently, they were called *yangban saram,* meaning "the wealthy people."

For the rest of the afternoon the primary subject of conversation continued to be the study of foreign languages. Mr. Cho maintained that a single world language would eliminate international conflicts and achieve world peace, since a unified language would promote communication among all nations, regardless of their respective customs and habits.

Agreeing, Shinkichi asked Mr. Cho, "Then what language are you proposing?"

"Oh, it has to be Esperanto. Each nation has its own history and pride, and people everywhere are attached to their mother tongues just as much as to their coins and currencies. Therefore a newly made language, Esperanto, should be used."

Shinkichi, impressed by the insight of a plantation owner, said, "I hope I can talk with you at length about this some day." Smiling happily, Mr. Cho replied, "At any time, please."

After he left, the principal said to Shinkichi, "You know, that man has guts. He's a true Korean!"

"What do you mean by a true Korean?"

"You'll soon find out. Some Japanese here think that we are benefiting this country culturally and economically by unifying Korea with Japan. But from the Korean point of view, our presence is a military invasion and the economic colonization of Korea. I don't want you to forget this."

Since the Mansei Incident in 1919, Japan's governor-general in Korea had been active in trying to reconcile Koreans and Japanese, but with little success. Shinkichi was very much aware of the situation, but he had no solutions to the problems.

After he returned to his lodgings, he told his landlady something about the conversation with the principal. Instantly she hissed, "Your principal is a liberal!" To himself Shinkichi acknowledged that different people with different ideas about how they wanted to live should be free to make their choices. But the thought that Japan had invaded Korea, and that he himself was here now, teaching in Seoul, filled him with feelings of guilt.

III

Just before the summer vacation, Shinkichi received a phone call from Cho Ch'ŏr-in's father, who said, "If you'd like, join me for a visit. Please come. Your principal will be coming too." Shinkichi gladly accepted the invitation. Later he remembered feeling some anxiety about the meeting. But, he reminded himself, if he had not accepted the invitation, surely he would not have met Yi Kŭm-ju, a kisaeng listed in the Korean Registry.

Unlike Japanese geisha, most of whom burdened themselves with heavy debts, all kisaeng operated independently. Yi Kŭm-ju worked mainly in the Korean-style restaurant called Myŏngwŏlgwan in Tonŭi-dong, a district of Seoul.

"Probably a restaurant like this is not new to you," Mr. Cho said to the principal as he took his two guests to the Myŏngwŏlgwan, "but no doubt it will be a new experience for Mr. Ikeda." The Myŏngwŏlgwan was once a historic place, he explained, because there the Declaration of Independence had been read at the time of the Mansei Incident.

The swooping curved eaves and gilded signboard at the entrance enhanced the restaurant's charm for Shinkichi. Indicating the ondol, the oil-papered floor, Mr. Cho remarked, "It feels cool and pleasant, doesn't it? But it will be warm in winter, just like the Russian pechka. Tonight, please enjoy the Korean dances."

Shinkichi was familiar with common dishes, such as cold noodles, but he had never tasted the traditional Korean foods. Seated near the front, with a kisaeng at his right side, Shinkichi tasted assorted hot dishes served by the kisaeng with her chopsticks. Something that looked like cooked green peas was actually green peppers, and the carrot-like strips were kkakttugi, sticks of radish preserved in red-hot peppers. They were so hot that he gasped for breath each time he put some into his mouth.

"Chinese mustard is nothing to us. But we can't take your Japanese mustard!" said the kisaeng with a laugh. After a while a musician appeared, holding a changgo, or long drum. She stood up to dance.

Mr. Cho leaned toward Shinkichi. "This dance is called Susimga, the Song of the Melancholy Heart. Korean dances use only a few gestures and body movements. But watch the hands and the toe movements." For some reason, Shinkichi was strongly affected by Yi Kŭm-ju's white pŏsŏn socks, with their upward-curving toes. Was it because her supple movements conveyed a subtle, almost coquettish, allure?

When she returned to her seat, Mr. Cho whispered to Shinkichi, "She speaks good Japanese. Talk to her."

"Please remember me," she said, handing Shinkichi her small name card, bowing formally.

She was beautiful, with fine features. Since first he saw her, Shinkichi associated her with the hibiscus blossom, whose beauty seemed to be so transient, so touched with sadness. She was nineteen years old. He wondered if her family's poverty forced her to be a professional kisaeng.

After they left the Myŏngwŏlgwan, Mr. Cho put the principal in a cab that would take him home. Turning to Shinkichi, he said, "I need another drink. Will you join me?" While walking toward a sulchip, Mr. Cho told him about the Korean custom of early marriage. A bachelor, a ch'onggak, no matter how old or how wealthy, never had more status than a married man. Moreover, since a wife was regarded as an additional pair of hands working in the family, often a fifteen- or sixteen-year-old youth would be given an older girl as his bride.

Shinkichi made a quick guess. "Then your son, Ch'ŏr-in, has a wife?"

"Yes, he has. His wife is six years older than he. Please forgive him. It's not his fault, but mine as a parent."

This was quite a shock to Shinkichi. He was still single at the age of twenty-eight, while his seventeen-year-old student already had a twenty-three-year-old wife! What a strange tradition that allowed a high-school student to be a married man. Shinkichi could not think of anything to say.

"I'm sorry, but I thought I had to tell you this," Cho's father continued.

"Well, if that's your custom, he can't help it, can he? Does everyone in the class know about this?"

"No, nobody except you and the principal. My son wanted me to tell you this."

"To tell me?"

"Yes. Ch'ŏr-in said that he felt he could trust you."

Shinkichi turned away to hide sudden tears. He was moved by the trust of this Korean student. But he really could not understand what trust meant in this case. Was it possible for the oppressed to trust the oppressor? Shinkichi knew very well that, in spite of elaborate pretenses, the Japanese were present in Korea as conquerors, not as friends. And there was no reason why the conquered people should obey so meekly their conquerors. So what was the meaning in Ch'ŏr-in's trust in him? Puzzled by this mystery, from that time on Shinkichi considered Ch'ŏr-in more than just an extraordinary youth. He began to feel more friendly toward him.

Two days before the summer vacation started, at the noon recess, Shinkichi invited Cho Ch'ŏr-in to walk with him on the hill behind the school.

"What are your plans for the future?" asked Shinkichi.

His brilliant student replied without hesitation. "I want to study abroad."

"Abroad? Why? Where?"

"Yes. In America. I don't think I would benefit much from study in Japan," said Ch'ŏr-in, looking straight at him.

"I agree. But in America I think you may have two great problems. One is that, as I have heard, the educational system in the new country of America is not yet well established. The other is your domestic situation."

"My father mentioned the same reasons. He thinks that I should go to England."

"To England?"

"But, you see, since America is the country called 'a melting pot,' I don't think the people there will despise me as a Korean. Whereas in England . . ."

"Well, you may be right about that."

"Besides, as you may have heard from my father, I want to go abroad to get away from my wife."

"You want to leave your wife?"

"Yes. She is six years older than I, and very jealous. I'm really annoyed with her, Sensei," said Ch'ŏr-in very seriously.

Ch'ŏr-in was fifteen years old when he was married to the twenty-one-year-old daughter of the foreman of the tenant farmers on his father's plantation. The marriage had been arranged even before he was born. Their sexual relationship had commenced in the following year. In the beginning, he was infatuated with his wife's body, which he enjoyed by day and by night. But gradually he became bored with her, especially as he came to believe that sex was intended primarily to provide one with descendants. The main purpose to which a man should devote his life, he believed, must be something greater than falling into bed with a wife.

"I see," said Shinkichi. He was not too much surprised by the Korean custom of early marriage because, after all, Japanese also made such arrangements. But he did not expect that a boy as young as Cho Ch'ŏr-in would be so advanced in his thinking. Shinkichi said, "With your ability, I think you will do well in America. You are already a fine man."

Ch'ŏr-in replied bitterly, "Thank you, Sensei. But my father does not think so. He still treats me like a child."

"You are not a child." Shinkichi revealed his true feelings. "Not many students of your age have thoughts like yours. I am much impressed."

IV
A year later, Cho Ch'ŏr-in sailed for America to attend Yale University. As his English teacher and supporter, Shinkichi did

his best to help him prepare for the journey. In July of the same year a rainstorm of a violence unknown for a century struck southern Korea. Usually rainfall is low in Korea, where even occasional precipitation is welcome. But the heavy rainfall of that year's storm caused the collapse of the Han River dikes and a great flood in the Yongsan district of Seoul. Two Japanese Navy destroyers were sent from Inchŏn to assist in rescue efforts. Although Shinkichi experienced some discomfort when the muddy water flowed into his lodging house near the Yongsan district, damage to that area was comparatively minor because of its elevation.

His high-school building, a two-story wooden structure, was assigned as a temporary refugee center, and Shinkichi helped to take care of people from the flooded areas. Among those refugees was Yi Kŭm-ju, the dancer he had met at Myŏngwŏlgwan Restaurant. While he was distributing freshly made rice balls to the refugees, a woman, most unexpectedly, did not take the proffered food. Quickly covering her face with her hands, she cried out, "Aigo . . ."

Korean women often say "Aigo." When written in Chinese characters, *aigo* means "a sad cry." Among Koreans, however, it is not used only on sad occasions but is a convenient exclamation for many different reasons, such as when one touches a hot object or hurts oneself. In surprise they shout "Aigo omma," in pleasure, "Aigo chok'etta."

"Ah, it's you," said Shinkichi, recognizing Yi Kŭm-ju. He put the rice ball into her hand. "Here, eat this. You'll feel better."

"My mother is not feeling well," Yi Kŭm-ju said. He saw beside her a old woman, soaked to the skin, shivering, with lips purple from cold.

"Come with me." Shinkichi took them to the school infirmary. After examination, the doctor decided that nothing serious was wrong with the mother; she was likely just catching a cold. Shinkichi brought a blanket. "Take off her clothes," he said to Yi Kŭm-ju, "and wrap her in this. Keep her warm." His kindness greatly surprised both the kisaeng and her mother.

Soon after the flood the summer vacation began. Just as

Shinkichi was thinking of going home to Japan for a visit, Yi Kŭm-ju called on him. She was dressed in Western-style clothing, for at that time it would have been indiscreet for a Korean woman dressed in the traditional costume to call upon a Japanese man.

"My mother wishes to invite you to our house, so that she can express her gratitude. I have come here to invite you to visit us—at your convenience."

Because he was thinking of going home within a few days, Shinkichi replied, "If I may go today or tomorrow, I would be delighted to call upon you."

"In that case, I will come to take you there, tomorrow, at noon."

After Kŭm-ju left, his landlady immediately wanted to know all about her. "She's a yobo, isn't she?" And when the landlady learned that the woman was a kisaeng as well, she scolded him. "How dare you, a schoolteacher! If you need a woman, plenty of good Japanese geisha are here!" Knowing that nothing would change her prejudice, Shinkichi ignored these objections and made no excuses for his conduct.

On the following day Shinkichi accompanied Yi Kŭm-ju to her house in Hyoch'angwŏn. Her mother, entirely Korean in upbringing, spoke no Japanese. But somehow, most remarkably, her true heart could communicate with Shinkichi's, even though he understood almost no Korean. When the mother said "Onŭl manhi tŏpsŏmnida," Shinkichi could sense that she was saying, "Today is hot, isn't it?"

They lived in an ordinary house in the Korean style, with several rooms surrounding a small courtyard. Shinkichi was led to the mother's almost bare sitting room, the size of a six-mat Japanese room. The room looked empty without the tokonoma, or alcove, that a Japanese room would have had. Yi Kŭm-ju explained that she had several younger brothers and sisters and that a few years before, their father had died of an illness.

Soon a girl of sixteen or seventeen, who strongly resembled Kŭm-ju, brought in a tray of food. Kŭm-ju offered Shinkichi a cup of warm sake, saying, "We tried our best to prepare food to please your taste."

"Thank you." Shinkichi took the sake cup. "In Japan, our custom called Returning the Cup invites the hostess to share the sake." Shinkichi filled the cup for the mother. Thus they happily passed the cup, continuing a delightful visit.

Later Shinkichi learned from Mr. Cho that a kisaeng rarely invited customers to her home. Because kisaeng were financially independent, they had no need to flatter their customers. If a customer asked whether he could come to her home on the following day, she would smilingly agree, "Please do come." But when the customer actually did visit her place, someone there turned him away with an obvious excuse, such as "She is out now" or "She has gone to the bathhouse," even though she was at home. In this manner, the kisaeng tried to maintain their independence. A persistent man might go to the house several times and eventually might be allowed to enter. But then he would be taken to a room where he received only a cup of hot water and some sweets. And then he would be dismissed. In spite of all this coy behavior, the customer could begin a relationship by discreetly shipping under his cushion five or so yen carefully wrapped in a piece of paper. He should never try to give money directly and openly to a kisaeng. If he did commit such a blunder, she would refuse it in order to maintain her status.

Completely unaware of the complicated etiquette observed by the Korean demimonde, Shinkichi acted naturally, simply thinking that Yi Kŭm-ju and her mother wanted to thank him for his kindness to them at the time of the flood.

However, after that visit, this innocent Shinkichi became more and more attracted to the beautiful blossoms of the hibiscus. To him they were reminders of the beautiful and fragile Yi Kŭm-ju.

V

At the time when, in Japan, the monthly salary of an Imperial University graduate was 80 yen, Shinkichi received 120 yen each month. This very high salary, which included a bonus for working abroad, was due mainly to the favor of Principal S. A teacher's pay was good in those days because only men with much learning and excellent character were chosen to educate children.

However, Shinkichi spent nearly half of his generous income in the Myŏngwŏlgwan, just to see Yi Kŭm-ju. Unsophisticated in the ways of a man and a woman, Shinkichi was unable to communicate his feelings to Yi Kŭm-ju. For her part, although she liked him, she was frustrated because she was not certain of his feelings. Thus their relationship remained an old-fashioned love affair, in which timid interest never led to joyful consummation.

Meanwhile, Shinkichi was invited by Mr. Cho to a Japanese restaurant, Chiyomoto, in Nanzanchō. There he found both Mr. Cho and Yi Kŭm-ju waiting for him.

"Let's drink and talk frankly tonight," said Mr. Cho, smiling. The purpose behind the invitation was to warn Shinkichi that gossip about him and the kisaeng had reached his students.

Mr. Cho began, "If one wishes to have a first-class kisaeng as his mistress, one must also take care of her family. The Korean custom is quite clear about this. Everybody in her family relies on the kisaeng. So if you are merely playing a game with her, please stop it."

Shinkichi became indignant. "I have no intention of just toying with her! I want to marry her." At this unexpected reply, Cho and Yi Kŭm-ju looked at each other, saying not a word.

Cho explained gently, "You see, Mr. Ikeda. She says that even now her monthly expenses are at least two hundred yen. If she marries, expenses will increase." Shinkichi had no answer to Cho's reminders of reality. Moreover, Kŭm-ju said she wanted to send her two younger brothers to college. Costs for their education would be great. If he married her, he would have to carry all her financial burdens as his own. He thought that he could increase his monthly income by seventy to eighty yen by working as a translator or by teaching night classes. But beyond that he could earn nothing more.

"So this is the end," thought Shinkichi, biting his lower lip. Tears glistened in his eyes. No laws prohibited a teacher from marrying a kisaeng. But many people, especially the Japanese, would criticize him. With a strong will he could bear such criticism, but he had no way to solve the financial problems.

To end the awkward situation, Mr. Cho changed the subject and talked about his son. Ch'ŏr-in was studying well in America, but his father feared that he might be getting involved in political organizations.

But Kŭm-ju wanted to return to her personal problems.

"Mr. Ikeda," she said, "let us go to Segŏmjŏng next Sunday."

"To Segŏmjŏng? What for?"

Shinkichi knew the place because twice he'd taken a class there on excursions. It was beyond the North Gate, which was reached by walking along a stream after passing beyond Hyoja-dong. The gate's formal name was Ch'angŭimun, but it was popularly called the North Gate, in relation to the three others, the Great East, West, and South Gates.

The high surrounding wall and the several gates of Seoul had been constructed by Yi T'aejo, the dynastic founder, to protect the newly established capital from external enemies. Records show that more than 118,070 laborers were involved in the preliminary work, from the ninth day of the first month to the twenty-eighth of the second month, in the year 1396, and that 79,400 laborers finished the construction between the sixth day of the eighth month and the twenty-fourth of the ninth month. Recruiting peasants for the construction project during the summer and winter agricultural breaks was a brilliant idea.

The result was the completion of the eight gates including the Sukchŏngmun; the Honghwamun, popularly called the Small East Gate; the Hŭnginmun, the Great East Gate; the Kwanghŭimun, or the Water Gate; the Tonŭimun, the Great West Gate; the Ch'angŭimun, the North Gate; the Sungyemun,

the Great South Gate; and the Sodŏkmun, the Small West Gate.
Segŏmjŏng was outside the North Gate and was a popular
scenic place for picnics and outings among residents of Seoul.
On the following Sunday, Shinkichi and Kŭm-ju met at Hyoja-
dong and moved on to Segŏmjŏng.

After the fifteenth ruler of the Yi dynasty, Kwanghaegun,
became king, he indulged in all kinds of dissipation with his
concubines and became increasingly despotic. One night in
1623, Prince Nŭngyang, later King Injo, and his supporters
gathered at the top of the cliff above Segŏmjŏng, sharpened
their swords with whetstones, broke into the Kyŏngbok Palace
through the North Gate, and overthrew the dissolute Kwanghaegun. In commemoration of the successful coup, Segŏmjŏng,
the Sword-washing Arbor, was erected.

Shinkichi and Yi Kŭm-ju ate a leisurely lunch while watching the clear waters of the stream flowing over the many
boulders and stones. Having finished their meal, Yi Kŭm-ju
said, "Over there, ahead of us, one of my relatives has a small
house. Shall we go there to rest for a while?"

Shinkichi was not so tired as to need to rest but, being
curious to see a typical Korean country house, he agreed. As
they walked up the hill beyond Segŏmjŏng, they reached a
small village of about twenty houses. They could see the typical
Korean laundry scene along the riverbank in the valley below.

"Here we are." Yi Kŭm-ju stopped in front of one of the
houses. "Please wait here." She entered the home, which had a
thatched roof, mud walls, and a rather shabby appearance.
Within a few moments an old woman came out, looked curi-
ously at Shinkichi, and walked slowly toward the haberdashery
in the village. Later Shinkichi learned that the house did not
belong to any relative of Kŭm-ju's, but was used for private
assignations by a number of kisaeng.

She would have invited a formal lover or patron to her own
house, but she must have felt that to receive a Japanese man in
her home was an indiscretion she could not risk, and so she
decided to use this place. She took him to a room with a thin

futon spread on the ondol floor and a tall, white porcelain vase
in the corner.

"What's that?" asked Shinkichi, pointing at the vase.

Kŭm-ju, plainly irritated, said, "Don't ask such a question
at a time like this!" Then, softening a bit, she continued, "I
cannot marry you. But because I like you very much, I have
brought us here." Swiftly she took off her clothes and lay down
on the futon, wearing only her white bloomers.

"Are you sure you want to do this?" Shinkichi asked,
sinking to his knees beside her.

"We have only two hours," said Kŭm-ju, drawing him
toward her, helping him to shed his clothes.

Shinkichi felt guilty about this furtive meeting but remembered an old saying from Japan: "Refusing an offered tray is
shameful for a man." So he lay with her. Her skin was as white
and smooth as porcelain, but her body was larger than his
limited experience with Japanese prostitutes had prepared
him for.

After they were spent, Shinkichi felt thirsty. "I would like a
drink of water."

"It's in a jar in the kitchen," replied Kŭm-ju, embarrassed
now.

The kitchen had a bare earthen floor, a soot-covered stove,
and a clay water jar with a ladle beside it. Shinkichi, inspecting
everything, saw how heat and smoke from cooking fires in the
stove passed into ducts under the ondol floor to warm it. He
scooped up water with the ladle and looked around for something to put it in, a tea cup, a glass, even an empty rice bowl.
All he could find was a dirty, chipped bowl lying on the floor in
a corner. It might have been used for feeding a dog or a cat.
Instantly his eye was drawn to the design on the sides of the
bowl.

While drinking his fill of water from the ladle, Shinkichi
picked up the dirty bowl and examined it. The simple design
must have been drawn in one swift stroke. The color of the
design was a most vivid blue. After studying it for a while, he

began to wash the bowl with more water from the jar. When it was cleaned, although chipped and slightly cracked, it revealed a free and bold beauty in both its color and glaze.

"What are you doing?" Kŭm-ju appeared in the kitchen.

"Look! This bowl! It's so beautiful . . ."

"You can see such bowls in any house in Korea. If you like this ugly one so much, I'll bring you some better ones from my home."

So, out of a kisaeng's act of kindness grew the fateful first encounter of the famous Yi dynasty painted porcelain and its Japanese discoverer.

VI

A few days later, as she had promised, Kŭm-ju brought some pieces of porcelain to Shinkichi's lodging house while he was away. That evening, watching Shinkichi take tea cups and vases one after another from their paper wrappings, the landlady sneered, "Such yobo chinaware isn't worth a sen." And Kim, the young Korean maidservant, said, "We have plenty of them in my home town." She came from the Kwangju county of Kyŏnggi Province, where her grandfather had been a potter.

Shinkichi was greatly disappointed by their low opinion of the pieces. But later, as he caressed the cups and vases in his room, they all looked so lovely with their lustrous glaze and delicate designs that he said to himself, "Whatever they think about this porcelain, it is beautiful to me. Especially because these pieces are a present from Kŭm-ju. As mementoes of our friendship, as a parting gift." Shinkichi displayed them all in the alcove of his room. He regarded each of those porcelain objects as representations of Kŭm-ju herself, and he greeted them each morning when he left for school and each evening when he returned.

He knew that his love for her could never be fulfilled in marriage, but his yearning for her still lingered deep in his heart. He felt miserable because even knowing the truth did not help to end his painful need. And, to compound his misery and his shame, each night he took a special one of the vases into his bed, to use it as he wanted to use Kŭm-ju, and tearfully remembered the fleeting moments he'd spent with her in Segŏmjŏng. The vase was as smooth as the skin of Kŭm-ju but, where she had been warm and living, the substitute was cool and unresponsive.

One night, while his passion was reaching its peak, he had an idea. "Since I have fallen in love to this extent with both Kŭm-ju and this vase, I might as well investigate the origins of this treasure." He desperately needed to do something that would help him forget Kŭm-ju's body. From that moment, his life took an ironical turn.

One of the vases that Kŭm-ju had given him was fairly large, 9.77 inches high and 9.45 inches in diameter. (Museum catalogues inform us that this very piece, known as "The Yi Dynasty Vase with Chrysanthemum Patterns of Iron Sand Painting, a masterpiece from the Sŏngch'ŏn Kiln," became very famous because it introduced the Yi dynasty painted porcelain to the world.)

Shinkichi asked his landlady to allow Kim, the maidservant, to take him to her family's village. Accordingly, on January 15 of the following year, he went with her to Kyŏngan-ri, a small farming village on the Kyŏngan River, a tributary of the mighty Han.

Kim's father, a tenant farmer, and other members of her family heartily welcomed Shinkichi and their homecoming daughter with a feast. While they ate, Kim interpreted for Shinkichi. In this way he learned much about the Kwangju county where, in former times, many government kilns had operated. "They must have fired pots and dishes at the king's orders," said Kim's father, with a shrug. From the family's storeroom he brought out many bowls and small dishes for Shinkichi to examine. "If you like any of these," he said, "please take them."

According to Kim's father, such "cheap porcelain" was abundant in his neighborhood. His comments about the "crudeness" of the pieces discouraged Shinkichi. He felt as if Kŭm-ju herself were being disgraced and devalued. He asked

Kim, "Don't you have a big vase?" using gestures to indicate the size he meant.

"Well, yes, we do. But we can't give it to you."

"But I just want to look at it."

"No, we have nothing like that to show," said Kim. Her embarrassment reminded Shinkichi of Kŭm-ju's when he asked her about the big white vase set in a corner of that room in Segŏmjŏng. Kim's father, more of a realist, told him that such vases were used as indoor toilets (what Westerners call "chamber pots"). Instead of going to icy backyard outhouses during Korea's severe winters, sensible Koreans urinated into such vases in their warm bedrooms. Being modest, both Kŭm-ju and Kim had refused to show them to him, or even to admit that they existed.

After lunch, Kim and Shinkichi visited the homes of several neighbors and saw many bowls, dishes, urns, vases, and flasks of various shapes and sizes. Most were used as food containers. Choosing pieces with simple designs, Shinkichi bought whatever he liked for five to ten sen apiece.

Although Shinkichi was far from expert in these matters, he did know something about the Japanese porcelain ware called Kiyomizu-yaki. Once, when he was a student in Kyoto, he had lived on the second floor of a porcelain maker's shop in Kiyomizu. Since then he had been attracted to that kind of porcelain, especially after he heard the master of the shop say, "You know, porcelain is very beautiful, very wonderful. People die in fifty years or so, but porcelain survives for hundreds of years." At that moment, the notion of the longevity of porcelain was strongly imprinted on his mind.

Life expectancy in those days was not very high; only a few attained the seventieth birthday celebration called the *koki,* meaning "a celebration for something rare." In comparison to such short lifetimes for humans, pottery, if properly treated, would last forever. What a remarkable situation! Moreover, his art in shaping and decorating his pieces would preserve forever the quality of the living, breathing, individual potter.

Shinkichi, ignorant of the significance of the government-subsidized kilns during the years of the Yi dynasty, collected many specimens of their work. Grunting under the weight of the heavy loads, he carried them all the way home to Takezoechō. There he placed all of them in and around the tokonoma in his room. He was like a miser, gloating over his hoard.

He started collecting these pieces during the winter vacation, when he had no classes to teach. He went to libraries, but he found no useful accounts to instruct him. Then he thought to visit a personage who was related to the royal family and from him learned that the government-subsidized kilns were referred to as "the official kilns of the Yi family." They had been constructed in the basin of the Kyŏngan River, which flows north from Namhansansŏng, about nineteen miles east of Seoul. Since the area was in the Kwangju county of Kyŏnggi Province, the kilns were generally called the Kwangju Kilns.

"In contrast to the pure white ceramics of Koryŏ, the porcelain ware from the Kwangju Kilns is relatively crude and was used for ordinary household utensils. The Kwangju products can hardly be called objects of art. To tell the truth, we Koreans pay no attention to them," explained the director of the fine arts department of the royal Yi family. Once again Shinkichi was disappointed. But as he gazed at the specimens arranged about his room, he was impressed all the more by their simple and unpretentious beauty—just as lovely, he assured himself, as are the large yet unscented flowers of the hibiscus.

The large vase that Kŭm-ju gave him was especially unusual, with its amber glaze casually covering the upper portion, leaving the rest in dark blue. An iron-hued chrysanthemum, deftly sketched, seemed to be dancing upon the belly of the vase. The more he looked at it, the more he liked it and, of course, seeing it reminded him of Kŭm-ju, and of how much he wished he could see her.

In February Shinkichi received a letter from his eldest brother in Japan, who told him to come home during the spring vacation to discuss something important. Scarcely bothering to wonder what the brother wanted to talk about, Shinkichi understood that of course he would have to answer the summons. And then he had a sudden inspiration. Recalling that Yamanoi Makoto, a high-school classmate who had gone on to major in art history, worked now in the Imperial Museum in Tokyo, he shouted, "That's the one!" When the spring vacation arrived, Shinkichi selected three pieces from his porcelain collection to show to Yamanoi.

Back in Tokyo, Shinkichi met with his eldest brother, who talked about two important matters. One was a marriage proposal for him; the other was an offer of employment in the Research Section of the Manchurian Railways. According to his brother, the Research Section with its generous budget would offer a higher salary than he was receiving in Seoul. But to Shinkichi it sounded like an espionage organization for the Japanese army in Manchuria, and he immediately declined the offer. As for the marriage proposal, he could not help but agree to an arranged meeting with the daughter of his brother's superior.

The daughter had good features but seemed quite distant, even snobbish. "Saa!" thought Shinkichi, borrowing the wisdom of his principal, "my Kŭm-ju is a hibiscus from Korea. This one is just a thorny rose from Ueno." After some hesitation, Shinkichi agreed to marry her because of the excellent dowry and the strong recommendation of his eldest brother, who had always taken care of him like a father. His brother insisted that Shinkichi should marry immediately and take his bride to Seoul.

"But I can't afford a wife just now. I am living in a small lodging house," Shinkichi argued. His brother persisted, saying, "Don't worry. I will rent a nice house for you in Seoul." Shinkichi yielded. He and Miwa Taeko had a quiet wedding and went to Ikaho for their becoming-acquainted journey.

Immediately upon returning to Tokyo from the marriage journey, Shinkichi called on Yamanoi. "So you finally got married," the eminent critic laughed. "And to a government official's daughter! Good for you! Well, let me look at your precious pieces." While examining the three specimens—the vase, an incense burner, and a wine flask—Yamanoi offered no opinion, saying only, "I see. Indeed. I see . . ."

"Well, what do you think?"

"Well, as you've guessed, these probably came from the Yi dynasty kilns."

"That's right. Even though they're plain, I think they're wonderful!"

"Yes, they're not bad at all. But somehow they convey low or depressed feelings on the part of the potters. A kind of despair . . ."

Yamanoi all but caressed the incense burner.

"Do you think they're only cheap trifles?"

"No. Far from that. Their simplicity of form and their obvious naturalness, a freedom from artificiality, make them very interesting. I would say," and here he allowed himself to sound like a Buddhist priest, "they convey a sense of desire growing out of non-desire."

"Indeed. That's why they're beautiful."

"The wares from Kiyomizu and Kutani are very rich in complex decorations, in the ornate geometric designs and patterns they favor. But this Korean vase is different: all those open spaces in the pattern create warm, relaxed feelings in the user. If I had the chance, I would definitely buy this vase," declared Yamanoi. Then Shinkichi told him a little about the official kilns of the Yi family. Yamanoi listened with interest. "Now I see why these Korean pieces are so distinctive. They reflect the true hearts of the people who were drafted to work in the official kilns. They were untrained, unself-conscious. They expected no flattering admiration. So they made these things for the king just as they would have made them for themselves. Despair may be hidden beneath their naturalness, but hope too enters into the colors of their glazes, the sweep of their designs. I would very much like to study these pieces further. Could you leave them with me for a while?"

VII
Shinkichi's wife Taeko delivered a baby girl in early
December of the same year, eight months after their marriage.
The midwife called the delivery premature. A week later the
infant became ill. Shinkichi summoned a doctor and, during the
examination, asked, "Is the baby premature?"
     "My goodness, no! She is so plump and round. She can't be
premature," said the doctor.
     "Ah, just as I suspected," thought Shinkichi, biting his
lower lip.
     His suspicions has been awakened when his eldest brother
so persistently urged him to go on their wedding trip immediately after the ceremony. He became more skeptical as he
thought of his wife's very generous dowry and of the rapid
change in her sexual responses. She complained greatly of the
pain on the first night, but as soon as they moved to Seoul she
began to demand frequent intercourse. And just about the time
he noticed this change, one night he clearly heard her say in her
sleep, "No, no, Masao-san!"
     "Masao-san?" thought Shinkichi, and his suspicions
doubled. Then the baby arrived—too soon.
     "So the child is not mine," he mused. "Having learned
about his daughter's pregnancy, her father must have consulted
my brother. And he pushed me into this marriage, just to help
his superior." Shinkichi became intensely angry as he understood how their scheming minds had trapped him. He said
nothing to his wife, but he released much of his rage in his
diary.
     Years later he learned that his wife Taeko had had an affair
with a son of the vice minister of internal affairs and become
pregnant. She turned for help to her mother, asking for an
abortion, but met strong opposition, for abortion was a serious
crime in those days. Her father consulted a trusted subordinate,
Shinkichi's eldest brother, who sacrificed his youngest brother
to save face for the Miwa family.
     Soon after the baby was born, the Taishō emperor died.
About that time Shinkichi told his wife, "I am going to spend

your money on my hobbies." He began to buy fine pieces of
Kwangju Kiln porcelain, frequented the restaurants of
Chongno, and entered into a patron's relationship with Yi
Kŭm-ju.

The more he learned about the porcelain, the more he
became passionately devoted to it.

For example, he found that during the time of Sejo, the
seventh king of the Yi dynasty, the Kwangju Kilns began to
produce a very handsome ware painted with designs in cobalt
blue. The costly blue pigment was imported from China. The
blue and white porcelain was valued as highly as were pieces
decorated with gold and silver. According to the Yi dynasty
National Codes, in the sixth year of Sejo (1460), government
officials were prohibited from using gold, silver, and blue and
white porcelain containers except for liquor cups.

As soon as Shinkichi learned the historical background of
Korean porcelains, he sent Yamanoi a long and detailed report.
In reply, Yamanoi sent him this opinion: "After kneading and
shaping the clay, they probably dried the piece in a shady place,
then painted it with the blue designs, glazed it, and baked it in
the noborigama [climbing kiln] at a temperature of seven
hundred degrees in the Serger Cones."

In the second year of Shōwa (1927), Yamanoi published
an important article entitled "The Beauty of the Yi Dynasty
Painted Porcelain." It appeared in a journal of fine arts and
immediately established his position as a critic of the fine arts.
At that time Shinkichi did not give much attention to Yamanoi's
debut in the academic world but, as the years passed and Yi
dynasty porcelain became well known, he felt that Yamanoi
had ignored his part in telling the world about Korean
porcelain.

Then one day Yamanoi suddenly arrived in Seoul and
sought out Shinkichi. "Buy me more of this porcelain," he
demanded. "Send me as much as you can." Shinkichi asked the
maidservant, Kim, and Yi Kŭm-ju to collect a number of
porcelain pieces and send them to Yamanoi. By that time Yi
dynasty porcelain, which had hardly been noticed before,

increased rapidly in value in Japan. Those crude bowls, dishes, and vases, which had been lying around in farmers' kitchens and yards for so long, were attracting the attention of collectors. When Shinkichi's interest in Korean porcelain started, he could buy an iron-colored liquor jar of flower-bird design for only fifteen sen. But as soon as Japanese connoisseurs appreciated their simple beauty, the price of these smaller Korean porcelains rose to two or three yen apiece. A large jar bought from a farmer at five yen was priced at twenty-two yen at an auction in Seoul, soared to a hundred yen when it reached Tokyo, and was resold there at seven hundred yen. From these reports, Shinkichi could imagine what a sensation these Korean porcelains caused. He did not mind in the least, because in the process he too became rich. Having money greatly changes a man's life. In the fourth year of Shōwa, Shinkichi quit his job as a teacher and acquired a house for his mistress, Yi Kŭm-ju. His wife tried to protest but was silenced by a single ruthless remark: "Why are you complaining? You married me just so you could have another man's child—and pass it off as mine." That quieted her.

Shinkichi traveled often between Japan and Korea. Now he became a dealer in antiques. Yamanoi advised him, "Dealing in Korean porcelain is good, but you should learn more about all the fine arts." Even so, in those early days, Shinkichi was the foremost expert in Yi dynasty porcelain. He took his pieces, bought in Korea at five to ten yen each, and sold them in Tokyo or Kyoto for several hundred yen each. Most of his profits he lavished on his mistress. Thanks to that enormous income, the beautiful kisaeng Yi Kŭm-ju opened a cafe-bar, named Arirang, in Meijichō.

At about that time, Shinkichi's former student, Cho Ch'ŏr-in, returned from the United States.

VIII

"Sensei, you have changed!" exclaimed Cho Ch'ŏr-in. He looked so strong and mature that Shinkichi felt tired and old.

"Have I changed that much?"

"Yes. You were more pure in those days."

"Pure?"

"As much so as is the porcelain to which you are devoted now."

Shinkichi was touched by Ch'ŏr-in's comment. He recalled a wise saying: "How much one is taught by a child whom one used to carry on one's back!"

The two were exchanging drinking cups in a tavern in Chongno. The floor was earthen and the yakchu drinks cost only five sen for a cup, served with a side dish.

Cho Ch'ŏr-in, serious now, changed the subject. "Sensei, Japan is now in danger."

"What do you mean?"

"I don't mean to blame you, personally, of course. I'm talking about Japan. The country will certainly be destroyed if it continues on its present path." Probably because he lived almost at the center of the whirlpool, Shinkichi did not comprehend what Ch'ŏr-in was saying. When a man left his native land for another country, usually he could see his own country from another point of view. Restricted to Japan alone, he would not be able to see matters objectively. Cho Ch'ŏr-in, who had lived in America for several years, could analyze Japan now from an outsider's point of view and judge the situation more objectively.

"In short, do you mean that leaving teaching and devoting myself to Korean porcelain is not good?" Shinkichi tried to sound as if sneering at himself.

Shaking his head, Cho Ch'ŏr-in repeated, "No, I don't mean that at all. I mean that Japan will destroy itself if it persists in its present course of action."

"Destroy itself?"

"Yes. But that destruction might benefit us here, in Korea." Whereupon Cho ordered another round of drinks.

"You seem to have become a real Korean after living in America." This time Shinkichi directed the sneer at Ch'ŏr-in. "Your father has been afraid that you might get involved in a political or social movement."

"I am already," admitted Ch'ŏr-in boldly, not even looking

over his shoulder. "I have returned to help liberate my country from Japan."

"I see," nodded Shinkichi. He sipped his drink and then continued quietly, "That's quite natural, I think, since we Japanese improperly forced Korea to join us." Neither one thought about the danger in such talk.

"And, Sensei, I have a personal request to make. Don't send too many Korean art objects to Japan, please."

Shinkichi stared at his former student. "You mean the Yi dynasty painted porcelain?"

"Yes."

"But your people have ignored it for hundreds of years. You have never appreciated its beauty because of the notion that keeping something old will bring evil to a household."

"That's true. A Confucian proverb warns that devils inhabit old things."

"Your people have abused these porcelains in your kitchens, your backyards, your toilets. You discard them when they're cracked or chipped, afraid that they will bring bad luck."

"I know."

"Well, I discovered them lying around on bare earthen floors and in courtyard mud and gave them a new life. I think you should feel grateful to me."

"But I've heard that you have made a profit of tens of thousand yen from them."

"Yes, but coincidentally. And selling them is my job now. My livelihood."

After this unsatisfactory exchange of opinions, in which neither convinced the other, they fell into an awkward silence. A short time later, they parted.

As Japan's connoisseurs began to prize the Yi dynasty porcelain, buyers and agents from foreign museums, too, were attracted, and the prices rose even higher. Rumors spread. Some people claimed, for example, that what looked like a mud-encrusted modern jar found in a remote village turned out to be a Yi dynasty painted porcelain and was sold for thirty yen. In and out of Seoul, people gravely assured others that brokers and agents were competing furiously for the porcelains and were killing each other without mercy.

By that time Shinkichi had opened a shop with a frontage of twelve feet in the second block of Hommachi. His wife, Taeko, still as beautiful as a rose, did not get along well with him. She was unhappy, no doubt because he spent most of the time with his mistress. Yi Kŭm-ju, no longer a kisaeng, was his very discreet and loyal assistant. Shinkichi disliked Taeko and knew that he could never love her.

As Cho Ch'ŏr-in had predicted, an incident took place in Manchuria that enabled Japan to establish a new country, called Manchukuo. Shinkichi's eldest brother visited Seoul on the way to a new position in Dairen, as a member of the board of trustees of the Manchurian Railways.

As soon as he saw Shinkichi at the station, his elder brother said, "You're doing well here, aren't you?" In the next breath he declared, "Don't hold a grudge from the past."

Immediately Shinkichi knew that his brother was referring to Taeko. Shinkichi did not bother to reply. As far as he was concerned, this interfering eldest brother had caused nothing but misfortune for him. Shinkichi remembered very well how this brother had tried to place him in the Research Section of the Manchurian Railways. Considering the present situation in Japan and Korea, everything relating to Shinkichi's life seemed to have arisen from his brother's self-centered efforts to benefit only himself.

His eldest brother stayed in Seoul for about a week, naturally as a guest in Shinkichi's home. Every night he came back late, smelling of tobacco smoke and drink. He must have been invited to geisha houses by high-ranking army officers and the governor-general of Korea.

Several days after Shinkichi's brother left for P'yŏngyang, Cho Ch'ŏr-in came to the house at midnight. "Is His Highness Ikeda your elder brother?" he inquired.

"Yes. But why do you ask?"

"Did he say anything special?"

Shinkichi responded frankly, "Since we don't get along, we hardly talked."

"That can't be possible." Cho persisted. "Did he mention a place called Kando?" At that moment Taeko brought in a tray with tea and sweet cakes.

"Oh, yes," she said. "I remember that name. He was reading a typewritten document about Kando or someplace like that. I saw the papers lying around in his room."

"Just as I thought," muttered Cho Ch'ŏr-in. "Please excuse me now," he bowed to Taeko first and quickly went out into the night.

While sipping the tea that Cho had not touched, Taeko said, "He is quite handsome, isn't he?"

"Well, he's young. And he has been to America, you know," snorted Shinkichi, not paying much attention to such womanly gush.

"I wonder why he's interested in Kando? Where is this island?"

"Don't be stupid! It's not an island. It's a village beyond the Yalu River, at the boundary between Korea and Manchukuo." Shinkichi, having only the vaguest memory of the place, talked as if he knew all about it.

According to Japanese military police, Kando was a base for Korean revolutionaries who wanted independence for Korea. They had organized a guerrilla band, attacked a border garrison, and stolen weapons and ammunition.

A man named Kim Il-sung was the leader of those guerrillas. Later he became the head of the Democratic People's Republic in North Korea.

IX

Shinkichi, recently returned to Seoul from Japan, noticed that his wife was wearing heavy makeup again, as she had before their marriage. In addition, she had a fashionable permanent wave for her newly bobbed hair. Many pairs of high-heeled shoes were neatly arranged in her shoe case. And she wore flesh-colored silk stockings, even inside the house.

While I was gone, assumed Shinkichi, I guess she's learned about all these fancy things from the movies. No doubt she's planning to seduce me. To his surprise, a surge of pity mixed with lust for this beautiful and unused wife weakened him. "Let's go upstairs," he said, yielding to the urge. After many months of absence, he embraced her; she was wearing only those sheer silk stockings. Taeko responded happily, but Shinkichi thought that something new and different marked their intercourse that evening.

He resumed his work, devoting himself daily to his interest in Korean porcelain. He planned to write a long article about Yi dynasty painted porcelain. He did research in libraries and archives and carefully assembled the fragments of a rare glazed vase that was inscribed with verses and had come from the Toma-ri Kiln. He discovered early ceramics of white porcelain and celadon enclosed in the ancient tombs at Kaesŏng and in Chŏlla Province. He supported conclusions expressed in his articles by excavating the ruins of official kilns. Leaving the business of dealing in art objects to Yi Kŭm-ju and her brother, Shinkichi concentrated on his academic work. Perhaps Ch'ŏr-in's plea, "Don't send too many Korean art objects to Japan," had been taken to heart, and he was concentrating on research as if atoning for earlier sins.

Shinkichi's long absences from home gave Taeko the opportunity to become involved in an affair of which he was unaware. His former student, Cho Ch'ŏr-in, became her lover. Dodging arrest by the Japanese military police, Ch'ŏr-in informed his colleagues of their activities. He visited the Ikeda house when Shinkichi was away, asking Taeko such questions as "How many pages were in those documents Mr. Ikeda was reading?" Taeko told him everything she knew, and in return he gave her up-to-date information about the ways of American women. Taeko's craze for short hair and Western dresses grew out of Ch'ŏr-in's instructions. They went out together to buy shoes for her and to see Western movies. At first their relationship was innocent enough, but soon, being young and in need, they forgot the standards of moral behavior and found consolation in Taeko's bed.

While her husband was in Japan, Taeko was unable to control her frustration. She became completely infatuated with the younger man, without knowing of his activities as a revolutionary. In those day, adultery by a woman was a criminal offense, especially among the Koreans, who had high standards of morality. Dragging an adulterous wife through the streets by a rough rope tied around her neck had official sanction. Knowing about that penalty may have given Taeko more thrills from her infidelity. Or she may have begun the affair in revenge for her husband's indifference, or to show her hatred for Yi Kŭm-ju.

One day, when Shinkichi was immersed in his studies in the Kwangju county, he received a message from Kŭm-ju telling him to return to Seoul immediately. Upon his arrival, he learned that Taeko had strangled her daughter and committed suicide by cutting her throat with a razor blade.

Appalled, Shinkichi was doubly shocked—first, by the autopsy report of the doctor who had examined Taeko's body and found her pregnant; and second, by her will, which declared that her lover was Cho Ch'ŏr-in. In that will she wrote, "Our marriage has been wrong from the beginning. That was my fault, and I made another mistake with Cho Ch'ŏr-in, who has gone to Manchukuo. I have no excuse to offer you. Since it would be a pity to leave my daughter behind, I've decided to take her with me."

For the first time in many years Shinkichi thought about all that he had done—or left undone. And he grieved at how the blossoms of the Korean hibiscus and the painted porcelain of the Yi dynasty had driven Taeko and her daughter to their deaths. On the night before the funeral, after all the visitors had gone, Shinkichi, alone in the empty house, sobbed with bitter tears. In his sorrow the death mask of the little girl, whom he had raised and loved as his own daughter, seemed to be crying out for vengeance. He even thought of apologizing to the dead by destroying his most cherished blue and white porcelain vase. But as he gazed upon the beautiful thing, saw its translucent glaze and the harmony of hues beneath its thin veneer, the bitterness that seethed in his heart subsided, and he found peace.

The vase was the product of nameless potters who worked silently, following orders from above. Their wages must have been so meager that they could barely support their wives and children. They did not intend to make objects of art, but just turned out utensils for common use in ordinary homes. Their products lacked the simplicity of Ming ceramics and the elegant touches of Japanese porcelain. Their skills as painters were imperfect. But precisely because of the crudeness of their work they had succeeded in conveying the fullness and largeness that to later generations characterized the painted porcelain of the Yi dynasty. The absence of arrogance and pretense only emphasized their strength and naturalness.

"Taeko and her daughter are gone," he muttered. "But this piece of porcelain is still fully alive. It endures. It survives. May it live forever." Shinkichi gently stroked the vase, as so often he had stroked Kŭm-ju's body. "Even when I am dead, you will be here, alive and beautiful." The tears he shed so vainly fell on the dry tatami.

On the following morning two detectives from the special police section visited Shinkichi and Kŭm-ju. After extending formal condolences, one said, "As a matter of fact, we've come here to ask about Cho Ch'ŏr-in."

According to them, Cho Ch'ŏr-in had been marked as a revolutionary ever since he returned from America.

"His affair with your deceased wife was a part of his scheme to divert our attention. I'm sorry to have to say this."

Irritated by their very presence, Shinkichi raised his voice, "Say whatever you want!"

"We wish to know if letters for your wife have come from him." Taking turns, the two detectives asked several more questions, justifying them by saying, "We are sure that he has run off to Kando."

"No, he hasn't sent her any letters."

"Unfortunately. Well, he has been very cautious, so . . ." Clicking their tongues, the detectives concluded their inquiry by trying to put Shinkichi under an obligation. "We will not publicize this affair," they said, bowing politely, and left. As far as Shinkichi was concerned, he preferred that the affair would be publicized, so that they could catch the treacherous Ch'ŏr-in when the tragic news brought him back to Seoul.

The solemn funeral ceremony was conducted as soon as members of the Miwa family arrived from Tokyo. After the funeral, full of polite lies from people he scarcely knew, Shinkichi felt so agitated that he hurried to Kŭm-ju. "Let me cry on your breast," he moaned.

Kŭm-ju held him close to her naked bosom and caressed him gently, as if stroking a baby. "I'm so sorry that I caused them to die. Forgive me," she sobbed. In the garden at the rear of their home, white blossoms of the hibiscus seemed to float against the night sky. Like ghosts . . .

X

With the start of World War II following the Japanese invasion of China, Shinkichi's antique shop, called Ikeda Art Objects, and the branch shop with the same name in the Nihombashi section of Tokyo, which had been managed by Kŭm-ju's younger brother, Chong-il, were often closed. The connoisseurs who had formerly frequented both shops stopped going to them. Art objects and antiques offered no protection against possible air raids.

Shinkichi was almost sixty years old. His former landlady, Itoman Tane, had been dead for many years, and Principal S, denied his hope to die in Korea, ended his days after retiring to his native Kumamoto Prefecture in Kyūshū. Yi Kŭm-ju was already fifty years old. Shinkichi had repeatedly suggested that they marry, but she always declined his proposals, saying, "I cannot do that when I think of your wife's suicide. Just to live with you is good enough for me."

Meanwhile, Shinkichi wished to write a worthy book in art history. He had already photographed most of the famous Yi dynasty painted porcelains in Korea, but not those in Japan. Shinkichi took a camera and rolls of film to Japan and began

his fieldwork by visiting old customers and taking pictures of
their ceramic treasures.

He soon found that those field trips were both difficult and
disappointing. Some customers had already sent their ceramics
to safe places in the countryside for storage. Other clients,
either greedy or needy, would not permit him to photograph
their porcelains unless he paid them for the privilege. Once,
as he wandered about a rural area with his camera, he was
stopped by a policeman who suspected him of spying and interrogated him most rudely. On another occasion, when he had
finally traced the route of a porcelain that had been sold and
resold, he discovered that the piece had been broken by a child
of the owner.

After all these troubles, Shinkichi had taken about fifty
pictures of the painted porcelains. Before returning home, he
closed his Nihonbashi shop, selling some art objects and
placing others in the earthen-walled storehouse of his relatives
in isolated Ibaragi. He returned to Seoul in 1942, the seven-
teenth year of Showā.

Life in Seoul was still casual and relaxed. Even meat dump-
lings were being sold in the streets, and the war seemed far
away. Shinkichi resumed his studies. He collected and edited all
the articles that he had presented at academic meetings or had
published in art journals. To these he added some unpublished
manuscripts. He spent nearly eight months in writing a major
work contributing new materials. The manuscript, which he
intended to publish privately, consisted of 1,200 pages of text, a
number of line drawings, and 120 pages of photographs.

Unfortunately, the time was wrong for such a work. In the
eighteenth year of Showā, all paper stocks were controlled by
the Japanese government. No publication was permitted unless
it related to national policies. Although Shinkichi had paid an
advance to the printer, government officials would not allocate
the paper, saying, "During this critical time, an art history book
to be published by a private press for the owner of an antique
shop is not essential to the war effort." Their logic was under-
standable, yet Shinkichi still hoped to publish his book. But

approval was never granted. At last the printer, unwilling to wait any longer, said, "We must destroy the plates." Shinkichi barely managed to retrieve his manuscript.

Then the government insisted that he close his antique shop in Seoul. Clasping his hands, Yi Kŭm-ju apologized: "If I hadn't given you those vases, you wouldn't be having these hardships. I am so sorry; please forgive me."

At this, he drew her into his arms. "That is not true. Thanks to the Yi dynasty painted porcelain you showed me, we have shared our lives. We have been happy together. But now, when conditions have become so trying, why don't we buy an orchard in the country, raise a few chickens, and live in peaceful retirement?"

He sold his shop in Seoul, donated most of his artifacts to the Museum of the Royal Yi Family, bought an orchard not far from the capital, and moved with Kŭm-ju into a house almost hidden among fruit trees. All their neighbors were Koreans, who at first rejected them. But after learning that Kŭm-ju was Korean, they changed their attitude and visited the newcomers, bearing gifts of fresh vegetables, and even taught them how to raise chickens.

The relaxed country life helped Shinkichi and Kŭm-ju to forget the war, most of the time. Soon, however, all the able-bodied males and younger women were drafted into labor service, and only the aged, the disabled, and the children were left in the villages. Finally, in the summer of 1945 Japan surrendered. The war ended.

Now the Koreans, suddenly transformed from a suppressed people into citizens of a nation restored to freedom, rejoiced in the prospect of independence. In the course of their outbursts of enthusiasm, many unfortunate disturbances occurred in local areas.

Three unforgettable incidents involved Shinkichi. The first happened when a crowd of youths broke into his orchard and threw stones at him, shouting, "Japanese go home!" Seeing this, Yi Kŭm-ju, dressed as a Korean housewife, stood before

the youths, shielding her lover. "Kill me first!" she shouted.
"But do not harm my husband." The young men, shamed by
her courage, went away.

The second was an unexpected visit by Cho Ch'ŏr-in, who
came in October of the same year. Shinkichi's former student,
now more than forty years old, appeared very dignified with his
uniform and splendid mustache. He told them that he had
returned to Seoul as soon as the war ended and that since then
he had been looking for Shinkichi.

"Sensei, I wish to make an apology," Cho Ch'ŏr-in said
immediately. Kŭm-ju yelled, "You villain! Go away!" Raising
his hand to stop her, Shinkichi said gently, "Kŭm-ju, please be
quiet. He comes in peace. The past is past. Don't say anything
more. My wife and daughter died of sickness. Long ago. . . ."
The passage of more than ten years had eased the pains of
regret, and Shinkichi knew the uselessness of cherishing hatred
for his former student.

"For your kindness, I thank you. Please let me pray for
them with an offering of incense."

After he had finished praying, Ch'ŏr-in talked about the
future. "Sensei, we are going to build a new country. I want to
play a part in that."

Shinkichi and Kŭm-ju wished him well when, in a hurry as
usual, he went back to the city.

The third incident was the most incredible of all. When all
Japanese who had been living in Korea were forced to return to
Japan, Shinkichi naturally thought that Kŭm-ju would accompany him. But contrary to his expectations, she said, very
firmly, "I shall stay here." Unable to believe what he'd heard,
he asked, "Why?"

"Because I am a Korean woman! I belong here. But you—
you are a Japanese man, so you must go back." But her true
heart was revealed in the sobs that shook her, as she clung to
Shinkichi, and in the hot tears that fell upon his chest.

Kŭm-ju went to the port of Pusan to say farewell to Shinkichi. Published orders of the American armed forces allowed

each departing Japanese to take only one rucksack. His manuscript about the Yi dynasty painted porcelain filled most of Shinkichi's rucksack.

When the signal for boarding ship sounded, the Japanese formed a line near the gangway. Kŭm-ju embraced Shinkichi tightly. "You are my husband," she said through her tears. "My beloved. I will never, never forget you. Not until I die." Among the people leaving for Japan from Pusan that day, some must have seen this pair of aged lovers tearfully clinging to each other, unwilling to part.

The two never saw each other again. Shinkichi's manuscript was never published, but his role in revealing to the world the beauties of the Yi dynasty's painted porcelain was remembered, principally through the efforts of Yamanoi Makoto.

As I conclude this short memorial account of Ikeda Shinkichi's life, I remember too how much he—the teacher I respected, the husband I betrayed—loved the Korean hibiscus flowers. The season of their blossoming is beginning once again in this new Korea that is, in so many ways, still ancient and unchanging.

The Remembered Shadow of the Yi Dynasty

I

ON A HOT and rainy night in the summer of 1940, made even more miserable by hordes of mosquitoes, Noguchi Ryōkichi met an extraordinary young woman in the pleasure quarter of Seoul. Kim Yŏng-sun was a kisaeng, the Korean equivalent of a Japanese geisha. In those days, both geisha and kisaeng were officially licensed to serve as entertainers in the pleasure quarters of Seoul.

Unlike the Japanese geisha, the Korean kisaeng had been decreasing in numbers for more than twenty years, and in 1940 the few who still appeared in high-class restaurants, such as the Kitei in Chongno, were scarcely aware of their profession's glorious past. When many of the kisaeng adopted the style and practices of geisha after the annexation of Korea by Japan in 1910, they forfeited their pride and lost much prestige among the men who sought their company.

Kim Yŏng-sun was one of the few women who resisted the trend and tried to preserve the traditions. Like the oiran, the first-rank geisha of the Yoshiwara, the famous pleasure quarter in Tokyo, the kisaeng in days of old had enjoyed a high position in Korean society and lived almost as comfortably as did the country's aristocrats.

Being an efficient former military man, Noguchi's father used to keep diaries of his activities. He also organized in a scrapbook all the name cards he received from people he met, with the correct dates and appropriate notes for each card. Among them, Noguchi, still a student in middle school, saw some small cards that bore such unusual names and titles as Wŏlgye from P'yŏngyang, of the Third Rank, and Ongnan from Chinju, of the Fourth Rank. Those were the cards of certain esteemed kisaeng.

"P'yŏngyang and Chinju used to produce good kisaeng," Noguchi's father explained. "Those two kisaeng were extremely beautiful; they were described as Number One in P'yŏngyang–Number Two in Chinju." The ranks shown on these name cards indicated the official status of the kisaeng; the third rank was equal to that of a district officer. In the time of the Yi dynasty, some kisaeng achieved a very high social standing, far above the reach of Japan's geisha.

During the Yi dynasty, administrators in the imperial palace appointed more than three hundred kisaeng, who served as officials in charge of the Wardrobe, the Department of Health and Medicine, and the Department of Welfare. This system, important in the nation's political affairs, was modeled after the Ministry of Music and Rites in medieval Koryŏ, and such women were indispensable to the functions of the court. According to old documents, those kisaeng entertained high government officials with music, dances, and refreshments at gatherings held in the several palaces. Quite probably they influenced indirectly the country's political affairs because of the control they gained over a few of the kingdom's important personages. They must have wielded great power in arranging promotions and in deciding lawsuits.

Special schools in P'yŏngyang and Chinju trained young girls in music, dance, art, and poetry, preparing them to become future kisaeng. Students in such schools were divided into three classes according to their accomplishments. Those in the third class were called "demi-kisaeng." The first-class kisaeng could work officially in the imperial court and were very difficult for ordinary people to approach.

If a man was interested in associating with a high-ranking kisaeng outside the court, he had to go through very complex procedures to arrange the liaison. He had to be properly introduced to her by someone who was familiar with the customs of the pleasure quarter. He had to offer gifts or fees to the go-between, who would accompany him on several preliminary visits to the kisaeng's residence.

After he became well acquainted with the kisaeng through the intermediary's good offices, he would be allowed to ask if she accepted his attentions. If she refused him, their association ended. If she accepted him, the man, as her patron, had to continue to offer gifts—including money, jewelry, and clothing—until the relationship ended. He also had to pay all her household expenses. In the case of a demi-kisaeng, a patron would stay at her place for a certain period of time, such as five or ten days. In any case, the kisaeng of old times were regarded as "flowers on the summit," which not many men could pluck. Even though a number of patrons, in turn, might support her, a kisaeng retained her high pride and great prestige. But, by 1940, modern trends had degraded the art and the life of the kisaeng, and many of the "flowers on the summit" had fallen, to become prostitutes, called kalbo. Kim Yŏng-sun must have lamented such debasing. Noguchi certainly felt that she did so on the night he met her.

Noguchi watched Kim Yŏng-sun perform her favorite dance at a restaurant called the House of the Red Dream, in Insa-dong of Chongno, a traditional dance from the court of the Yi kings. The restaurant had a connection with the Mansei Incident (about which Noguchi knew nothing). The chance to see Kim Yŏng-sun was provided accidentally by Tawara Haruyuki, a friend of Noguchi from his student days at the School of Fine Arts in Tokyo, who visited him in Seoul on the way to a job as an assistant in the art department of a newly established film company in Manchukuo.

Noguchi's father had married a daughter of a Japanese who owned the Chiyoda Inn at the foot of Namsan. Mr. Noguchi had concentrated on managing the inn after ending his term of military service in 1920. Ryōkichi was the only child of this marriage. His father wanted him to enter either the Imperial Army or the Imperial Navy. But Noguchi was too nearsighted to be accepted as a candidate for a military career. Instead he entered the School of Fine Arts, more agreeable to his interests. After graduation, he returned to Seoul, became an art instructor in a private girls' school, and enjoyed painting in oils.

The main subjects of his painting in those days were the interesting native customs that were rapidly disappearing as life in Korea was Japanized. In the old New Year's season, for example, Korean boys enjoyed a game called yutnori, tossing four cylindrical sticks of hardwood into the air and determining success or failure according to the five different ways in which the sticks would land, while girls played a game of seesaw called nŏlttwigi. The young girls, especially, rising and sinking while their colorful skirts flared in the cold air of the New Year's season, created a genuinely beautiful scene, which Noguchi depicted in many fine paintings. However, recently he could not find such charming yutnori or nŏlttwigi players unless he visited country villages. Noguchi truly regretted their disappearance from Seoul's neighborhoods.

Seoul is surrounded by many mountains, including Paegak, Nakt'a, Inwang, and Mongmyo; the river Han, like a moat, lies to the south. In earlier times, Seoul was a fortresslike city enclosed within a massive protecting wall. Eight huge gates pierced the great wall, ten meters high and sixteen kilometers long, raised during the reign of the great founder of the Yi dynasty and by Sejong, the fourth sovereign of the line. Ancient documents state that in all 429,870 people and 2,211 masons were involved in constructing the wall. These ramparts, the symbol of Seoul, after enduring rains, winds, and frosts for more than five hundred years, were removed during the expansion of the city after Japan annexed Korea, and only the two great gates in the south and the east walls remain as memorials to vanished glory.

One August afternoon in 1940, Noguchi, sketchbook in hand, walked along the space left by the razed city wall, accompanied by his friend Tawara. As they waited for nightfall,

Noguchi said, "This evening I shall show you some true Korean places." Sounding like an expert on Korea, he led Tawara toward Chongno. Noguchi liked the sights along Chongno Street between Kwanghwamun Square and Great East Gate. Only this street, where trams were still running, retained much of the old Korean atmosphere. It was a typical Korean street, in vivid contrast to the Honmachi, which could be regarded as a sort of Ginza for the Japanese.

The Hwashin Department Store at the entrance to Chongno Street; Poshingak, with a large bell in its southern corner, opposite the department store; Pagoda Park, with its splendid thirteen-story marble pagoda; and the many stores along both sides of the street—this was the familiar setting that Noguchi had known since childhood, and from which he had gained much varied knowledge about Korea. The names of shops and stores delighted him. He found that a pawnshop was called chŏndangp'o, and a haberdashery, obangjaega. During frequent sketching sessions in Chongno, he learned that a most unusual wholesale store selling things for decorating horses' manes and tails was called mami toga. In Chongno, he encountered interesting scenes to be painted, such as the paper shops that sold yellow oiled paper for the heated floors and rooms in homes, the fish shops with stacks of dried codfish and packaged roe, the writing-brush shops offering different kinds of stationery and implements for calligraphy, and the shoe stores displaying all sizes of the characteristic boat-shaped, thick-soled footwear.

Among all those fascinating things to see, what most captivated Noguchi were the street peddlers and vendors. Some cut soft sweets and hard candies with strong shears that made a sound like "gacha, gacha." People paid for those delicacies with scraps of iron rather than with the usual copper coins. Porters called chige carried travelers' luggage on their backs, and the muljangsu, or water carriers, worked their way through the crowds, selling five-gallon cans of water for three sen each.

Wearing the kat, the Korean straw hat, and turumagi, flowing robes, vendors of medicinal herbs awaited their customers while leisurely smoking long, slender pipes. Other vendors' shrill cries, seeming to be produced from the tops of their heads, offered cool, juicy cucumbers in the summer and hot roasted chestnuts in the winter. Those many changing scenes in Chongno showed Noguchi the ways in which the Korean people lived—a style that was rapidly disappearing. Chongno still revealed the smells, the colors, the excitement, and the poetry of the waning culture. This was precisely why Noguchi chose to portray an old Korean couple resting in Pagoda Park near Chongno for his final student work, presented as a requirement for graduation from the School of Fine Arts in Tokyo. As if possessed by a demon warning of decay and death, he had tirelessly sought Korean customs, habits, and types since returning to Seoul.

In Chongno, that lively section of Seoul, Noguchi never met any antagonism from Koreans as he sketched them and their setting, while he observed everything from the street. But on reaching the suburbs or the rural areas, cold glances as sharp as icicles pierced his body. Such antagonism was most strongly felt when he met groups of young men of his own age. Their dislike seemed to hit his face, strike his back, and definitely stopped the movements of his sketching hand holding the soft-lead pencil.

In the beginning he tried not to feel that antagonism, but gradually he began to wonder about it. "Why?" he asked himself. "Why me?" He knew that some Japanese residents treated the Koreans almost as slaves and abused them with names like yobo. But Noguchi, born and raised in Seoul, had always held friendly feelings toward Koreans and had been fascinated by their customs and habits. Why did they look at a pro-Korean man like him so coldly and hatefully? Noguchi could not understand such an attitude. The Korean dancer Kim Yŏng-sun finally answered this question. For that reason Noguchi felt most fatalistic about what had happened on that particular night—and in the months that followed.

After they'd walked about four blocks from Chongno,

Noguchi led Tawara to a sulchip in an alley off still another block. Such a small, shabby tavern would be one of the best places in which to enjoy typical folk food and drink. The environment in any alley was entirely different from that of the main street with its trams. The humid air in the dark, winding, narrow alley stank of filthy gutters and stale urine. The tile-roofed houses with small windows and low eaves stood side by side, shops and homes intermixed. The only way to distinguish a sulchip was to find the red poles at its entrance, on which were written good-luck verses such as "Fortune like the mountains, Wealth like the seas" or "Thousands of calamities have departed; hundreds of happinesses have arrived."

The verses on the red poles before Noguchi's favorite sulchip declared, "The red shadows poured into the jade decanter are the reflections of flowers; the purple lights floating in the silver jar are the glances of the moon." Passing beneath the curved eaves supported by those red poles, Noguchi and his friend stepped into a wide room with a bare earthen floor. Two men sat before two small earthen ovens placed upon a platform opposite the entrance. Smoke from braised meat and the sharp smell of burning garlic filled the room.

As Noguchi expected, Tawara turned in surprise, exclaiming, "A terrible place!"

"This is a typical sulchip. Those in the country are worse than this," replied Noguchi, proud of his knowledge. He also explained that the character for chip in the ideograph sulchip originally meant a small hut, but that in cities it indicated a restaurant; in the countryside, it identified an inn, or sometimes a brothel with kalbo prostitutes. Three typical Korean drinks were served in such places: makkŏlli, yakchu, and soju. A saek-chuga was a tavern that both served drinks and provided prostitutes, while a naewoe chujŏm only served drinks.

"I see. Noguchi, you are a real Korean expert—but I can't stand this smoke and heat!" Smiling bravely, Tawara wiped his sweaty cheeks and forehead.

Cows' and pigs' heads hung from the rafters in the left corner of the room; under them, piled high in baskets, lay hunks of red meat and coils of white intestines. Several Korean men sat at tables in the center of the room, talking and laughing. Noguchi and Tawara chose a table near the entrance.

"What would you like to eat?" asked Noguchi. "A dish of meat or a bowl of soup will be brought with our drinks." Peering through his thick glasses, he said, "Over there you'll see the usual fare eaten at a sulchip: kalbi (barbecued ribs), and komt'ang soup." He pointed toward them, set on the table before the other customers.

In the kitchen area at the right side of the room, white steam rose from a huge iron pot, two arms' length in circumference. A soup made with pigs' feet and cows' intestines was simmering in the pot. The barbecued ribs and the boiling intestines released a delectable aroma. Greasy smoke hung above a big iron grill placed over glowing charcoal.

"Let's try the ribs, along with kimchi," Tawara decided, hungry even while blinking because of the smoke.

"Sorry, but there's no kimchi in summer. The best you can do is to have sour preserved radishes." Noguchi told the waitress to bring some kalbi and yakchu liquor.

As soon as they heard Noguchi's order, the two men in front of the ovens stood up, removed the lid from a great liquor jar, and, with iron ladles, dipped some of its contents into shallow, dish-shaped pans. They tossed a handful of dry pine needles into each oven. The needles blazed up in red flames, over which the men placed the shallow pans, slowly stirring the yakchu with the ladles. Their unhurried movements and interesting way of warming the liquor reminded Noguchi that he was not in Japan but on the continent. For the moment he forgot the war being waged in China, so near to Korea.

Tawara, annoyed by their slowness, repeatedly urged them on, calling, "Isn't that yakchu ready yet?" But as soon as the drinks and the food arrived, he became happy again. Grasping a barbecued rib in both hands, he gnawed at it, showing his front teeth like a monkey, uttering such comments as "Good" or "Hot!" Everything about the meal must have been unusual for a newcomer like Tawara. As he and Noguchi talked loudly

in Japanese, the other customers became very quiet. Noguchi
began to worry. Worry made him tired. By the time Noguchi
ordered some makkŏlli for their third drink and barbecued
intestines for a side dish, all the other customers had left,
except for one middle-aged gentleman, dressed in a white suit,
who sat in a corner by himself, drinking beer.

"Well, everybody's gone," said Tawara. Only then did
Noguchi notice his friend's head, with hair cropped short, like
that of a military man. Because of thinning hair and a natural
tendency to baldness, Tawara always had his hair cut close to
his skull, even while he associated with long-haired types in art
school.

Smiling, Noguchi said, "You with your round head like a
Japanese soldier's and your loud talk in Japanese—you scared
them away."

"Me?" Tawara laughed. "Me, a military man?"

"Sure. They must have thought you were a military policeman, trying to hide in a civilian's business suit."

"Ah, that's too bad," said Tawara, quite cheerful after
several drinks. Holding the makkŏlli jug by its neck, he crossed
the room to the gentleman in the white suit and asked in
friendly fashion, "Do you think I am a military man?"

Noguchi hurried after Tawara, scolding like an embarrassed mother. "Don't bother him. He is enjoying his beer,
quietly and alone."

The gentleman smiled and addressed Noguchi in fluent
Japanese. "Is this your first time here?"

Having lived in Seoul for more than twenty years, Noguchi
could distinguish at a glance a Japanese from a Korean. And
hearing them speak always supported his assumption, because
Koreans could not pronounce clearly the sounds of Japanese
speech. And, of course, Japanese did not do proper justice to
Korean speech.

"Saa!" thought Noguchi, looking closely at the gentleman.
Men wearing neckties and jackets were not rare in Seoul's
sulchips. Usually they were sons of wealthy families or members of Korea's intelligentsia. Naturally Noguchi assumed

that the gentleman belonged to such a high social level. But a doubt rose in his mind when he heard him speak such excellent Japanese. "I wonder if he's a Japanese?"

Noguchi replied, "Yes. This is the first time for him. But it's the fourth time for me," and, observing the gentleman's high cheekbones, square jaw, and the mustache made of hair as fine as Tawara's, concluded that this must be a Korean face.

"I can tell easily that you two are neither military men nor policemen. Well, then, let me treat you to a cup." Whereupon the Korean gentleman, probably in his early forties, introduced himself as Pak Kyu-hak, a professor at Severance Medical School. The name card he presented bore the identification Kinoshita Keigo, printed in small Japanese characters, showing that he had converted his name into Japanese.

"In Korea," he explained with a smile, "when one drinks yakchu, one should pour what is left at the bottom of the cup on the ground, as an offering to the god of wine. And in drinking makkŏlli, one should hold the sabal container with two hands and drink in the taiho style. These are drinking manners, you see."

To Noguchi all of Pak's remarks were new, interesting, and intelligent. And the manner in which he expressed them was both forthright and pleasant.

"Since the old days, we've had a proverb here in Seoul: 'Southern liquor and northern rice cakes.' Good liquor must have been produced in the foothills of Namsan, South Mountain, while tasty rice cakes come from the north."

"Really? I live at the foot of Namsan," said Noguchi.

Pak knew the name of Noguchi's home, Chiyodaro, which already had a long history. Noguchi's maternal grandfather had taken over the inn in the twenty-seventh year of Meiji, or 1894. After further conversation, Pak invited both Noguchi and Tawara to go with him to Hongmonggwan, the House of the Red Dream, in Insa-dong.

II

Noguchi's remarks about the rapid disappearance of genuine Korean subjects for his painting caught Pak's interest.

"Then you are an artist?"

"Yes. I like this section of Chongno. But I am sad because everything's changing. We no longer see bird cages with larks in them hung in front of barber shops, for instance."

"You remember them well?"

"Yes. I used to see them every day on my way home from middle school."

"For your paintings?" After a moment's thought, Pak's eyes shone. "Wouldn't you two be interested in seeing a dance?"

"A dance? What kind of dance?" asked Noguchi.

"A court dance from olden times."

"I see . . ."

"It's a dance performed by kisaeng, who in the old days used to serve at the court of the Yi kings. Most of the performers have disappeared, but one good dancer is still with us. She learned the kisaeng tradition and dances very well."

"Oh, like the dancing by the famous Ch'oe Sŭng-hŭi?" asked Noguchi.

"Yes. Ch'oe Sŭng-hŭi's traditional court dance has some aspects of modern ballet. But this kisaeng's dance is the original dance with its traditional beauty. The air of courtly times."

"Sounds interesting," nodded Noguchi. While agreeing, Tawara made a strange point. "How interesting that she is not an ordinary kisaeng."

The House of the Red Dream was a typical Korean restaurant of the more elegant kind. As they stepped through the ornate gate, they entered a bare courtyard, without plants or fountains, enclosed by the house's wings, each with several rooms. A patron could enter and leave a private room by passing under the low eaves, which curved upward slightly.

According to Pak, this kind of restaurant had been established in Seoul during Japan's Meiji period, between 1868 and 1912. In earlier times, a kisaeng owned her own house, which her customers would visit. Another such restaurant, called the House of the Bright Moon, on a street near the House of the Red Dream, was the best in Seoul. Pak and his guests were conducted to a room in the wing to the right of the gate.

Generally, wooden houses in Korea were constructed to

keep people warm during the very severe winters. These one-story dwellings had thick outside walls made of packed earth and gravel, held in place by wooden panels. Inner walls, also made of earth, were most often covered by two layers of thick paper. Doorways within the house were just tall enough to allow adults to pass through by stooping. Because there were few windows, there was little sunlight or fresh air. Floors in these houses were warmed in winter by the ingenious heating ducts called ondol. Such houses were ideal for retaining warmth in winter. But they did not suit most Japanese people, because they provided neither alcoves nor closets and very little sunlight. Such houses might be expected to be unpleasantly hot in summer, but actually they were rather cool because they received less sunlight and because the ducts in the ondol floor permitted air to circulate.

Pak and his guests sat in a twelve-by-twelve-foot room, the floor of which was covered by straw mats made in the Korean style. Pak spoke a few words in Korean to a young servant, who soon brought in an electric fan and chilled beer. Small trays holding several dishes of assorted foods followed, one after another. All these were simple and essentially vegetable foods, such as fried seaweed, cooked bean sprouts marinated in vinegar, soybean curd with gingko nuts, vegetable soup, and braised dry fish meal marinated in soy sauce with sesame seeds. Each had the typical Korean flavor. Food and beer were brought in almost continuously, but still the kisaeng did not arrive.

Feeling impatient, Noguchi said, "She is late, isn't she?"

Pak chuckled. "That's usual. Don't worry. She must go to a few other restaurants, too, some at a distance from here. She has to visit them in sequence, you see."

Because of his father's strictness, Noguchi had never before had a chance to step into the pleasure quarters of Seoul. Only after entering the School of Fine Arts at Ueno, in Tokyo, did he even taste cigarettes and strong liquor. Some of his classmates in middle school frequented the brothels in Yayoichō and Shimmachi in Seoul or the house for kalbo prostitutes on the slope

of Hatsunechō, but not Noguchi. Now that he was an art
instructor at a girls' school and his father was operating the
family's inn, if he took even a single drink at a restaurant in
Seoul the information would reach his father's ears in no time.
But the obedient and naive Noguchi could see at once that the
House of the Red Dream was a high-class establishment, and
that inviting the kisaeng dancer to appear was more difficult—
and more expensive—than bringing in a popular geisha would
ever be. He thought that, for once, his father would approve his
having these new experiences that would contribute to his
growth as an artist.

After waiting nearly two hours, they heard the notes of a
musical instrument, the t'ungso, coming from a room across
the courtyard. The sounds mingled with the patter of raindrops
that had just begun to fall, conveying suggestions of loneliness.

"So, finally they are here." Pak pushed open the paper
doors. They saw the room across the yard being lighted, and
dark shadows moving. Pak, familiar with everything, explained, "Since they were caught in the rain, they're probably
changing their clothes and tuning their instruments."

Soon four old men, in their sixties, perhaps, appeared with
musical instruments. All wore black-lacquered tall hats and
Korean turumagi made from black silk over white chŏksam.
The turumagi resembled the Japanese haori, or short coat.
Koreans' clothes included upper and lower garments over
which men wore the turumagi coat and women wore the
ch'ima skirts. Some of those upper garments were lined, others
quilted, and still others unlined. The chŏksam, an unlined
upper summer garment, was replaced in winter by the chŏgori;
the koi, an unlined lower skirt for summer use, by the paji.
Men wore the tall hats and the turumagi as formal attire.

These old men placed their rare and unusual instruments—
such as the kayagŭm, t'ungso, changgo, chaeng, and chŏnggo—
on the mats in the corner of the room and sat beside them with
one knee lifted, obviously waiting for someone.

Judging by these old codgers, the dancer must be an old
dame in her fifties, thought Noguchi, resigning himself to an

antique performer as well as to antiquated musicians. But his grim imaginings were soon corrected.

The kisaeng who entered the room was a young woman in her twenties. She wore a tall crown with metallic decorations, an iridescent costume with full, rounded sleeves, and a narrow brocade sash bound high across her bosom, its long ends hanging gracefully down on either side. Her white socks, the pŏsŏn, ended in pointed, upturned toes.

After exchanging a few words in Korean with the kisaeng, Pak turned to his guests and introduced her: "This is the person who can show us the court dance." That was when Noguchi first heard her name: Kim Yŏng-sun.

"The first piece," Pak continued, "is a kwŏnjuga, a song commending drinking. It has been regarded as very important for opening a drinking party. She will sing and dance this song." Both Noguchi and Tawara felt that they were most fortunate to have met Pak, who interpreted each word of the lyrics sung by Kim Yŏng-sun in her beautiful voice.

The song praised the pleasures to be found in drinking and prayed for good fortune and long life for the drinkers. Pak's translation revealed much of the poem's beauty: "The liquor brewed with immortal herbs fills the cup for ten thousand years. Each time the cup is raised, one prays for the blessings of Mount Namsan. Sipping from this cup will bring immortality. Accept the cup, accept the cup, oh, please accept this cup. This is not an ordinary liquor, but is made from dewdrops taken from the Urn for Collecting Dews that belonged to Emperor Han Wu-ti." The complicated lyrics, enriched with a number of classical Chinese words, flowed forth to the perfect accompaniment of raindrops falling in the courtyard.

The four solemn old musicians, sitting in the corner of the room, played as if they still served in the palace of Yi. The sounds of their music and the motions of the dancer filled the chamber with elegance and beauty. The sad melodies and the varied tones, with their burden of remembrance of times long past, were created by wrinkled old men who would never forget the complicated rhythms they achieved by delicately interchanging double and triple beats, matching the meanings of the poems they sang with the graceful movements of the dancer.

"Ahh," sighed Noguchi, recognizing this Korean music's resemblance to Japan's ancient treasured court music from olden times. But, he thought, this music from Korea's past conveys much more pathos. Even so, what impressed him most was not the sadness in the music but the beauty of the dancer. Grasping his cup as if it held indeed the elixir of immortality, Noguchi sat entranced, gazing at Kim Yŏng-sun—until, suddenly, becoming aware of the company, he blushed, lowered his cup, and carefully placed it on the tray.

Kim Yŏng-sun's second dance, The Song of the Spring Nightingale, fascinated Noguchi. All his artist's sensibilities were involved. He felt as if every movement of her hands and feet entered his mind through his eyes. Her motions were beautiful. By waving her gauze sleeves, fashioned from pale blue silk, she drew delicate lines in the air, giving the effect of a nightingale flitting from one plum tree's branch to another's. Her foot movements, slight and restrained, suggested larger sweeps, filling the entire space of the room. The dance became more bewitching as she expressed her natural feeling for the nightingale. Here Noguchi recalled the Japanese Nō dance, in which performers create effects of largeness through the slightest of movements.

In her dancing, Kim Yŏng-sun vividly depicted the happiness of the joyously singing nightingale, delighting in the sunshine of spring. Noguchi was deeply moved. It was more than a strong impression, something about which he could say, "This is wonderful! This is important! Without question." In other words, coursing through him surged—no, not a feeling of love for the dancer, but rather a desire to paint her. He was seized by the kind of flashing inspiration that is born when one looks into an unknown world or perceives a theme for painting.

Kim Yŏng-sun performed another dance, Musanhyang, and then withdrew immediately. She had spent only forty minutes with them.

"How did you like that?" asked Pak.

"Oh, she's quite a beauty, isn't she!" said Tawara in his honest way. Noguchi did not feel like talking just then, and so said nothing.

Tawara's comment made Noguchi think about her white complexion, her deep-set black eyes, all those other fine features. "Judging by her dark eyebrows," he thought, remembering the old wives' tale from Japan, "she must be a strong-willed woman. Why does she have such a mystifying darkness?" Recalling her sharp features, those dark, heavy eyebrows, and the proud, curved nose, he felt that he had been shown the image of an unhappy woman, with those straying black locks and earlobes that seemed to be carved in ivory. As if she had been captured in a photograph of a fox-spirit taken at twilight. . . .

"How about you, Mr. Noguchi?" Pak would not let him go.

"Well, I believe that tonight I have seen a hidden and unknown Korea for the first time. Both the dance and the music convey a loneliness and a beauty that appeal to my heart." His comment revealed more than he intended. The beauty of the dancer had ensnared him. Thus began Noguchi's awareness of Kim Yŏng-sun.

Saying that everything they had enjoyed at the House of the Red Dream was his gift to them, Pak called a taxi for Noguchi and Tawara. "This is to show my gratitude to you two young Japanese men, who appreciate the beauty of Korea." In the taxi driving through the rain, the young men, still excited, talked about Kim Yŏng-sun and Pak's graciousness, even while they scratched the mosquito bites on their hands and necks.

The following morning, Tawara seemed to have forgotten all about the magical evening. But in Noguchi's mind, the graceful lines of Yŏng-sun's body actually being the Spring Nightingale were unforgettable. Long after Tawara left Seoul to go to his position in Manchukuo, the picture of Yŏng-sun did not fade, but grew ever stronger in Noguchi's memory.

"Japanese still do not know the beauty of Korea. I must try to put it on canvas," he told himself. As time passed, an image formed in Noguchi's mind. In the corner of a dark room in the House of the Red Dream, the low and elegant court music was being played. Keeping the rhythm, Kim Yŏng-sun danced, her white face as impassive as a Nō mask, delicately curved lines extending from shoulders to outstretched hands. An ornate lamp suspended from the ceiling shed soft light on her. Moonlight passing through a window fell on the pale faces of old musicians, sitting on the floor, tapping changgo drums. Was he fascinated only by the elegant court music and by the delicate lines of the dance? Or was he not personally attracted by the kisaeng herself, by something cold and dark and mystifying about her? He himself could not be sure. Not yet. . . .

Two weeks after he'd said farewell to Tawara, Noguchi went again to the House of the Red Dream. This time he went alone. He waited for three hours before Kim Yŏng-sun appeared in the room he'd rented. She danced three numbers, for him alone, and retired without even granting him a smile. Noguchi, who wanted to ask her to be his model for the painting he envisioned, had no chance to speak to her before she hurried away, guarded by the four old musicians.

On his third visit, Noguchi was able to speak to her. "You need not dance tonight. But please drink with me." The suggestion of a smile—or of a grimace—showed on only one of her cheeks. In Japanese, she said, "Call for another kisaeng."

"But you are a kisaeng, aren't you?"

"Yes, of course I am. But I only dance. Nothing else," she replied angrily. She flatly refused his plea to allow him to paint her, and, still indignant, left the room. Her curt manner told him, clearly enough, "I won't yield to the wiles of a Japanese artist!"

III

Noguchi became depressed and frustrated because the Korean dancer misunderstood him. He was a hard-headed young man of twenty-four. He swore to himself that he was going to make her his model. He felt all the more irritated because he thought that he was the only one in Seoul who could capture in paint the beauty of her dance. He made about ten visits to the House of the Red Dream within the next two months, and so accumulated debts that he could not pay. His monthly salary of eighty yen could cover only three visits to the restaurant. Yŏng-sun's dancing and the accompaniment of the four musicians for her three numbers cost twenty-five yen each time. Even if he were fortunate enough to be able to spend all of his salary just as he wished, twenty-five yen for a performance of less than an hour was much too expensive. His mother spoiled him, of course, and gave him ten or twenty yen whenever he asked her. But for larger sums, he had to ask his father, who had recently said, more than once, "Aren't you overdoing your nightly carousing?"

At a loss for a solution to his problem and yet unable to cut his perverse attachment to the kisaeng, Noguchi telephoned Pak at his office, asking for advice.

"So you are much involved." Pak's amusement carried over the telephone wires. Still chuckling, he promised that he would speak with Yŏng-sun, to recommend that she agree to be Noguchi's model. "But people say she is the most stubborn kisaeng in Seoul. I cannot promise you anything."

"I'm willing to pay her for modeling, although I can't afford twenty-five yen per hour."

"I see. I shall talk to her anyway."

Pak called Noguchi on the following Sunday night. "Right now I am at the House of the Red Dream. She says she doesn't wish to model at all."

Tightly gripping the receiver, Noguchi begged desperately, "Wait! Please wait there. I'll be there right away."

He caught a taxi and ran into the restaurant. Pak and Kim Yŏng-sun were exchanging wine cups, while the musicians entertained themselves in the next room. Noguchi felt jealous to see the two happily drinking, when she had spurned the cup he had offered her once. Her prejudice hurt him. "She despises me just because I am Japanese," he sulked.

When Noguchi stepped into the room, Yŏng-sun turned her head away, as if still angry. Pak spoke quickly to him. "I talked about your request. She doesn't care to pose. But she says you can sketch her while she is dancing." Pak added that this was as far as she would go. "A few months ago, she was so difficult that she threw her fan at the governor of Seoul when he tried to photograph her. So please understand."

While listening to Pak's fluent Japanese, Noguchi glanced at Yŏng-sun, still turned away from him, showing her profile. Not many women of this country have high-bridged noses, Noguchi thought, admiring those beautiful features while dismayed by her coldness. "So she'll allow me to sketch her, then?" he said.

"Yes. She says that she cannot stand still, posing for a long time. That would be too tiring."

"I understand. I very much appreciate your trouble." Noguchi expressed his gratitude to Pak, even though he was not completely satisfied with the arrangement.

Autumn was stealthily approaching the city of Seoul. Mornings and evenings became quite cold. Soon the severe winter of the continent would reach Korea. To mollify Noguchi after leaving the House of the Red Dream, Pak took him to the sulchip where they'd first met and told him a number of things about Kim Yŏng-sun. She was, to begin with, a stubborn woman. She was twenty-seven years old, three years older than Noguchi himself, and had vowed that she would never sleep with any man. No one knew why she had become a kisaeng or how she had learned the art of the court dance. She lived with her mother in Wŏnnam-dong, near the royal shrine. Naturally, she was still unmarried. And those four old musicians also lived in that neighborhood. Her reputation was not based on beauty alone, but also on the quality of her dancing, which faithfully transmitted the art of the almost forgotten court dances and the music of the Yi dynasty. The rich Koreans, the yangban, especially appreciated her dancing. Moreover, her stubborn attitude in presenting that art without flattering the wealthy or the powerful seemed to have attracted several Japanese patrons.

But when she said that she would neither sleep with any man nor flatter the powerful, Noguchi felt that she really meant

she would not sleep with any Japanese man nor flatter powerful Japanese officials, including military men, and that her
attitude toward them was deliberate, not emotional. He
suspected this from the subtlety with which Pak touched upon
the subject.

"By the way, what do you expect to accomplish by painting her?" asked Pak as he poured out upon the floor the dregs
from his cup of yakchu.

"I am going to compete in the Korean Exhibition."

"Oh, that new one, established in rivalry with the Japanese
Exhibition?"

"Yes. Since the deadline is the end of next January, I don't
have much time."

"True. I suppose the decisions will be announced by the end
of February."

"Yes. And if I win a prize—if, I say—please go and see my
picture."

Unfortunately, Noguchi could not submit the picture he
planned to show because Yŏng-sun became ill. Even though he
already had in mind the picture he wanted to paint, he was not
confident that he could depict the four old musicians in the
background without sketching them first. Instead he sent in
another work based upon a sketch he'd made in a remote
temple in the Outer Diamond Mountains of Kangwŏn
Province.

In contrast to the feminine charm of Inner Diamond Mountains, the Outer Diamonds were known for their bare and vast
masculine contours, enhanced by bold summits and deep
gorges. When Noguchi visited there at the end of October, the
leaves were turning red and the gorges were spotted with
patches of icy snow.

What impressed him most during the two days he spent in
that lonely mountain temple was the rare drink called igangju,
made from the best soju, or low-grade distilled spirits,
produced in the Chinnam area. The heavenly mixture—
prepared with five pounds of raw sugar, 0.6 ounce of cinna-
mon, 0.6 ounce of saffron, 6.6 ounces of ginger, five whole

pears, and 4.7 gallons of soju—was sealed in an earthen jar for
about ten days and then slowly filtered through a clean hempen
bag, to yield a light amber liquor. A single sip of this incomparable fluid would fill one's mouth and nose with the flavors
of all those ingredients, blended with the strong scent of jinchoge flowers plucked from the mountain slopes braced by
the severity of the cold north wind sweeping through nearby
gorges. Its full, sweet taste, gliding over one's tongue, reminded
the lucky imbiber of sweet white wine fortified with a strong,
fragrant brandy. That was igangju—the Pear-Ginger Spirit.

A castrated monk living in the mountain temple, who
looked like a nun, offered Noguchi his first taste of this nectar.
He tried to toss it down in a single gulp, as if drinking Japanese
sake, and choked on the unexpectedly strong fragrance.
Noguchi imagined the effect in a painter's colors: the fragrance
like ultramarine blue, the taste like the strong red of azalea-
lake. For no clear reason, the image of Yŏng-sun appeared in
his mind. He could see no connection between the two, the
drink and Yŏng-sun, but he felt that they shared very unusual
attributes. Furthermore, both annoyed him because they did
not behave as he expected.

"But someday I certainly will paint her! I vow to do so!"
Imbued with a strong fighting spirit, not to mention generous
sips of igangju, Noguchi sat on the veranda of the mountain
temple and busily sketched the granite cliffs and peaks,
sparkling with varicolored mica, of the Outer Diamond Mountains. From these sketches he did a spectacular oil painting,
sixty-one by seventy-three centimeters, which he entitled Late
Autumn in the Outer Diamond Mountains. This entry won him
a prize for the first time in the February exhibition. The award
boosted Noguchi's self-esteem and made his father very happy.

"If you were in military school," the father reminded his
unmilitary son, "you would have been commissioned a second
lieutenant by now. No matter. You have done well in your
chosen field."

In this roundabout way, Noguchi's father approved of his
only son's exceptional ability as an artist. But the satisfaction in

receiving the award did not equal Noguchi's happiness when once again he saw Yŏng-sun in the House of the Red Dream. This new sequence of meetings began as the deep snows started to melt.

As long as his money allowed, he continued to visit the restaurant, waiting impatiently for the dancer to appear, meanwhile nibbling at the vegetarian dishes and sipping cold beer. As soon as the drumming foretold her arrival, he took out his sketchbook. As usual, she was aloof and silent. Believing that she showed him such hostility simply because he was Japanese, Noguchi sometimes almost choked with rage.

After June arrived, Noguchi created all his paintings from those sketches. If the sketches did not solve technical difficulties, he visited the restaurant for new impressions. Then, invigorated, he returned to his studio, to shut himself in with work. Gradually he developed a study that he thought was good, completing it just before the summer vacation started. During all those hours of work, he had been inspired by memories of Yŏng-sun.

One Sunday morning at about ten o'clock early July, Noguchi left home holding this study carefully under his arm. He was going to visit Yŏng-sun at her house in Wŏnnam-dong. The strong sun blazed above the city, making people feel as if they lived at the bottom of a vast cauldron. Nanzanchō and Wajōdai were two of the new sections that the Japanese had developed at the foot of Mount Namsan. The official residence of the governor-general and the offices of the naval command were in Wajōdai.

He felt slightly cooler when he descended the pine-covered slopes of Nanzanchō. But by the time he crossed the main street, Hommachi, heading toward Meijichō, the back of his shirt was soaked with perspiration.

Large buildings of brick and stone, among them the Bank of Korea, the Mitsukoshi Department Store, the Central Post Office, and the Shokusan Bank, marked the square at the entrance to Hommachi. Noguchi climbed aboard a tram heading north. The tram crossed Chongno to reach Ch'anggyŏngwŏn, where crowds of people streamed toward the zoo and the botanical gardens. Wŏnnam-dong was just south of Ch'anggyŏngwŏn.

When Noguchi asked for directions the policeman in the neighborhood kiosk did not know of "the kisaeng of the court dance." But he could identify the house of "the kisaeng who worked with the four old musicians." A short walk south from the tram stop called Wŏnnam-dong and another ten-minute walk after turning left brought him to an area filled with the unmistakable odor of the folk who lived in the small, crowded houses made of stone and clay.

Noisily gossiping housewives dressed in white were beating their laundry with heavy sticks, called kinuta, as they gathered around the wells scattered throughout the community. This activity was called the "water-pounding laundry." Because Koreans always wore white clothes, Korean housewives did a lot of laundering. In addition to using water from rivers and wells, they spread their soiled clothes over flat stones at any available pond and beat the dirt out of them. After that vigorous attack, they spread the washed clothes over green grass or bushes to dry in the sun.

Noguchi thought he was following the policeman's instructions, but he could not find the designated landmark, a Chinese date tree. Since this part of town had grown rather haphazardly from a small village, the narrow lanes were utterly confusing to any stranger.

Noguchi stopped a primary-school boy who understood some Japanese and asked about the house of Kim Yŏng-sun. The boy had a swollen belly, as if he suffered from hunger, and could not identify Yŏng-sun by name even when Noguchi scratched in the dust the Korean characters for it. Then Noguchi uncovered the painting he was carrying and showed it to the boy. A quick glance was enough. The boy immediately said, very respectfully, "Oh, yes. I know her," and walked ahead to guide him.

Noguchi imagined that she lived in a large house set in a garden, surrounded by a high, tile-roofed earthen wall—in fact, just like the houses of rich yangban, since she must have a considerable income from her several patrons. But what he found was a small, Korean-style cottage of the kind in which people of the middle class lived. He stepped through the broken gate and saw a small yard and the spreading Chinese date tree almost hidden by the cottage's thatched roof. An old woman was drawing water from the well. As he began to speak, she took fright and ran into the house, leaving him alone and helpless.

With the painting under his arm, Noguchi simply stood in the yard. Soon he heard the low voices of neighbors gathering outside the gate. For a moment he thought he had made a mistake and reached the wrong house. But when he read the nameplate beside the entrance to the dark kitchen, he was relieved to see Yŏng-sun's name.

"Excuse me." Raising his voice, Noguchi called out. At about the fourth call, Yŏng-sun appeared—thoroughly angry, of course.

"Hello," he managed to say. "This is so unexpected . . ." Noguchi blushed as he wiped perspiration from his brow. Nearly an hour's walk under the hot sun had soaked his shirt with sweat. In the bright sunshine, and without her usual coating of white cosmetic powder, Yŏng-sun looked like another person, not as cold and forbidding as she did at night. Without her heavy dancing costume, simply dressed like an ordinary girl in a pale blue chŏksam top and a pink ch'ima skirt, she was beautiful.

"What's your business here?" she demanded, putting both hands on her hips. Noguchi didn't know what to do. He felt so stupid! To have been so naive! Simply to have assumed that he would be treated nicely if he made a personal visit, even though she had always been so unfriendly in the restaurant. Only later did he learn that her attitude was assumed out of necessity.

She was not forgetting the rules governing relationships between men and women that had been established for generations. Even a married couple would be severely criticized if they went out together. Tradition required a man and his wife to have separate quarters unless they were members of the lowest class. Generally, a woman who received a male visitor was thought to be guilty of shameful behavior. Accordingly, no matter how closely related the visitor might be to her husband or to other members of the family, she would try to avoid him entirely or else treat him coldly and formally. Naturally, then, everybody regarded Noguchi's sudden visit to her household as very impolite, almost insulting.

The old woman who had fled into the house glared at him as if he were an enemy. She stood on the bare earth just outside the door, protecting her daughter. Even worse! At his back, a crowd of hostile women was gathering.

Carefully taking out his canvas, he spoke to Yŏng-sun: "I thought I would show you this painting—and ask your opinion. . . . If this is an inconvenient time, I'll leave it with with you . . ."

Looking down at her own dancing figure on the canvas, not at dismayed Noguchi, she said not a word.

Pushing his way through the mob at the gate, he fled—most unheroically.

This disastrous visit filled him with the same kind of uneasiness that seized him when he went alone to sketch people and places in rural villages. The people there made him feel like an intruder because he was different from them.

Now a new anxiety was added to the old discomfort as he hurried away from Yŏng-sun's house. "What if she tears it up and throws it away?" Caught between fretting and worry, he stood at the tram stop. Since the picture was only a study, it would not be too great a loss if she destroyed it. Nonetheless, he did become depressed when he feared that the piece, the very heart of his hope and efforts, might be treated as cruelly as she had treated him.

The next morning, while he puttered around in his atelier, a maid from the inn came to inform him that Pak had telephoned.

"Can you come to the restaurant the day after tomorrow?" Pak asked, when Noguchi returned the call. "The time will be—well, the earlier the better."

"What's this about?"

"Good news. Until about six o'clock then." He hung up.
Noguchi thought the call must be about the haughty
Yŏng-sun, since he could think of no other reason for being
summoned to the restaurant. On the appointed evening,
Noguchi arrived at the restaurant at exactly six o'clock. The
familiar maid, grinning happily, took him to a room different
from the one he'd seen on previous visits. Nervous, but also
curious, Noguchi stood outside the door, almost afraid to enter.
The maid motioned him to go in, then left him alone. Night
had not yet fallen and the maid, dressed in white, looked like a
ghost crossing the courtyard.

In the room he found no one but Yŏng-sun, sitting in the
dusk. Startled by the presence of this second ghost, he switched
on the light. A sign from Yŏng-sun bade him sit opposite her.
She was not yet in costume, but her face was painted white for
dancing.

"I am sorry about the other day," he said softly, bowing his
head. Yŏng-sun smiled slightly. This was the first smile she had
ever granted him.

"I am returning your painting." Yŏng-sun brought out
the study, wrapped in cloth. After a moment's silence, she
explained that, according to Korean custom, it was improper
for a lone man to visit a woman, or even a family of women;
the neighbors would misunderstand his intentions.

"I apologize. I did not know. I thought only that daylight
would be better for looking at the painting."

"I looked at your painting."

"And what do you think? Is it good or bad?"

Yŏng-sun gave him a challenging look. "Mr. Noguchi, do
you want to paint the Korean dance or me? Which?"

Her sharp tone and direct question intimidated him. Avoid-
ing her glance, he tried to win her good will. "Both! And more,
much more. What I want to paint is neither the court dance
alone nor you alone, but the beauty of Korea expressed in the
dance and in you. And in you yourself I want to depict the sad
beauty in Korean things that are dying away . . ." he faltered,
"before they are lost forever."

Later Yŏng-sun told him that she was impressed by what he hoped to do, for she, too, grieved over the pathos and the beauty in Korean things that were in peril. Yet did his words tell her the truth? How could he be sure? Didn't he really mean the beauty of Kim Yŏng-sun, when he spoke of the beauty of Korea? Yŏng-sun was the kisaeng who had declared that she would never sleep with any Japanese man and had been resisting the attentions of even the powerful ones. She was a Korean woman who embodied the sensuous aroma and the warming taste of the igangju spirit. Wasn't he attracted to her precisely because of her cold attitude, her cold look, and the dark shadows in her face, rather than by the grace of her dancing? And the clear-cut features so unusual in a native Korean? Wasn't he trying to probe into the mystery of her past? Even as he raised these questions in his mind, his heart told him that all this analyzing was both unfair and unkind.

What he really wanted to know was much simpler and far more important: did he love Yŏng-sun? Or did he merely play with the idea of being interested in her because she represented the mystery of Korea?

"The dance you show in your painting is dead," said Yŏng-sun bluntly. Then, having hurt, she soothed. "That's because your sketches were made inside such a small room as this, and one with a heated floor." The court dance of the Yi dynasty, she believed, could be appreciated only when it was performed in a great hall or in a broad open space. Its beauty could never be caught unless it was seen in bright sunshine. Its beauty would never be born in a dark six-mat room like this.

"Then where can I see it?"

"The best place is the Kyŏnghoeru Hall in the Kyŏngbok Palace."

The Kyŏngbok Palace had been constructed in the southern part of Mount Paegak after Yi Sŏng-gye, founder of the Yi dynasty, moved the capital to Seoul. Later destroyed by fire after a battle, the palace had been rebuilt in 1867, the third year of the Keiō era, by Regent Taewŏngun.

The palace built at that time covered about 130,000 tsubo

(one tsubo equals 1.33 square meters) and was surrounded by a wall three kilometers long. Its main gate, the Kwanghwamun, was still remembered in the name of a place. Since then, many buildings in the great compound had been destroyed, but Kŭnjŏngjŏn, Sajŏngjŏn, and Kyŏnghoeru still survived. Now the large, white office building of Japan's governor-general sat where the palace had soared.

The Kyŏnghoeru stood behind the governor-general's building. Extending thirty-five meters from east to west and twenty-seven meters from north to south, it was used as reception and banquet halls on its upper and lower floors. Forty-eight stone columns four and a half meters in height supported those beautiful levels. Like a gorgeous faerie island, it rose in the midst of a broad moat, where its magnificent tiled roof and great height dominated the scene and gave testimony to the unforgettable style of the Yi dynasty. Noguchi had visited it twice, and each time he wandered through it in awe.

"I want to dance there! I won't mind being your model when I dance there!" declared Yŏng-sun. Hearing this, Noguchi wanted to kiss the hem of the long, pale blue skirt that fell in flowing lines from her lifted knee.

IV

Sketching her while dancing in a banquet hall of the former royal palace proved to be impossible. Because the palace was within the compound of the governor-general's building, many visitors went to see it every day (except Monday) at three appointed times: eleven o'clock in the morning and one-thirty and three in the afternoon. Guides led the visitors by an invariable route, spending an hour on each round. If the number of arriving and departing visitors differed by even one person, a big fuss was made. Under such circumstances, giving permission for the four old musicians to bring in all those rare musical instruments and arranging enough time to allow Kim Yŏng-sun to dance and sing without interruption on the top floor of the Kyŏnghoeru lay beyond the power of the bureaucracy to conceive.

After discussing the problem, they decided to stage the dance at the Tŏksu Palace, on T'aep'yŏng Avenue in central Seoul. This palace, once the residence of the late King Kojong after his abdication, had been called Kyŏngun for the past nine years. Koreans still regarded it as the Royal Palace. It was the ideal place for performing court dances. Furthermore, it was under the supervision of the Royal Yi Office and was open to the public for an admission fee of five sen per person.

So Yŏng-sun, wearing her dancer's costume, stood on the green lawn of the Tŏksu Palace for an hour on fifteen mornings during the summer. Noguchi could easily sketch her while he sat before his easel, but it was difficult for Yŏng-sun to keep the same pose, stretching out her arms for a whole hour. In the afternoons, the four old musicians came, mostly to earn one yen per hour. Noguchi placed them in front of the palace, as part of the background for his painting. Sometimes Yŏng-sun stayed late, to sit with them. Thus she worked as his model for fifteen days, except when rain fell on Seoul.

One day, when rain did begin to fall just after she had put on her costume, they gave up their work at the palace and took a taxi to his atelier. His parents had rented this house for his studio. It was near their inn, and he went home only to eat and to bathe.

Interested in the atelier, Yŏng-sun asked many questions. "What is this?" "What is it for?" "How do you use it?" Her sentences were always very short—not because she could not speak Japanese well but because, as he learned later, she refused to speak Japanese. Her friendly interest made him very happy, and he explained to her the theories of colors and the uses of his implements. Those hours of the rainy day spent in his atelier seemed to remove all the obstacles that had reared like a great wall between them. The cold look and the distant manner disappeard from her eyes and her speech. She seemed more relaxed, much as he'd seen her when only Pak sat with her at the restaurant.

After the summer vacation ended and the fall semester commenced, he could paint only on Sundays and holidays. He decided to do an oil painting, seventy-two by ninety-one centimeters, based upon his completed sketches. While working on this painting, he realized how strongly her appearance had been imprinted in his mind. Standing in front of his class, which included many Korean girls, he often thought about her delicate waxen ear lobes, her proud curved nose, the straying dark locks.

"Have I fallen in love with this Korean kisaeng? This dancer who is three years older than I? This woman who has treated me with such disdain?" Often he asked himself these questions, trying to laugh at himself, to cure himself of this obsession. But he could not laugh her away. He could not drive her image from his mind. It was breathing, swelling, growing in his heart.

Finding all this unbearable, he sometimes visited the restaurant when she was there. But he found no comfort: she was just as cold, just as severe, as she'd always been in that setting, completely different from the times when she posed for him at the palace and in his atelier. He became almost desperate to see her smile.

One Sunday at the end of September Pak visited him at his atelier. As soon as Pak came in, he went straight to the painting. For a long time he stood before the canvas, inspecting it from top to bottom. Finally he turned to Noguchi. "Last night I went to the restaurant and heard much from her. I understand that she finally agreed to be your model."

"It's about half finished," said Noguchi. "I wish she'd pose for me some more."

Taking a European watch from his vest pocket, Pak asked, "She's not here yet?"

"What? Is she coming here? Today?"

Pak smiled. "Well, we decided to visit you here today. To look at the painting. And to encourage you."

Noguchi rejoiced at the astounding news that she would be coming. He remembered at this further evidence of Pak's kindness that the meetings with him, first at the sulchip in Chongno and then at the House of the Red Dream, had led to his associ-

ation with Kim Yŏng-sun. Whether or not it would be a
friendly association he could not say. Certainly the course of
human relationships was beyond predicting. But, as far as he
was concerned, always full of hope . . .

Noguchi ran home and asked his mother to help him at the
atelier. As he left the inn, he saw Yŏng-sun walking up the
slope of Nanzanchō, carrying a basket of fruit, her purple
ch'ima skirt flaring with each step. He rushed to greet her.

"Hi! Professor Pak has come already," Noguchi told her,
almost dancing for joy.

"Oh, this walking is so tiring! Last time I came here in a
car. I thought it was closer." Her pale forehead glistened with
perspiration. Even in the Season of Red Dragonflies the city of
Seoul is still hot. In Korea summer seems to flow into winter
with no easy transition.

"Here, let me carry this." He took the fruit basket, moved
ahead with long strides, and then loped back to be with her.
Because one of his female students lived in a house facing the
slope, he was very conscious of gossipy neighbors. His studio,
at the very end of the alley, was in a small house with a foreign-
style room, eight mats in size, a Japanese six-mat room, a
kitchen, and a small porch. He used the foreign-style room as
the atelier.

"I met her on the way," Noguchi scarcely needed to tell
Pak, as he hurried to place cushions on the tatami mats in the
Japanese room.

"Mr. Noguchi," said Pak, "these old musicians look rather
lonely, tucked away, off to the side. Does that have any
meaning?" Leaving Yŏng-sun standing in front of the canvas,
he stepped into the tatami room.

"Nothing really important. But to me they always seem to
be thinking about the old days as they play. I wanted to show
their lonely and yearning expressions, their nostalgia. And,
of course, Miss Kim must be the center of attention—in the
painting as in life."

When Noguchi's mother appeared, Yŏng-sun sat respectfully, on her heels, in the Japanese style. As Noguchi introduced

the two, his mother immediately recognized her, saying, "Oh, yes; she is your model, is she not?" She had seen his painting in progress whenever she came to clean the studio.

Mrs. Noguchi, having to hurry back to the inn, left after five minutes of polite—and meaningless—conversation.

Pak had a good knowledge of the fine arts. He and Noguchi did most of the talking, although the artist would much rather have given all his attention to Yŏng-sun. But with her he could only chat foolishly about how his summer vacation had ended and about how now he could paint only on holidays. Late in the afternoon the three went to Meijichō, shared an early supper, and then separated. At parting, Yŏng-sun said to Noguchi, really smiling this time: "Since I am anxious about the way you will show my face in your painting, I'd like to come to see it now and then." The message was just as simple as that, but how happy it made him! He couldn't sleep at all that night.

What Yŏng-sun said at parting was not just a pretense. On the following Sunday afternoon, she came again to the studio, bearing some pale apples from Taegu. The autumn sun was quite different from that of the summer. The tone of her skin was also quite different from what it had been in summer. The soft sunlight brought out a hue that was much more suitable for the painting. Noguchi explained this to her and asked if she could come to his atelier every Sunday afternoon so that he could try to capture that tone on his canvas. He felt a little worried, because the request sounded so contrived. He hardly dared admit to himself that he just wanted to have more time together with her. Unexpectedly, and pleasantly, she consented to come. After that he eagerly waited for every Sunday. His mother worried about what the neighbors would say, but she didn't oppose the visits after she understood that Miss Kim came only to be his model, while he worked on his great painting.

Yŏng-sun sat quietly on a chair while he worked. To keep her from being bored, he set on a table beside her a number of art books and some of his old photograph albums. In the beginning, she posed for an hour, rested for a while, and then resumed sitting for another half hour. By her third visit, however, she sat for only about thirty minutes and spent the rest of the time talking.

During these casual conversations, in which they discussed many things, Noguchi usually led the way. But when he started to ask about her life as a kisaeng, she answered quite straightforwardly.

"So you charge twenty-five yen per hour? That must be the highest entertainment fee charged by the kisaeng."

"No, it's not an entertainment fee. The money pays for the music and the dances—performed, don't forget, by five people."

"When you are paid so well, why are you living in a house like that?"

Her reply was as honest as his question was impertinent: "Well, we charge twenty-five yen only to yangban and Japanese."

This answer amused Noguchi very much; from it he could see, behind the curtains, so to speak, much about the Korean kisaeng's history. According to her, only rich Koreans and Japanese paid such high fees. Members of the intelligentsia like Pak, who appreciated the court dances but were relatively poor, paid only five yen. Moreover, when she did receive twenty-five yen, she gave ten of them to her agent, and the rest was divided equally among the five performers, leaving her with only three yen. If they performed at a government function, each of the five received only one yen. If these claims were true, then when she performed for three different groups of Japanese customers in one evening, she received only nine yen.

"Some evenings I get only one yen. But all the tips are mine."

Now Noguchi understood why these old musicians were willing to come to the palace on those hot summer days. Yŏngsun was paying her obligation to them, from whom she had learned the ancient court music and dances.

When November arrived, the people of Seoul prepared for

winter. Light snow began to fall toward the end of the month. On the Sunday afternoon before she arrived, Noguchi brought a brazier into the studio to warm them while he applied the final brush strokes to her face on the canvas. The composition portrayed a sorrowful dancer looking up at the somber autumn sky while four old musicians played their instruments against the splendid background of the Tŏksu Palace. Two of the musicians appeared to be yearning for times past, another was admiring the dancer, and one had lowered his eyes, staring at nothing—or, perhaps, into his memories. The dancer, in quarter-profile, lifting her pale right hand, gazed beyond the palace, beyond the things of earth, toward the gathering darkness.

The color in the iris of her eyes was difficult for Noguchi to find. He strove to achieve the right hue.

While he mixed pigments on the palette, Yŏng-sun suddenly raised her voice. "Who is this?"

"Who?" he responded absentmindedly. She was turning the pages of an old family album he had brought from his parents' house.

She stood up and came closer, pointing to a figure in a photograph, browning with age. "This one! This man!"

Glancing at the man she indicated, he laughed. "Oh, that's my father. When he was in the army."

"Your father? This man?" Suddenly her voice became sharp, on the edge of anger.

"Yes. He was a military man, long ago. Before I was born. He left the army after he married my mother."

Crying out as if in pain, she threw the album at the canvas.

"Hey! What are you doing?" he shouted. The easel was sliding to one side, and he sprang from his chair just in time to catch the falling canvas. Sighing with relief, yet dismayed by her violence, he looked up to ask why she was so upset. But she was gone, and the open door showed only the gray sky of autumn.

"Hey! Wait! Where are you going?" He ran out of the house, barefoot. But he dared not chase after her. The cold sharp stones, the watchful eyes of curious neighbors, the feeling of loss—all drove him back. He had to let her go.

Swift and surefooted, the Korean dancer fled down the hill, into the gathering dusk, her long, purple skirt billowing as she ran.

V

Soon after that strange afternoon, Noguchi finished his painting of Kim Yŏng-sun. He never saw her again, not even when he asked her to join him in the room he rented in the House of the Red Dream. Always she sent a servant to say, "She cannot come tonight." And he, seeking the wailing call of the t'ungso flute and throbbing beat of the changgo drum, wandered about in the districts from Chayachō to Chongno, hoping to meet her in one or the other of those place where she might dance. Once he caught up with one of her old musicians, who had just left a restaurant, and asked him to arrange a meeting with Yŏng-sun. But she would not come out of the restaurant.

By that time Noguchi had realized that he was out of favor with her. But he wanted to know why she had turned against him. He suspected that the photograph of his father must have had something to do with her antagonism. The picture showed his parents, recently engaged, standing side by side somewhere, either in a suburb of Seoul or in a town nearby. His mother was dressed in a Japanese kimono, while his father wore an army officer's uniform with a samurai's sword at his side.

"Why did that picture upset her so? Does she hate military men?" Her behavior worried Noguchi day and night. If he could only see her, talk to her, he might be able to clear up the mystery.

Showing his mother the photograph, he asked her to tell him where and when it was taken. But she gave him no help at all. "Perhaps it was taken when we went near Suwŏn," she said vaguely. "For a picnic or something. But I can't be sure. . . ."

Now he had to rely on his father's memory. Because his father was the chairman of the innkeepers' union, he rarely stayed at home during the day. Noguchi had to wait for a suitable night. At last it came. Never would he forget that occasion. It was the night of December 7, 1941, the night before the Pacific War began. Seeing his father sitting at the counter near the inn's entrance, Noguchi laid the photograph album before him.

"Father, I want to ask you something."

Handing the ledger to the clerk, Mr. Noguchi turned to his son. "What about?"

"This picture."

"Let's see it."

Putting on his spectacles, his father glanced at it, and then closed the album with an embarrassed smile. The clerk was not supposed to see how the years had so sadly changed a slender and young army officer.

"This is the first photo you took with mother, right?"

"Yes, I guess so. Unless there's an older one somewhere."

"Mother said that it was taken near Suwŏn."

Stern now, Mr. Noguchi asked, "Why are you so concerned about this? About such far-off times?"

"Since the scenery looks so interesting, I'm thinking I might take my students there for sketching."

"In this cold December weather?"

"No. Next spring sometime," the son lied. "I'm making up our schedule now for next year."

The trusting father put on his spectacles again, flipped the pages of the album, and examined the photo under the desk light.

"Suwŏn, eh?" he murmured, trying to call forth old memories from black and white and gray images of low hills and a wooden structure resembling a village office building at the left side of the picture.

"Oh, yes. This is Paranjang," he said in a low voice.

"Paranjang?"

"Now it is called Paran-ni. It's not a scenic place. A bit west of Osan." Mr. Noguchi removed his spectacles.

"Why did you go to a place like this?"

"Well, in those days there was a garrison in Paranjang. Maybe we went there for a picnic. Or to pick apples or pears. The picture must have been taken at that time."

His father's answer was convincing enough. Noguchi, hoping to hear something that would explain the reason for Yŏng-sun's behavior, was disappointed.

"Didn't you gather peaches and grapes perhaps?"

"In the old days, more apples, pears, and plums were grown around there. The Paranjang garrison, I should add, had acted meritoriously during the Mansei Incident."

"The Mansei Incident? What was that?"

"Maybe you were not born yet . . . or was that the year when you were born?"

His father, taking an Asahi brand cigarette from its packet, lit it against the hot chimney of the stove.

"That was the time when some young and foolish Koreans caused a great deal of unrest by shouting out 'Mansei!'—ten thousand years!—when they gathered in the street. Many Korean students assembled at Pagoda Park in Chongno and read a declaration of independence that caused a great commotion throughout the whole country."

"Did such a thing really happen? I've never even heard of it."

"Sure it did. Because it happened on the first day of March, our military leaders called it the 'March First Agitation.' They also issued pamphlets warning against future incidents of that kind."

"Then the garrison is related to this photo?"

"Yes, the garrison subdued the rioters. . . . Isn't this enough, now? I'm busy."

Noguchi thanked his father and left. The Chiyodaro Inn was so designed that the maids' quarters were in the left wing of the first floor, which extended from the front porch. His parents' rooms were upstairs. Noguchi went straight to his father's study, where the notebooks holding name cards, diaries, and inn registers were arranged in chronological order on shelves attached to one wall. On another wall were the shelves containing books needed during his father's military career and additional volumes acquired for the business of managing the inn.

Without hesitation, Noguchi searched among the old books. Finally, among the pamphlets, he found one entitled *Outline of the Progress of the Korean Agitation.* Its yellow cover had begun to fray. Quickly he scanned the first paragraph: "On the first of March, as planned, about three to four thousand students gathered at the Pagoda Park, and read the Declaration of Independence. As they started their demonstration march, the mobs joined them. . . ."

"Ah! This is what I want!" Noguchi slipped the pamphlet into his pocket, left the study, and ran down the road to his castle, the atelier. Since the *Outline* was written in the old military style of the 1920s, with many Chinese characters, he had difficulty in understanding much of it, but he managed a hurried scanning.

In the peaceful Korea of his time, he could scarcely believe that such great agitation had occurred some twenty years before. Yet it must have happened, because the pamphlet described it baldly, presenting fact after fact, date after date. But contemporary textbooks about Korean history completely ignored the Mansei events and emphasized how peaceful the country had been since its annexation by Japan.

According to the *Outline,* the leaders of the independence movement included some Christians, several Ch'ŏndogyo followers, and some students. The declaration was drafted by a Korean historian named Ch'oe Nam-sŏn. All the student allies cut classes on the first of March and gathered at Pagoda Park. According to their original plan, the declaration would be read by Son Pyŏng-hŭi, the head of Ch'ŏndogyo, and the demonstration march would begin after participants raised three shouts of "Mansei!"

However, at sight of all those excited young students in the park, the adult members of the movement feared a riot, changed their plan at the last moment, and moved to the Myŏngwŏlgwan in Insa-dong. There they read the declaration,

raised the three shouts of "Mansei!" and phoned the director of
the metropolitan police to accept their voluntary surrender.
The students, enraged at being "betrayed" by the elders,
passed the written declaration to people in the gathering crowd
and set out on their demonstration march in two groups, one
going to the east, the other to the west. This provoked the first
of the fierce demonstrations that continued for nearly nine
months throughout the Korean peninsula. As the several thousand students left Pagoda Park, they resembled a small stream,
but by the time they reached Tŏksu Palace, where the body
of the late King Kojong lay, the stream had grown, flowing
around the palace like a river in flood. Their shouts of
"Mansei" stirred the people of Seoul, and soon the entire city
was filled with maddened hordes rushing through the streets,
shouting their hope for freedom and their hatred for Japan. The
madness spread to P'yŏngyang and Wŏnsan during the first
day; to Hwangju, Chinnamp'o and Anju on the second day;
and to Kaesŏng, Kyŏmip'o, Sariwŏn, Sŏnch'ŏn, and Hamhŭng
on the third day. Thus the rebellion spread and the Japanese
authorities hastily put all of Korea under martial law. But that
decision came too late.

As he read, Noguchi kept wondering what all this had to do
with Kim Yŏng-sun. Trying to make sense of the chapters in the
Outline, with their sober accounts covering a period of three
months, exhausted him. Learning about such an incident as a
fact of history was a shocking surprise.

Unable to sleep that night, Noguchi was reading a maga-
zine in bed. Suddenly an idea flashed in his mind: what had
upset Yŏng-sun was not his father, but rather the background
of the photograph—the town of Paranjang and its garrison.

Again he studied the pages of the *Outline*. The progress of
the incident was recorded by months and districts. He read
with increasing alarm the section about the Kyŏnggi Province
in April:

> The agitation within Seoul had been controlled by the police
> and military, and order was superficially maintained. However,

the local districts were much affected by the disturbances, which
hit their peak at the beginning of April. The rioters attacked the
government buildings, district offices, police headquarters, and
military police stations; destroyed and set fire to civilian houses,
offices, and bridges; and committed all possible violence. Moreover, about two thousand rioters attacked and seized the police
station of Hwasu-ri, Ujŏng-myŏn, in Suwŏn County. One policeman tried to defend himself by firing but was unable to cope with
the far more numerous rioters and was finally murdered. His
corpse was abused. Under the circumstances, the Japanese in that
area evacuated their women and children. The situation was like
a civil war, causing commotion and confusion among the people.
The newly arrived captain of the garrison in Paranjang saw the
need to eliminate the leaders of the riots. He led his soldiers to
Cheam-ni village on April fifteenth, gathered twenty-some Christians and Ch'ŏndogyo followers who admitted that they were the
leaders, killed them all, and burned down most of the village.

The garrison at Paranjang was mentioned only once in this
statement. Noguchi read again the part that said "gathered
twenty-some Christians and Ch'ŏndogyo followers and killed
them." It was written in a plain military style. However, a most
cruel retaliation for the single dead policeman was acknowledged. It had been a massacre. Did the soldiers use machine
guns to kill more than twenty Koreans at one time? Or did they
shoot them with rifles, one by one? What was their purpose in
burning the village afterward? Noguchi sat up in bed and
stared in horror at the telltale report.

He imagined the scene in that remote village of Cheam-ni,
where frightened villagers, including the elders wearing white
turumagi coats and straw hats, were gathered. Some might
actually have been leaders of the rioters who had attacked the
police station in Hwasu-ri, but others would have had nothing
to do with the riots and been only devout Christians and
Ch'ŏndogyo followers. And all of those "twenty-some" living
men had been killed to eliminate the few leaders; and then, to
teach the survivors a lesson, their village was burned down.

"I wonder if my father was the captain of the garrison?"

This possibility frightened Noguchi very much. He simply could not think of his father as such a brutal murderer. But when he remembered the fury in Yŏng-sun's face on that terrible Sunday afternoon, he could not avoid the conclusion that his father must have been the cause of her anger.

On the very next day, December 8, Japan started the Pacific War. The people of Seoul were much excited by the news that Japan had attacked Pearl Harbor. All the students and teachers in Noguchi's school went to the Shinto shrine in Namsan to pray for Japan's victory. The 384 stone steps leading up to the shrine were crowded with primary- and middle-school students going to offer respects to the gods of Japan. But in his heart, Noguchi was much more concerned about Yŏng-sun than with the war.

After returning from the shrine, he telephoned the office of the union for geisha and kisaeng and asked for information about the registration of Kim Yŏng-sun. A female clerk spoke from the other end of the telephone line, "Please wait a while," and did not return. He waited, as instructed—and as experience with clerks had taught him long since.

About five minutes later, a male voice spoke on the phone and said, indifferently, "We are short of personnel and cannot check on her. We are at war now, you know." Noguchi barked: "This is the military police! Find it right away!" The command succeeded: the man checked immediately and reported the facts about her. Just as Noguchi had feared, Yŏng-sun came from Cheam-ni, Hyangnam-myŏn, Suwŏn-gun in Kyŏnggido. As he put down the receiver, he felt sweat rolling down his sides, even in the cold of winter. "So she is from there," he mumbled hopelessly.

At home Noguchi examined a map and learned that Cheam-ni, situated near Paranjang, was a small village with only fifty-four families. The map indicated that the Korean words *ŭp* and *myŏn* were equivalent to the Japanese terms for town and village. A *ri* was the same as the Japanese *aza*, meaning hamlet.

"So Yŏng-sun was born in the small village where the

massacre took place during the March First Agitation. And she was about four years old then. She remembers it!" Noguchi was much disturbed, thinking that he too would hold a grudge throughout his whole life if his father had been killed in such a massacre. Cheam-ni and Paranjang were so close. If he had been told constantly by his mother that his father had been murdered by soldiers of the garrison at Paranjang, certainly he would have grown up hating the soldiers, their barracks, and even the very hills and valleys around Paranjang.

Yŏng-sun must have recognized the background in the photo and believed that the smiling man in a Japanese officer's uniform was the one who ordered the killing of her father. To her that officer was not the father of Noguchi Ryōkichi, but the murderer of her father. Now he understood why she said that she would never sleep with any Japanese man. If her father was one of the leaders who were executed in Cheam-ni, then certainly she would hate all Japanese, including himself—and, hating him, would refuse to be a model for his painting. The sudden death of her father must have been a great misfortune, causing her to live in that shabby old house with her mother, forcing her to become a dancer, earning only a few yen per night. Desperately, he wanted to see Yŏng-sun, to ask her all kinds of questions, to try to comfort her for years of loss and misery. Yet the thought that his father had been in the army at the time of the Mansei Incident filled him with dread.

"What if my father was the captain of the garrison? And the very man who killed her father?" Taking upon himself a guilt that was not his own, Noguchi brooded over this curse of fate. Day after day, he thought about it, even while he tried to teach.

VI

Noguchi's painting of Kim Yŏng-sun, *The Remembered Shadow of the Yi Dynasty*, was ready for the Korean Exhibition. More than a year had passed since he'd met her. During much of that time he had concentrated on representing her dancing figure on canvas. He had great confidence in his work.

After the New Year of 1942, he sent the painting to the Fine Arts Museum for the spring exhibition. It need not have been sent so early, but he could not bear to stack her portrait in a dark corner of his atelier.

If anything, Noguchi was an introspective man, the type to worry about things, but to keep those worries to himself. He could have asked his father directly about the times of the March First Agitation, but he could not bring himself to do that. He remembered that once his father—or someone else, perhaps—said that the garrison in Paranjang had done quite a good job of controlling the area. Noguchi found another reason why he preferred not to ask his father directly. After the disturbance and its consequences, even a military man would have been brought before a court-martial, charged with killing civilians. And, he knew, immediately after the March First Agitation, his father had retired from the army with the rank of captain of the infantry.

"Did his retiring have anything to do with the Cheam-ni incident?" he wondered. Just thinking of that possibility made him despondent, reviving the memory of Yŏng-sun's coldness toward him and her cruel opinions about Japanese in general. He would not go any more to the House of the Red Dream. Before discovering his father's possible role in her tragedy, he might have gone in search of her. But now that he could guess the cause of her anger, he did not dare to see her. Yet he yearned to see her.

Then he would quarrel with himself. What's wrong with you? he'd snarl. What do you want from her? She's just a Korean kisaeng! He tried hard to forget her, recounting all her faults. She was older than he, for one thing. He had never even held her hands, for another. And, above all, she was a fatherless Korean kisaeng. Without family to speak for her, without honor, without money—and so, of course, the more he tried to forget her, the more he remembered her, asleep or awake, by day or by night.

In the city, all victorious actions of Japan's army and navy were reported over the radio every morning, to the accompaniment of vigorous marching songs. Japan's achievements in those weeks were glorious, stunning the whole world. Dive-bombers sank the two most prestigious British battleships in the seas off Malaysia. On January 3, 1942, Japan's soldiers occupied Manila, utterly defeating the U.S. forces in the Philippines. That event was followed by the fall of Singapore on February 15. With such brilliant military conquests one after the other, the people of Seoul were much involved in celebrating victories and advances. But Noguchi could never rejoice over his country's triumphs because the plight of Yŏng-sun and her oppressed country weighed heavily on his mind.

Toward the end of February, when the naval engagement off Surabaya was in the news, a reporter from the *Keijō nippō* visited Noguchi at his school.

"What is this all about?" wondered Noguchi as he went to the principal's office, where, beaming happily, that eminent personage received him.

"Congratulations!" said the principal.

"What for?" Noguchi glanced at the name cards handed him by the reporter and a photographer. The reporter, peering at a note in his hand, said, "Your painting has won the special award. Tell us how you feel about it."

"The special award?"

"Aren't you the Mr. Noguchi Ryōkichi who entered the painting entitled *The Remembered Shadow of the Yi Dynasty?*"

"Yes, I am . . ."

"So, then, tell us how you feel?"

Noguchi spoke modestly about his surprise and gratitude on this occasion, and the photographer took his picture. Upon hearing the news, everyone in the office congratulated him, some with pleasure, a few with envy well hidden.

"So my painting has received the special prize!" thought Noguchi, wishing that he could tell Kim Yŏng-sun all about it. Then he had second thoughts, wondering if she would really feel happy about a *Japanese* man's recognition. So he telephoned only to his parents at home and to Pak at the medical school.

The great exhibition opened on March 5 at the Fine Arts Museum of Korea and was supposed to last for a month. On the third day of the show, Noguchi took some of his female students to the museum. Many spectators had gathered in front of his painting. Assuming a nonchalant air, while inwardly proud, Noguchi felt sad that he could not view it with Yŏng-sun. After all, the painting was the tangible result of all the energy, hope, tenacity, and expense that had made him seek Yŏng-sun at the House of the Red Dream for more than a year.

The one who valued this award the most was his father, whose sense of family honor had become increasingly strong ever since he'd ended his military career. "This award has finally made my son known to the world as a professional artist," he said more than once. His father wanted Noguchi to meet all important guests who stayed at the Chiyoda Inn. This represented quite a change in his father who until now had considered a military man to be much more valuable to society than a mere artist. A number of congratulatory messages and gifts were sent to the artist by his friends and neighbors; among the gifts was a whole bream fish from Pak, very knowledgeable about the customs of Japan. But such a joyful mood lasted only a short while.

On the eighth day of the exhibition, General Tazawa Kaichirō, the Chief of Staff of the Japanese Army in Korea, went to see it. While viewing Noguchi's painting, he questioned one of his aides. "Isn't this that Korean kisaeng, Kim Yŏng-sun?"

"Yes, it looks like her," replied the aide.

"It does not just look like her. She *is* the one. Check this out!"

Not long before, General Tazawa had seen Yŏng-sun dance; he had been very much interested in her ever since. But in spite of his staff member's diligent efforts, neither Yŏng-sun nor her agent would ever consent to establishing a relationship with the general. Tazawa's pride must have been hurt at seeing how Yŏng-sun allowed herself to be an artist's model after having refused his attentions.

On the afternoon of the same day a military policeman went to Noguchi's school while he was teaching his watercolor class. As soon as Noguchi appeared in the principal's office, the policeman asked him directly, "Who is the model for your painting?"

"A Korean lady," replied Noguchi softly, observing the mark across the policeman's brow made by his cap.

"We can see that. What's her name and address?"

"I do not know the exact address, but I think she lives in Wŏnnam-dong. Her name is Kim Yŏng-sun."

"She's a kisaeng, isn't she?" The military policeman's voice hardened, and Noguchi matched him with a harsh "Yes."

"A schoolteacher who uses a kisaeng as a model does not make sense."

"Doesn't it?"

"Of course not! What ignorant conduct at such a critical time as this! We are now at war."

Amazed, Noguchi simply stared at the policeman's cruel expression. "But she was my model last year. Before the war."

"You're trying to be impudent?"

"But that is the truth!"

"At any rate, you come with me. We want to ask more questions."

Noguchi was taken to the military police headquarters. By evening, cold and hungry, he'd become very cross. At last he was led into an interrogation room, which was warmed by a stove. A man wearing the insignia of a lieutenant sat at a desk near the stove. Noguchi bowed. The officer was polite. "Sit down," he said. After listening to Noguchi's explanation about his painting, and why and when it had been started, he asked different questions concerning Noguchi's personal relationship with Yŏng-sun. Noguchi's answers were simple and clear.

"I see. Then nothing has happened between you and Kim Yŏng-sun."

All this prying irritated Noguchi. "Of course not. Why do you ask such a question? Now, let me go home."

"I will let you go as soon as our business is over. By the

way, what was your intention in giving your painting a title like that? Tell me your reason."

"I had no particular reason."

"No particular reason?"

"That's right. Its theme is an ancient court dance of the Yi dynasty."

"You say you had no particular reason, but the title of your painting, *The Remembered Shadow of the Yi Dynasty*, would give people in general the impression that the Yi dynasty is still in existence. Furthermore, the scene is Tŏksu Palace. Your intention is quite obvious to me."

"What do you mean?"

"Don't try to make a fool of me!" Shouting, the lieutenant stood up, slapping the desk loudly. So began the hard technique of interrogation, as compared with the soft approach he'd tried earlier.

"I'm not."

"Don't lie to me! What's this?"

The lieutenant shoved a pamphlet across the desk. Noguchi winced. It was the one he'd taken from his father's study, *Outline of the Progress of the Korean Agitation*.

"We searched your atelier and found this! Do you still keep saying that you had no deliberate purpose in choosing that title?"

"Yes! That pamphlet had nothing to do with the painting."

"Then why was it in your atelier?"

"I don't quite remember how long it's been there." Noguchi was trying to protect his father, who had obtained it during the years of his military service. He feared that telling this to the lieutenant might cause trouble for his father. As the lieutenant questioned him further, Noguchi decided to make a false statement, saying that he had picked up the pamphlet in a schoolyard some time ago. If he said that he'd bought it in a secondhand bookstore, the bookstore would have been investigated.

The interrogation ended at about ten o'clock that night. Frustration and hunger made Noguchi very sullen.

"Since your father is a former military man, I think I will overlook your fault this time. But don't ever again dig up the past. Mind your own business from now on. Do you understand? Furthermore, don't ever make a kisaeng your model for a painting."

"I won't."

"And lastly, change the title of your painting. Right away!"

"Change it? Why?"

"Of course. Unless you're a nationalist, you can easily change it, can't you?"

Now Noguchi added anger to frustration. To think that a mere lieutenant, flaunting his power, was making so unreasonable a demand! Just for a whim! Only a military policeman would be stupid enough to think that the Yi dynasty still existed when he read a title meant to be poetic. What else could *The Remembered Shadow of the Yi Dynasty* be?

"Then what are you going to do? Are you going to change it or not?"

"Since I seem to have no choice, I will change the title."

"You mean you voluntarily wish to change it, is that it?"

Noguchi resented the arrogance of this strutting cock on a dungheap, forcing him to commit himself, trying to break his spirit. But he wanted to go home. So he yielded. "Yes, I think I would like to do that."

"Fine. And what's the new title?"

"I won't give it any title at all."

"What?"

"If it has to have something, then *Untitled* will be just fine."

The lieutenant stood up and punched the middle of Noguchi's face. His spectacles fell to the floor. His nose filled with warm blood.

"What—what are you doing?" Even as he tried to regain his balance Noguchi received another blow, this one to the jaw. He fell to the floor, taking the chair with him. The lieutenant stepped on his glasses, shattering the thick lenses.

"What an insult to name it *Untitled!* You must be a

Communist! And you'll see what happens when you insult an officer in the Imperial Army."

That night, they kept Noguchi in a very cold cell at the military police station. Even though the middle of March had arrived, Korea still endured its long winter. He hated the despot who had hit him and broken his glasses and confined him in an icy cell because somebody did not approve the model he had used and the title he had given his painting. Now, at last, he understood all too clearly how brutal Japanese soldiers could have committed that massacre at Cheam-ni, and burned the helpless village, too.

See, Yŏng-sun: see how I, too, am treated like an enemy. How I am beaten, thrown into a freezing cell, given nothing to eat or to drink. . . . As he shivered and raged, he remembered the beauty of her ears, the curve of her proud nose. Overcome with misery, he clutched the thin blanket around him and wept for sorrow and longing. Now that she was lost to him, he knew that he loved her.

In the morning they took him back to the interrogation room. While stumbling nearsightedly along the corridor, holding up his pants because the belt had been taken away, he thought he saw his father sitting on a bench. For the first time he felt a rush of hope, thinking that he must have come to pick up his son. Fortunately, Mr. Noguchi, straight of back, an upright military man, did not see his miserable, bloodied, disgraced son.

The lieutenant, well fed and warm, sipping delicious hot tea served by a soldier, resumed the attack at once. "So, Noguchi, what about that title?"

"Well . . ."

"You're not going to waste that hard-earned special award, are you? Don't forget the family honor. Your father distinguished himself for his service at the time of the March First Agitation. The pamphlet belongs to him, doesn't it?"

"Yes."

"Then why did you hide that fact? Because you did so, rather stupidly, I point out, you spent the night in one of our comfortable rooms. You had no need to doubt the merits of your father, the distinguished captain of the garrison in Paranjang."

Noguchi sagged.

"My father? Captain of the garrison?"

"Sure. Didn't you know that? As a matter of fact, he's in the colonel's office now, returning to active duty. As a major. We've always thought he retired too soon."

The lieutenant's expression accused him of being an unfilial son. He drew from its pack a cigarette of the Homare brand, meaning Honor, shook it at Noguchi so he could not miss the lesson, and finally got around to lighting it. His manner, very different from that of the night before, seemed almost friendly.

"Soldier!" he called. "Another cup of tea." The lieutenant, returning his attention to Noguchi, stiffened with embarrassment. This fool of an artist! This weak son of an honorable military man, was crying!

Noguchi wept without shame. His honor was shattered, his pride broken. What he had most feared was true. Now he knew who had killed Yŏng-sun's father.

"Tell me. What will the new title be?"

The soldier brought him a cup of steaming tea. Suppressing the impulse to reach for it, Noguchi shook his head. "No. Still no change. I don't want to change it."

"What?" the lieutenant snarled.

"Instead, I'll ask them to cancel the special award."

The next moment, Noguchi lay again on the floor. The pain in his head was unbearable.

But behind it, through the mist of tears, he saw the face of Yŏng-sun, glowing like the moon in autumn. Like a remembered light from kinder times. . . .

A Crane on a Dunghill:
Seoul in 1936

I

MANY RED DRAGONFLIES were hovering about as Akutsu
Minoru left the great, white building that housed the governor-
general and his staff. Depressed by everything, he sighed, "This
will be my second autumn in Korea." The thought of yet
another hard winter was the worst affliction of all.

Because he'd been raised in Kyūshū, the southernmost of
Japan's large islands, he could bear the heat of summer well
enough, but not the cold of winter. The biting cold of Korea's
winters penetrated his very bones. The usual alternation of
three absolutely frigid days followed by four days of relative
warmth that characterized Korean winters was quite different
from what he had been told at home in Japan. He could toler-
ate the brief exposure to cold as he rushed from his lodgings to
his office near the government building but, because he was a
newly hired journalist, constantly sent out to gather information for the paper, he was not allowed to take refuge (least of
all a comfortable nap) in the warm editorial office. When the
new year of 1937 arrived, his company would begin to print
the evening paper in a large six-page edition. That meant even
more misery for shivering Akutsu.

When he went out into the city, he wore two layers of camel's hair underwear, two pairs of mittens, a pair of rabbit-pelt ear muffs, arctic boots over two pairs of cotton and wool socks, and two overcoats atop the usual woolen suit and sweaters. He slipped and fell many times on the frozen roads and could not move fast because of all those heavy layers of clothing. On one occasion, he even lost consciousness for a few moments when he fell on his back. At such times, he felt that he really lived in a foreign country, somewhere north of Siberia perhaps, although Korea was supposed to be a part of Japan. Nothing made him happier than the return of spring.

He usually walked from his lodging house in Eirakuchō to his office, only two tram stops away. In any case, he had to walk from the stop at Koganechō. Seeing the fresh sprouting grass beside the road delighted him. He found pleasure in watching the yellow shoots emerge from the moist earth, then gradually change color to light green as the blades increased in size and number. He felt like pressing his cheeks against the young shoots just because, like him, they had survived the severe cold and, like him, could respond to the warmth of spring.

But now this second summer of comfort had passed, and dismaying autumn was bringing its mixture of beauty and threats. The bachelor journalist enjoyed only a brief sentimental moment at the sight of the dragonflies, which had reminded him of home in Kyūshū. He decided to return to his office leisurely on foot, by way of Kwanghwamun Avenue with its lines of plane trees still decked in fading yellow leaves. To him the interval between summer's end and autumn's midpoint was the best season in Korea.

As he worked on the draft of a news article in the office, Tazaki, a senior journalist, tapped his shoulder.

"Hey, you should treat me one of these days."

"What's this all about?"

"It's not going to be cheap, you know— The madame of the Midori wants to have a private talk with you."

"Really?"

The Midori was a new cafe-bar in an alley in Meijichō, which was becoming a pleasure quarter, much like the Asakusa district of Tokyo and the Shinsekai of Osaka. It used to be called the Myŏngye-dong, or the Myŏng-dong, since it was near Myŏngye Palace. The name was changed to Meijichō after the Sino-Japanese War. Japanese settlers had been living there for quite some time. Along the main street it looked like a financial district. The stock exchange stood among other small shops, including many stockbrokers' offices. But on stepping into the alleys and back streets, one found numerous cafes, saloons, and small restaurants, not to mention popular billiard places and the new movie theater of the Shōchiku Company, which had just opened during the past summer.

The police station at Hommachi controlled the whole neighborhood. The police survey showed that 542 girls worked as waitresses in the 116 cafes and saloons in the area, including those surveyed by the police stations at Chongno and Yongsan. The two top cafes were the Marubiru Kaikan and the Kikusui. The former, which had been in business for fifteen years in a three-story building, employed more than fifty waitresses. The Kikusui, formerly the Biliken, was developed into a larger and more refined cafe by a female proprietor, who boasted that her waitresses, in their white aprons, would never sit with any customers in the cafe. Together with those two establishments, the Hanada in Hasegawachō, the Sanyōken in Asahichō, and the Rakuen in Chongno represented the five major cafes of Seoul in 1936.

According to Akutsu's colleagues, Seoul had had only a few coffee shops until recently. They included the Meiji Seika and the Honjōya in Hommachi and the Rakurō in Hasegawachō. Then, in the Meijichō area, many new ones—such as the Hollywood, the Eliza, the Dinah, the Prince, the Falcon, the White Dragon, and the Troika—suddenly appeared, like new bamboo shoots popping up after a heavy rain, and the number of cafe-bars also increased.

"Many of them have come out just as if to welcome you," said Tazaki, to Akutsu. "You should visit them sometime."

With such encouragement, the lonesome bachelor began to visit the cafe-bars near his lodging house. The Midori, with ten waitresses, was one of the smaller ones. It had opened only two years before Akutsu came to Seoul. Akabori Midori, quite a good-looking woman, was the proprietor.

American jazz music was very popular in those days, and in the Midori, as elsewhere, customers and waitresses danced to the tunes from phonograph records. Akutsu became a regular customer at Midori because he and the proprietor came from the same hometown and also because he was attracted to Kaoru, one of her waitresses. Kaoru was a small, quiet girl with a somber expression that revealed, perhaps, her subdued life. She wore little makeup. She had eyebrows resembling crescent moons, slightly slanted dark eyes, a straight nose, and a small mouth. She could handle her liquor very well, and she never got drunk. Because of her short hair, she looked rather childlike. Akutsu had never heard Kaoru laugh aloud. Somehow, when she smiled she seemed to be crying. The sympathy of the lonely bachelor in a foreign country may have been aroused by the forlorn appearance of this waitress, and that may have led to his interest in her. Usually he walked straight home from his office, ate supper, and then went out to the cafe in Meijichō.

II

Dancing in the Western style was prohibited in Korea in those days. The authorities regarded it as unpatriotic (as well as ridiculous) for a man and a woman to put their arms around each other and to dance in such bizarre ways during a time of war. But the more the authorities opposed this foreign music, the more did human beings want it. Dancing and jazz music went together, and so even geisha danced in public in the half-world of Asahichō. One evening, when a policeman entered the Midori while the patrons and the waitresses were dancing and the proprietor was about to be questioned, Akutsu had showed his name card to the policeman, thus saving her from considerable trouble. Since then she had accorded him "special treatment," charging him less than she did other customers.

One night, as he stepped into the cafe, she met him almost at the door and guided him to a corner booth, saying, "Oh, Mr. Akutsu. Please help me."

"What's the trouble?"

"I have a problem with my boy, Ichirō," she whispered. "I can't ask anyone else."

Ichirō, the proprietor's only child, was in his first year of junior high school. A handsome and bright boy, he had placed second in the entrance examinations for a famous school in Seoul. Usually a boy with only one parent, especially a mother who managed a cafe-bar, would be rejected by such a school, but the principal happened to be very much interested in special education for talented students and accepted Ichirō because of his good record. Akutsu knew the boy slightly, having taken him to a swimming pool in Ttuksŏm during the summer.

"So what's happened to him?"

"Well, today someone in the school office telephoned to tell me that he has cut classes for ten days this semester, without any excuse."

"For ten days?" Akutsu repeated. For a young student in a prestigious school to cut classes so many times was unthinkable. "Why did he do that?"

"I asked him, but he wouldn't tell me," said the proprietor, beginning to weep. At that moment she looked like Kaoru did when she smiled.

"Not much help . . ." Akutsu sipped the Sakura beer that Kaoru had brought him.

"I am sorry to bother you, but will you please take him out with you next Sunday and try to learn why he's behaving this way?"

As he lit a cigarette, he studied the mother's lovely face. For a second, he saw Ichirō's young features superimposed upon hers.

"Yes. I'll do that."

Midori and her son lived in a rented three-room house in Nanzanchō, which had a strange combination of demimonde and residential characteristics. The monthly rent was thirty yen, including the water they used. The cost of electricity was not included, but the tatami mats and the paper sliding doors were renewed each year. Compared with Akutsu's rent of twenty yen per month for one six-mat room, with meals, the madame's rent was not at all cheap. But she liked her landladies, two sister geisha who operated out of the main geisha call-office in Nanzanchō. They had saved money, bought land, and built houses to rent.

The geisha offices in Nanzanchō and Asahichō were more prestigious than were the east office in Shimmachi and the south office in Yayoichō of Yongsan. Being a journalist, Akutsu was quite familiar with the geisha houses of Asahichō, such as the Chiyomoto, the Izumi, the Chiyoshin, and the Kiraku. He remembered some beautiful geisha, including Motoya and Momotarō of Yoshimoto, Azuma and Kotsune of Daikoku, Hidechiyo of Yoshinoya, and Chiyoyakko of Kikunoya, all of whom, at one time or another, captured his young heart.

Thinking about those geisha, he asked, "Madame, if I learn something helpful from Ichirō, will you give me a special treat?"

"Which do you prefer, the crane dish of Kyōkiku? Or the snapping turtle of Kagetsu?"

"Neither. I've never had any fun anywhere in Nanzanchō."

Frowning, the madame said decisively, "Fine. Then I'll treat you to an evening at a geisha house, such as Seizansō or Gingetsusō."

"No, no. I'm just joking! But you're really worried about Ichirō, aren't you?"

Inviting a geisha through a main call-office was not inexpensive. Generally a geisha charged steady patrons one yen fifty sen per hour; a new customer had to pay two yen twenty-five sen, excluding food and drinks.

On the following Sunday, Akutsu left his lodging house early and went to Madame Midori's home. Ichirō was having a late breakfast, served by a Korean maid. Madame Midori was still in bed. "Omoni," said Akutsu, "bring me some, too." He sat at the low table, opposite Ichirō.

In those days Japanese in Korea called Japanese maidservants *jochū* and referred to Korean maids either as *omoni* or
as *kijibe*. Kijibe meant a young girl. Japanese maids were paid
twenty yen per month, as well as room and board. Omoni
received ten yen, and kijibe only six yen. Most Japanese
families kept either omoni or kijibe.

During the meal Akutsu did not say a word about Ichirō's
cutting classes. But when they'd finished eating, he said, "Let's
go hunting for old books."

Ichirō became noticeably suspicious. He was very much
aware of his mother's devotion. She managed a cafe-bar for
their livelihood, rented a house, hired a Korean maid, and
retained a tutor for his instruction. Because of these burdens on
her, his cutting classes for ten days amounted to a serious act of
disloyalty. Moved by guilt, Ichirō reluctantly agreed to join
Akutsu for book hunting. Assuming that what Madame Midori
said was true, the only male visitors to her house were Akutsu
himself and the tutor, Kozuki, a poor, disconsolate university
student who gathered a few neighbors' children at her place
and tutored them for a fee. Madame Midori could have asked
Kozuki for help, but she preferred to consult with Akutsu
rather than with the doleful tutor.

Nanzanchō had developed at the foot of the northern side
of Mount Namsan, a small hill about three hundred meters
high, where the Korea Shinto Shrine, the Seoul Shrine, the
Onshi Science Hall, and the Nogi Shrine had been constructed.
Akutsu and Ichirō walked down Namsan's winding road, with
the Seoul Post Office on their left and the Mitsukoshi Department Store on their right, and came to Hommachi Street. On
the right were the Shinozaki Stationery Store and the Yamagishi
Pharmacy; on the left, the post office, Japan Musical Instru-
ments, and the Hirata Department Store. After passing assorted
shops and stores, including the Seoul Athletic Goods Company,
Osawa Camera Shop, Chichibuya Clothing, Kanebō Service
Station, Maruichi Clothing, Tajimaya Shoes, Tsukatani Goods,
Hinomaru Store, Minakai Department Store, and Hinode
Picture Postcards, they turned right to reach Meijichō, and
Cafe Midori.

Akutsu spoke at last about the important subject as they
approached Meijichō. "You see, Ichirō, . . ."
"Yes? See what?"
"I'm wondering if you're in trouble? If anything is bother-
ing you, why don't you tell me about it? You won't find a way
out if you keep it all to yourself."
"I have no problem."
"No problem?"
"None at all," Ichirō insisted, looking straight ahead.
"Then why have you cut classes for ten days, with no
excuse? Your mother is very much worried."
"Yes, I know." Ichirō, obviously annoyed, looked to
the left and to the right, rather than at Akutsu. In silence
they passed the Kumahiro Security Company and the Saeki
Furniture Store, opposite each other. The Kameya Candy
Store, Kongōsan Coffee Shop, Muraki Watch Store, Yama-
guchi Tea Instruments, and Meiji Confectionery lined the
street.
"Why did you cut classes?"
"I cannot talk while walking," said Ichirō.

III
Carrying caramel candies and sweet bean-paste rolls,
Akutsu took Ichirō to the Tŏksu Palace. After paying the five
sen entrance fee, they walked through the imposing structure
that the signboard identified as "The Great Han Gate." The
palace had been built as a residence for Wŏlsan Taegun, the
elder brother of the ninth Yi sovereign, Sŏngjong. Later, when
it served as the residence of King Kojong after his abdication, it
was renamed Tŏksu Palace.
While they reclined on the palace lawn, nibbling at their
sweets, Akutsu urged the boy, "Why don't you begin to tell
me?" Persuading Ichirō to talk seemed more difficult to Akutsu
than drawing newsworthy facts from government officials. At
first Ichirō did not say anything useful, but chose instead to
express unhappiness with his mother, his home, his school. He
did mention, however, that recently he'd spent a day in Ch'anggyŏngwŏn Park.

In former times, Ch'anggyŏngwŏn was the Sugang Palace, but it became a public park after Japan annexed Korea. The park contained a botanical garden, a zoo, and a museum. "What's so wrong about a day spent in Ch'anggyŏngwŏn?" wondered Akutsu.

Ch'anggyŏngwŏn was famous for its cherry blossoms. During the season it was crowded day and night with spectators who were much cheered by "flower-viewing-drinks." A visitor entering Honghwamun, the main gate, would see the botanical garden on his right and the zoo on his left. The path was bordered by ancient cherry trees, each with a trunk nearly a foot in diameter, whose extended branches created a flowery arcade. Trees bearing double blossoms were more abundant near the central square, while the single-blossom Yoshino trees were more numerous near the pool and along the path to the inner region of the park. When they were in season, the five thousand blossoming trees attracted about seventy thousand spectators each evening. The admission charge was ten sen for an adult and five sen for a child. Akutsu wondered—but never really calculated—how much income the government received during the twenty days of the season, from about the end of April until the middle of May.

Akutsu guessed that something must be wrong when a middle-school student spent a day in the park when the cherry trees were not blooming. He pressed Ichirō with question after question, until the boy burst into tears. "That sister!" he blurted. "It's all the kisaeng's fault!"

"What? What kisaeng?" Akutsu's surprise made Ichirō wipe the tears away.

"We'd better have a man-to-man talk," said Akutsu. "And, believe me, I will never repeat what you say to anyone."

Slowly, reluctantly, Ichirō told his story. He often took a roundabout way home from school, which was on Sŏdaemun Street. The most direct route went past the First Girls' High School, then near the Seoul Broadcasting Building and the newly constructed Pumingwan, a music hall, to the Seoul Post Office in Hasegawachō, coming at last to Nanzanchō from Asahichō. But that familiar route was boring, so sometimes he

took another way, leaving by Kwanghwamun Gate, going
through the Insa-dong, turning right around Pagoda Park,
crossing Koganechō and Hommachi, and finally reaching Nanzanchō. He liked this slower route because it offered greater
variety and the sort of sights that stimulated his interests when
he went through the Korean section in Chongno and the Japanese section in Hommachi.

One day, after parting from a classmate, Ichirō felt the need
to urinate while walking alone through the Korean section in
Chongno, so he turned into a back alley to empty his bladder.
Suddenly a young woman rushed out from one of those taverns
with black hangings in the doorway, pushed something into his
cloth shoulder-bag, grasped his hand as if to thank him, ran
into another tavern a few doors farther down the alley, yelled a
few words in Korean to someone inside, and then sped away.
To the amazed Ichirō, all this seemed to happen in a split
second.

Small taverns, called sulchip, numbered 220 in Chongno
alone. Ichirō dared to venture into the one from which the
young woman had come. Standing on the bare earthen floor, he
looked around, seeing the inside of a sulchip for the first time
in his life. It had a counter on the right side with dishes of
assorted vegetables, beef, and fish, and, on the other side, a
brazier with burning charcoal.

A young man standing near the counter asked, in accented
Japanese, "You are Japanese?"

"Yes."

"You stay here for a while. You understand?"

"Why?" Ichirō quavered.

Shrugging his shoulders like a Westerner, the young Korean
replied, "I don't know. She say keep you here for a while."
Ichirō felt relieved that no customers were present. Even so, he
was very uneasy at being in such a forbidden place.

In a sulchip, three kinds of drinks—hwaju, yakchu, and
makkŏlli—were served, and most customers drank them while
standing near the food counter. In another kind of tavern,
naewoe chujŏm, young waitresses served the yakchu in black

mugs, charging forty sen a drink. They tried to run up a big bill for Japanese customers by bringing them one drink after another. Customers in sulchips were exclusively Korean, and even Akutsu did not have the courage to go into one alone. He could easily imagine how helpless Ichirō must have felt.

When Ichirō tried to leave the tavern, the Korean man at the counter gave him a stern look, shut the door, and said, "You stay for a while." Ichirō realized that the package pushed into his bag by the young woman must be the reason why he was being detained. Half crying, he begged the Korean, "I'll give you the package. Please let me go!" The Korean replied harshly, "No! Cannot take it. You must give to her."

Just then, several men came in; they stared at Ichirō, backed against the wall. While the counterman served them, Ichirō dashed out and ran to the tram. Nobody chased him. At home he examined the package. Firmly sealed, it felt like it held a book.

On the following afternoon, Ichirō went back to the tavern, where he found the same Korean. Seeing the package in his hand, the man said quickly, "No! Cannot take that. You go Ch'anggyŏngwŏn Park, near Myŏngjŏng Hall, tomorrow in morning, between ten and eleven o'clock. Understand? You must give to her hand, or you in much trouble. And your parents go jail. Understand?" The Korean's worried expression and the strange behavior of the woman on the previous day filled Ichirō with alarm. "Oh, what a mess I'm in!" he thought.

On the next day, after considerable distress during the night, Ichirō decided to report to school late. He went instead to the Ch'anggyŏngwŏn. The young middle-school boy was being caught up in a great adventure.

IV

As soon as the Honghwa Gate of Ch'anggyŏngwŏn opened at ten o'clock, Ichirō, hiding his school cap under his jacket, entered the compound. The Myŏngjŏng Hall rose opposite the gate. It was a one-story irimoya-style edifice, with a throne placed in an unusual location—on the eastern side within the building. Two splendid phoenixes and elaborate clouds, all carved in deep relief, decorated the ceiling. The building's exterior was so neglected that no tourist could imagine that it held a king's throne. Ichirō passed the time by looking at the ancient sundial and at images fixed under the great curving eaves to ward off evil spirits.

When his watch, a gift from his mother on entering middle school, pointed to eleven o'clock, Ichirō decided he'd better go to school. As he started on the way, the young woman called to him. She looked so different in Western-style dress that he did not recognize her. She had been wearing the Korean woman's chŏgori and ch'ima skirt the day his adventure began.

He was so glad to see her that he reached immediately for his shoulder-bag. She said harshly, "Wait! Not here! Follow me. But stay five meters behind me." While he started after her, she went off in the direction of the botanical garden. Impressed by her beauty, Ichirō followed her without hesitation. When they reached a place where bushes and trees hid them from view, she stopped and commanded, "Sit!" When Ichirō did not obey her promptly, she yelled, "Sit down quickly!" Finally he settled on the grass.

"The package?" she demanded. "Where is it?"

"Here."

"Did you open it?"

"No."

She asked a number of questions—his name and address, his mother's name, and even Midori's telephone number—all of which she recorded in a small notebook. Then, just like an interrogating policeman, she took the textbooks and notebooks, and the mysterious package, from his bag to double check his answers.

"Did you mention this package to anyone?" Suddenly she grasped his wrist, pulled him closer, and began to choke him with both hands.

"Please! I didn't tell anybody!" Ichirō cried out, shocked by the sudden change in this beautiful woman.

"Are you sure? Do you swear by the god of the Korea

Shrine!" Ichirō could only raise his eyebrows. She released her
hold on his throat. She smiled, then, showing her white teeth
for the first time. "I am sorry I doubted you." Ichirō, close
enough to being a man to harbor this thought, wondered,
"How can such beauty be possible in this world?"

He wanted to give the package to her, but she would not
accept it. "Wait!" she said. "You are a good boy. Will you help
some more? If my younger brother were still alive, he would be
your age. Won't you become my younger brother?" She drew
him into her arms and held him tightly. Intoxicated by her
perfume, Ichirō nodded his willingness to be anything she
wished.

"So you will be my brother! Then cut the rest of your
classes for today and stay with me this afternoon." They stayed
in the park until two o'clock, eating the foods packed in his
lunch box and the jam rolls she bought at a tea shop in the
park.

She told Ichirō a little about herself. She was a kisaeng, a
dancer trained in the style of the Yi dynasty (about which
Ichirō knew almost nothing). And her name, he learned, was
Ch'oe Kŭm-ju. After that she entertained him with a romantic
Korean tale, the *Ch'unhyangjŏn*. Yi Mong-yong, a son of the
magistrate of Namwŏn county of Chŏlla Province, fell deeply
in love with a young kisaeng called Ch'unhyang. But when
Mong-yong's father was transferred to the capital city, the
young lovers had to part. After Mong-yong left for the capital,
Ch'unhyang gave up her profession as a kisaeng and worked
as a maidservant, waiting only for the day when Mong-yong
would return for her. The new magistrate of the district became
interested in her. When because of her love for Mong-yong she
would not yield to the magistrate's wishes, he had her jailed on
a false charge.

Meanwhile, Mong-yong was promoted to a government
post, with the duty of investigating the behavior of district
officias. When he went on his official rounds to the Namwŏn
county, he learned that his sweetheart had been imprisoned and
that the people were suffering under the magistrate's despotism.

Mong-yong heard that the magistrate planned to hold a great feast for his birthday. On that day, Mong-yong brought in official agents from other districts, disguised himself as a beggar, and mingled with the spectators at the banquet. When he saw his sweetheart, ashamed in chains and fetters, he loudly recited these verses:

> This sweet drink in golden goblets,
> The blood of ten thousand people!
> This fancy food on jade dishes,
> The bones of ten thousand people!
> As candles drip their melting wax,
> The people shed their falling tears!
> When the singing voices rise,
> So do the anguished cries!

"Here comes the official investigator!" Mong-yong shouted. With this declaration, he ordered the arrest of the magistrate, released all the innocent prisoners, and took Ch'unhyang as his wife. This tale is said to be an adaptation of a famous Chinese work, the *Xixiangji,* and is the most popular stage play in Korea. It always draws large audiences, just as does the Japanese drama *Chūshingura,* about the forty-seven faithful retainers.

Just before two o'clock in the afternoon, Kŭm-ju asked, "Will you do me a favor?" Naturally Ichirō agreed, and again she held him close, saying, "Then let's meet again here the day after tomorrow, Ichirō. But don't tell anyone. This is our secret." Meanwhile, that very afternoon, he was supposed to give the package to a middle-aged man, who would be standing with a newspaper in his hand at three o'clock sharp in front of the Kirakukan on First Street in Hommachi. Ichirō did exactly as he was told. Then the man gave him a small box, saying, "This is for her."

Eager to be embraced by her, Ichirō went to the Ch'ang-gyŏngwŏn on the appointed day and delivered the box. They spent the hours happily enough until two o'clock. This time Kŭm-ju gave him a large envelope and told him to hand it to a

young girl who would be standing at the head of the stairs leading to the second floor of the Hwashin Department Store. Kŭm-
ju made him promise to meet her again two days later, in the
usual place.

Noticing that he was a bit hesitant, Kŭm-ju moved closer
and hugged him. "Remember, I'm your kisaeng sister. Now just
close your eyes and stand still." Slowly, gently, she fondled his
crotch. The boy arched his back and soon breathed rapidly.
"There now, doesn't that feel good? No one else can do
this. . . ," she whispered, skillfully unbuttoning the front of his
trousers, putting her fingers in a place he himself had not yet
learned to touch. A few minutes later the boy quivered and
sighed, then slumped back against a nearby bush.

"Don't open your eyes. Just stand still." From a pocket she
drew out a piece of soft cloth, wiped him dry, carefully tucked
his limp organ back in his pants. Once again she embraced him
sweetly. "Now if you want to enjoy something pleasant like this
again, meet me here the day after tomorrow."

For the next two days, all day long and far into the nights,
Ichirō simply could not put the bliss of that first experience out
of his mind. As if possessed by a fox-spirit, he hurried out to
Ch'anggyŏngwŏn to meet Kŭm-ju earlier than he needed to
when that second day arrived.

After hearing Ichirō's story, Akutsu felt that something was
very wrong about the whole affair. The kisaeng could have
retrieved the mysterious package from Ichirō when she first met
him in the park, but she chose instead to send him to the
middle-aged man standing in front of the Kirakuen. Why did
she do that? Was she being cautious? She had asked Ichirō all
kinds of questions about himself but said hardly anything
about herself, except for calling herself his kisaeng sister. To use
sex so obviously to entrap an innocent boy was unforgivable.
Akutsu decided to investigate this kisaeng and to bring charges
against her if she was involved in any kind of criminal activity.
Being a journalist, he was swift to associate her strange behavior with the traffic in opium or illegal prostitution.

Akutsu decided to talk like a father to the lad who, having

lost his innocence, needed to be warned about the wiles of certain kinds of women. "As that Korean in the tavern said, 'If you see her again, you'll be in big trouble.' So stay away from her!" And he preached to Ichirō about the harm from masturbation, as if he were some kind of reverend moralist rather than a worldly father.

V

Akutsu decided not to tell the truth to Madame Midori, who, if she knew it, would undoubtedly worry a great deal about her son. He told her only that Ichirō had been involved, very briefly, with some irresponsible boys and that he would not get into such trouble in the future. Madame Midori was very much relieved by Akutsu's report and completely forgot about the promise she had made about treating him to a party in the pleasure quarter.

Akutsu himself went to the place in the botanical garden where Ichirō had met the Korean kisaeng. For three days, at about ten o'clock in the morning, Akutsu roamed about in the shrubbery, but he did not find any such beauty there. When he told the story to his colleagues, the office superior laughed. "He must have made up the whole business as an excuse. These days, you can't trust a kid!" Akutsu thought he should try to verify the story, but he could not find time to go see Ichirō at Nanzanchō.

A few nights later, when Akutsu visited the Midori, the madame had another worry. "Both the tutor and our maid say Ichirō comes home late, about eight o'clock, when I'm working over here." Apparently Ichirō came home late every other night, saying that he was spending time with his friends. Akutsu suspected that he was still being used by the kisaeng after school.

When Akutsu questioned him, Ichirō confessed that the kisaeng waited for him at the school's gate and made him run errands for her. The next task she imposed on him was to receive an article from her at a Chinese candy store near Taihei Street. Akutsu arranged to meet the boy at the newspaper office on the next day so they could go together.

Akutsu accompanied Ichirō to Chinatown. Kŭm-ju, standing in front of a shabby Chinese candy shop, reminded him of the old saying about, "a crane on a dunghill." His heart beat faster at this first glimpse of her. He took out his name card and, as he presented it, said politely, in the usual formula, "I ask your favor."

For a moment, she seemed to wilt, then, turning upon Ichirō, she cried, "This is the end of our sister and brother relationship!" Ichirō, much distressed, backed away. Still scolding, she followed him. And Akutsu followed her, admiring her shapely legs sheathed in silk stockings and her high-heeled shoes. He steered her and Ichirō into a small Chinese restaurant nearby. When they'd settled at a table, Akutsu asked for her name and address.

"Why do you want to know?" Kŭm-ju asked, in fluent Japanese.

"Why? Because I know you are using an innocent Japanese boy for some suspect purpose. That's a terrible thing to do, isn't it?"

"But we are just friends."

"Just friends? How can a friend make him cut classes, teach him an obscene habit, and use him for secret errands?"

"I am sorry. I won't do it again."

"I hope not. What in the world are you using him for?"

She began to sob bitterly. "What did Ichirō tell you? Does anyone besides you know about us?"

Irritated because she would not answer his questions, Akutsu tried to grab the package, wrapped in brown paper.

"Open it!" he commanded. "What's in this?"

As they fought over the package, it slipped from her hands to the floor. The paper wrapping broke, releasing a flow of white flakes. Frantically pushing his hand away, she stamped on the package, scattering even more of the flakes upon the floor. Because they were in Chinatown, where crimes relating to opium, prostitution, and gambling were frequent, Akutsu instantly associated the white powder with opium from China. Ignoring her protests, he picked up some of the powder and put it in one of the restaurant's paper napkins.

"Aigo," she said, "please forgive me. I promise I won't use Ichirō again."

Believing that she was involved in the opium traffic, Akutsu seized her arm. "No, I won't give in. I'm taking you to the police."

"Oh, please! Don't do that. Please come to my house. There I'll explain everything."

A beauty in distress is almost impossible to resist. He agreed to listen to her story. They got rid of Ichirō easily enough by sending him off to school.

As Akutsu's colleagues had told him more than once, an invitation to a kisaeng's home was the first step toward a romantic liaison. Unlike a low-class prostitute, such as a kalbo, a kisaeng never became involved with a stranger. And, unlike the geisha, since the kisaeng were usually free from debt, they worked independently. A kisaeng would go from her home to her call-office, but she had no other obligations, either to customers or to the call-office. Nearly a thousand kisaeng were registered at the three major call-offices in Seoul: Hansŏng, Chosŏn, and Chongno. They charged one yen ninety sen for the first hour, and one yen thirty sen for each additional hour. The Hansŏng office had some elite kisaeng on its rolls, and Akutsu was happy to learn, later, that Ch'oe Kŭm-ju was one of the most popular registered in that office.

VI

Koreans had long observed an old Confucian maxim that a boy and a girl should not sit side by side after they reached the age of seven. Consequently, a good wife would never speak directly to a male visitor, not even to a friend of her husband, unless her husband was present. Even with a married couple, proper behavior required them to speak only while one was inside the house and the other was outside. During the hot summers, if their room had no dividing partition, the wife would listen to her husband speak without looking at his face, as if she were his servant. That was why the word *naewoe*, within-without, was used to denote a chaste wife. In such a strict social order, great courage and decisiveness were required of a kisaeng if she invited a man to her house at their first meeting. This was especially true because the kisaeng's primary concern was not to sell herself, but to entertain her customers with her artistry in music and dance, developed during many years of training.

Usually a first-class kisaeng remained faithful to her patron until he ended the relationship. Even if a customer wished to become romantically involved, and she invited him to her house, on his first visit they would share only light conversation, and he would depart after a few minutes, discreetly placing some five- or ten-yen notes wrapped in a piece of white paper under the cushion upon which he sat. After that he could visit her at any time he wished, without paying the registry's fee. But when a physical relationship was established, he was expected to leave twenty to thirty yen under the cushion. Akutsu learned all these details about the manners of the Korean demimonde from his colleagues and older journalists in his office. That was why he was astonished to be invited to Ch'oe Kŭm-ju's home in Tonŭi-dong.

The house was small but well built, with a tiled roof and thick, earthen walls. Her room, furnished with a dresser and a writing desk, both gorgeously decorated with inlays of mother-of-pearl, revealed a high standard of living. Sitting opposite him, she showed him a photograph of herself and bowed formally.

"I am Ch'oe Kŭm-ju, a kisaeng registered in the Hansŏng call-office. Because I think Ichirō is very cute, I invented some errands as an excuse to see him. I like boys who will soon be men. And I like men!" Then she closed and locked the door to her room.

"I'm not lying. If you doubt me, I will prove with my body that I am telling the truth. Be my lover. Now!" She threw herself into his arms. Surprised by such boldness, Akutsu—who was not much older than Ichirō—fell back on the floor. Responding to the same excitement that had aroused Ichirō, he sucked wildly at her lips.

Her closed eyes and small nostrils, the beauty of her face, stirred his lust, robbing him of self-control. He mumbled into her ear, his voice hoarse and eager, "Are you sure you want me? I am not rich." "No matter," she whispered. "Quick! Let's make love. Take me! Take me . . ."

To him, such fantastic luck was a veritable gift from heaven. Swiftly he stripped off her blouse, skirts, and underwear, then tore off his own clothes. Naked, he joined her on the hard, heated floor. He was so excited that, naturally, their union satisfied only himself. But she did not mind. Kissing him repeatedly, she muttered, "We are lovers. Aren't we? Aren't we? And please don't tell anyone about Ichirō, because I am ashamed . . ." Assuming that she was ashamed of the way she had played with Ichirō, Akutsu agreed. "I won't tell anyone. Now that I have a wonderful lover like you, your shame is my shame."

Making him even happier, Kŭm-ju decided to stay at home all the rest of the day instead of going out to work. She sustained them with beer and foods ordered from outside. As evening closed in, she begged, "Please stay and spend the night with me." He was easily persuaded, much preferring the more delicate lovemaking in her soft bed to the quick bout on the hard floor.

That night, the kisaeng amused the young journalist by telling simple jokes and funny tales. A ginger seller lost his last sen while involved with an elderly kisaeng of P'yŏngyang and said, "Even with no teeth in her lower mouth, she gobbled all my ginger!" Another merchant, who also lost all his money to a kisaeng, could not return home, became her house servant, and was burning firewood one day to heat the floor. Meanwhile, a new customer came and stayed for a long time with the kisaeng. The servant said to himself, "What a fool! Another servant to burn firewood!" A soldier fell in love with a very young kisaeng at his place of duty. When his assignment there ended and he was ordered to leave for the capital city, he shed bitter tears over their parting, while the young kisaeng felt quite indifferent. Her anxious mother told the girl to place her hands over her eyes and at least pretend to weep, but the kisaeng was still unmoved. The soldier became angry at her coldness and struck her cheek. The kisaeng cried out from pain. As her tears flowed, the soldier shed more tears saying, "Don't cry, my darling. The harder you cry, the sadder I become." All these innocent tales rather amused Akutsu. Having fully enjoyed her body, he left the house at about two o'clock in the morning. The experience was the most wonderful he'd known since arriving in Seoul.

Akutsu was by no means a virgin; once or twice a month he had accompanied his older friends to a kalbo house in Nami-kichō and to the pleasure quarter of Yayoichō. He especially favored certain brothels, which charged him as little as three to five yen for the night. But he had never even dreamed of embracing a beautiful, officially registered kisaeng.

He really was happy after he met Kŭm-ju. She said she wanted him to visit her at any time he wished. But when he heard his older friends talking about the complicated manners and rules applied to a kisaeng's patron, Akutsu did not feel easy about visiting her. Accordingly, he tried to bring their relationship to an end by staying away for five nights in a row. But of course he missed her very much, and, giving in, went to the restaurant where she danced on some evenings. In Chongno he found many first-class Korean restaurants, such as the Tenkōen, the Shokudōen, the Chōsenkan, the Taiseikan, and the Shōchikuen.

One evening he reserved a ten-yen table in a Korean restaurant for a dinner with her. Although he was accustomed to popular Korean dishes, such as onmyŏn, pibinbab, and sŏllŏng-t'ang, he had never tasted any of the highly spiced traditional foods, and that night he could not eat much of the restaurant's offerings: they were much too hot for him.

Kŭm-ju, feeling sorry for him and his fiery mouth, moved closer, saying, "Why don't you come to my place?" Her sympathy pleased him. So once again he fell under her spell.

VII

Akutsu enjoyed a very happy life from the late autumn of
that year to the following spring. After work he relaxed at the
Cafe Midori or in some small snack shop, such as the Kyō-
getsu, the Izutsu, or the Nimonji in Meijichō. Then he went to
Ch'oe Kŭm-ju's house by taxi, paying eighty sen for the ride. In
her warm room, naked, they made love, then slept in each
other's arms till morning. He ate breakfast at her place and
then went to his office.

She never charged him a sen. Not only that: she made him a
Japanese kimono-style dressing gown and also a business suit
at the beginning of spring. Because she worked as a dancer in
the evenings and wanted to avoid the gossip of neighbors, she
asked him to come to her house about midnight. The peculi-
arities of his job did not allow him to go to her every night.
Besides, being a man, he was also dallying with Kaoru, the
waitress at the Midori. So now the once-lonely bachelor felt as
if he were holding a fragrant flower in each hand.

One April night, after getting out of the taxi half drunk, he
was attacked outside Kŭm-ju's house by a man he never saw,
who hit him with a club on the head and legs until he lost
consciousness. When he awoke, he found himself lying in
Kŭm-ju's room, with a doctor setting his broken leg. The
doctor warned him not to walk for several days. Kŭm-ju, all
concern, said, "I shall report the incident to your office. You
just stay here and let me take care of you." Akutsu nodded,
groaning at the terrible pain in his head and back.

His life changed greatly after the attack. When Kŭm-ju
was not home, her old Korean servant looked after him. But
because the maid did not understand Japanese, he fretted a
good deal. And, on the fourth night after the beating, Kŭm-ju
did not come home.

He waited for her all the next day, but she did not return,
even after midnight. Wondering if she had become involved
with another man, or had gone back to her family's village,
Akutsu was frustrated and bored.

At last, after nearly half a month had passed, the doctor

told him he could walk with the help of crutches. He went back to his lodging house by taxi and telephoned the newspaper office. His boss answered the phone. "What in the world are you doing?" he yelled. "You've been away for two weeks, without giving us any notice!" Akutsu tried to calm him down with an account of the attack, and explained that Ch'oe Kŭm-ju had reported it. The boss snarled that he had received no such phone call, had not known a thing about the attack, and was thoroughly disgusted with such an irresponsible fellow as Akutsu had shown himself to be. Completely mystified, Akutsu could not understand why Kŭm-ju had lied to him about reporting the beating or why she had disappeared. He could not understand her at all.

His landlady told him that an important political prisoner had escaped from the Great West Gate Prison. She also mentioned that Miss Kaoru of the Cafe Midori had come to see him a few times while he was away. Akutsu paid very little attention to the landlady's chatter. Several days later, however, one of his newspaper colleagues made an unexpected phone call to ask if he had gone to Manchukuo during those two weeks of absence. He replied, with considerable annoyance, that he'd never left Seoul. Little did he realize that the inquiry had great bearing on a matter of serious import.

An hour after the colleague's phone call, two military policemen came to his lodging house and arrested him on the charge of assisting a political offender to cross the border to Manchukuo.

"What does this mean?" the incredulous Akutsu asked.

"Don't be a fool!" one of the policemen barked. "We know all about your affair with Ch'oe Kŭm-ju. An intellectual like you must have made all the escape plans."

"What? Me? Helping a prisoner?"

"Yes. Don't tell us that you don't know about this Korean political offender, Ch'oe Hong-sik, who broke out of prison with outside help. From you!"

While Akutsu protested innocence, he wondered if Ch'oe Hong-sik might be related to Ch'oe Kŭm-ju. The military policemen, not unwilling to talk, told him how Ch'oe Hong-sik cut the iron bars on the window of his cell with a metal saw, climbed a wall three meters high, and vanished. The military police, of course, were in full pursuit. Meanwhile, the Antung Station on the border between Korea and Manchukuo reported that a Japanese journalist from Seoul, named Akutsu Minoru, had presented his identification papers at the border crossing and that his features resembled those of Ch'oe Hong-sik. He was accompanied by a beautiful woman, his wife, and his purpose was to tour Manchukuo from south to north. Police and customs officers tended to be casual about journalists, so Mr. and Mrs. Akutsu were permitted to enter Manchukuo.

Limping along on his bad leg, Akutsu was taken to Seoul's main police station. There he tried to defend himself, but the military policemen would not believe him. Fortunately for him, at that critical time, vigilant border guards caught Ch'oe Hong-sik and his younger sister, Kŭm-ju, at a border station between Manchukuo and the Soviet Union. If that interception had not occurred, Akutsu himself would have been condemned to prison.

Ch'oe Hong-sik had been deeply involved in the Korean independence movement since his high-school days. After he was imprisoned, his younger sister, Kŭm-ju, moved to Seoul and became a kisaeng. She dreamed of freeing her elder brother from prison and of sending him to safety in the Soviet Union. She studied the structure of Seoul's prison and was convinced that with outside help, Hong-sik could escape. She planned every detail, down to the least incidental. She thought that she had everything under control—but failed to account for the waywardness of human beings. That's when innocent Ichirō entered the plot.

She hid a small metal saw in the spine of a book intended for Hong-sik, planning to pass it to a sympathetic prison guard with whom she had established a friendly connection. By mistake, another guard went to the appointed place and attempted to seduce her. Being afraid that he would guess her plan and expose it, she ran away from him. In the next moment she encountered Ichirō in the alley. Clever Kŭm-ju decided to use the naive Japanese boy to cover her movements. She tempted him with words and deeds, and with her beauty. He submitted easily, especially when she awakened his budding lust. With that he became her willing messenger.

When he was detected at the border, Ch'oe Hong-sik insisted that he was Akutsu Minoru and showed them Akutsu's old suit from Tokyo, with the tailor's label in it. That almost convinced the guards. But one of them had an idea. "If you are a Japanese, take off those shoes and socks and show us your feet."

Japanese who have worn thonged zōri or geta since childhood develop a wide space between the first and second toes. That is why Koreans call Japanese by the derogatory term chokpari, 'hoofed pig feet'.

At the guard's request, Ch'oe Hong-sik gave up. "Chokpari!" he muttered. "The Japanese people are separated from their emperor, as are their first toes from their second, while we Koreans are all the same, like our toes together in our pŏsŏn socks."

When the police in Seoul told Akutsu how Ch'oe Hong-sik and his sister Kŭm-ju had been apprehended in Manchukuo, everything about his strange relationship with the kisaeng became clear. All that lovemaking, which he had believed was so genuine—and so satisfying!—had been nothing but pretense, a play full of lies. "All shibai," he sighed, regretting the end to memories so full of joy. The new suit she had made for him was only a device to lay her hands on his old suit with his name sewn in it. His being beaten by "an unknown assailant" was another scheme to confine him in her house in order to gain time for "Mr. and Mrs. Akutsu" to flee from Seoul. But, clever as she was in all those arrangements, she failed.

Because the Confucian precept of filial piety had been greatly honored among Koreans for hundreds of years, Kŭm-ju regarded Hong-sik, the elder brother, as the head of her family and was fiercely loyal to him, even to the point of putting herself in jeopardy. She did not succeed in helping Hong-sik to escape across the border into the Soviet Union. Even so, Akutsu was much impressed by the brilliance with which she freed Hong-sik from Seoul's prison. She is so young, he marveled, no older than I. And she is so smart!

Kǔm-ju's confession proved Akutsu's innocence, and he was released near the beginning of May. At that time he was still using a crutch. About two months later, in early July, the Marco Polo Bridge Incident took place in China, starting the Sino-Japanese War. By then the broken bone in his leg was completely healed. Soon after the incident in China he was summoned to serve in Japan's army. Being young and healthy, he passed the physical examination.

The day before the army ordered him to report for duty, Akutsu obtained permission to visit Ch'oe Kǔm-ju in prison. Standing stiffly in the visiting room, he said, "The war has begun, you know."

"I know," replied Kǔm-ju, coldly, half turning away from him.

"I have been drafted. I may be killed . . ."

How could she not be touched? "Yes," she nodded. "Many people will die— My brother and I tried to prevent this war from happening." Looking directly at him, her eyes shining with tears, she whispered, "Annyŏnghi kashio."

"What does that mean?"

"It means 'Go safely.' In Korean."

"I see. 'Go safely' . . ." Akutsu repeated the phrase, saying it slowly, wanting to remember it. Tears gathered in his eyes, too. How could he hate her, even though she had fooled him? Even though she had betrayed Ichirō?

"Well," he faltered, looking upon her beauty for the last time, "I will go safely."

Later in the war he was transferred to central China from north China. Whenever he was exhausted and worried from all the horrors of combat, he remembered her lovely face. And her parting words, "Annyŏnghi kashio," lingering in his mind, touched his heart.